PENGUIN  CLASSICS

THE VICTIM

Saul Bellow is the author of thirteen novels—including, most recently, *Ravelstein*—and numerous novellas and stories. He is the only novelist to receive three National Book awards, for *The Adventures of Augie March, Herzog,* and *Mr. Sammler's Planet.* In 1975, he won the Pulitzer Prize for his novel *Humboldt's Gift.* The Nobel Prize in Literature was awarded to him in 1976. In 1990, Mr. Bellow was presented the National Book Award Foundation Medal for distinguished contribution to American letters. A longtime resident of Chicago, Mr. Bellow now lives in New England.

The Victim

a novel by

Saul Bellow

PENGUIN BOOKS

PENGUIN BOOKS

Published by the Penguin Group

Penguin Group (USA) Inc., 375 Hudson Street, New York, New York 10014, U.S.A.

Penguin Books Ltd, 80 Strand, London WC2R 0RL, England

Penguin Books Australia Ltd, 250 Camberwell Road, Camberwell, Victoria 3124, Australia

Penguin Books Canada Ltd, 10 Alcorn Avenue, Toronto, Ontario, Canada M4V 3B2

Penguin Books India (P) Ltd, 11 Community Centre, Panchsheel Park, New Delhi – 110 017, India

Penguin Books (N.Z.) Ltd, Cnr Rosedale and Airborne Roads, Albany, Auckland, New Zealand

Penguin Books (South Africa) (Pty) Ltd, 24 Sturdee Avenue,
Rosebank, Johannesburg 2196, South Africa

Penguin Books Ltd, Registered Offices: 80 Strand, London WC2R 0RL, England

First published in the United States of America by
The Vanguard Press, Inc., 1947
First published in Great Britain by John Lehmann 1948
Published in a Viking Compass Edition 1956
Published in Penguin Books 1988
This edition published in Penguin Books 1996

20 19 18 17 16 15 14 13 12 11

LIBRARY OF CONGRESS CATALOGING IN PUBLICATION DATA
Bellow, Saul.
The victim.
I. Title.
[PS3503.E4488V5   1988]   813´.52   88–17981
ISBN 0 14 01.8938 6

Printed in the United States of America
Set in Baskerville

To my friend
PAOLO MILANO

It is related, O auspicious King, that there was a merchant of the merchants who had much wealth, and business in various cities. Now on a day he mounted horse and went forth to recover monies in certain towns, and the heat oppressed him; so he sat beneath a tree and, putting his hand into his saddle-bags, he took thence some broken bread and dried dates and began to break fast. When he had ended eating the dates he threw away the stones with force and lo! an Ifrit appeared, huge of stature and brandishing a drawn sword, wherewith he approached the merchant and said, 'Stand up that I may slay thee even as thou slewest my son!' Asked the merchant, 'How have I slain thy son?' and he answered, 'When thou atest dates and threwest away the stones they struck my son full in the breast as he was walking by, so that he died forthwith.'

'The Tale of the Trader and the Jinni'
from *Thousand and One Nights*

Be that as it may, now it was that upon the rocking waters of the ocean the human face began to reveal itself; the sea appeared paved with innumerable faces, upturned to the heavens; faces, imploring, wrathful, despairing; faces that surged upward by thousands, by myriads, by generations . . .

DE QUINCEY, *The Pains of Opium*

I

ON some nights New York is as hot as Bangkok. The whole continent seems to have moved from its place and slid nearer the equator, the bitter gray Atlantic to have become green and tropical, and the people, thronging the streets, barbaric fellahin among the stupendous monuments of their mystery, the lights of which, a dazing profusion, climb upward endlessly into the heat of the sky.

On such a night, Asa Leventhal alighted hurriedly from a Third Avenue train. In his preoccupation he had almost gone past his stop. When he recognized it, he jumped up, shouting to the conductor, 'Hey, hold it, wait a minute!' The black door of the ancient car was already sliding shut; he struggled with it, forcing it back with his shoulder, and squeezed through. The train fled, and Leventhal, breathing hard, stared after it, cursing, and then turned and descended to the street.

He was bitterly irritated. He had spent the afternoon with his sister-in-law, his brother's wife, in Staten Island. Or, rather, he had wasted it because of her. Soon after lunch she had phoned him at the office – he was an editor of a small trade magazine in lower Manhattan – and immediately, with terrible cries, she implored him to come out, to come at once. One of the children was sick.

'Elena,' he said as soon as he was able to make himself heard, 'I'm busy. So I want you to control yourself now and tell me: is it really serious?'

'Come right away! Asa, please! Right away!'

He pressed the tip of his ear as if to protect himself from

her shrillness and muttered something about Italian excitability. Then the connection was broken. He hung up, expecting her to ring again, but the phone remained silent. He did not know how to reach her; his brother was not listed in the Staten Island directory. She was calling either from a store or from a neighbor's house. For a long time, Leventhal had had very little to do with his brother and his brother's family. Only a few weeks ago he had received a card from him postmarked Galveston. He was working in a shipyard. At the time, Leventhal had said to his wife, 'First Norfolk, now Texas. Anything is better than home.' It was the old story; Max had married young and now he was after novelty, adventure. There were plenty of shipyards and jobs in Brooklyn and Jersey. Meanwhile Elena was burdened with the care of the children.

Leventhal had told her the truth. He was busy. A pile of unchecked proofs lay before him. He moved away the phone after waiting a few minutes and, making an impatient noise in his throat, picked up a piece of copy. No doubt the child was sick, probably seriously sick, or she wouldn't have carried on so. And, since his brother was away, it was somewhat in the nature of a duty to go. He would go this evening. It couldn't be so urgent. It was just beyond Elena's power to speak calmly about anything. He told himself this several times; nevertheless her cries continued to sound in his ears together with the windy thrum of the long-stemmed electric fans and the tick of typewriters. What if it were really critical? And suddenly, impulsively, meanwhile condemning himself for it, he got up, pulled his jacket from the back of the chair, went to the girl at the switchboard, and said, 'I'm going in to see Beard. Buzz him for me, will you?'

With his hands in his hind pockets, pressing against his chief's desk, bending toward him slightly, Leventhal announced quietly that he had to go out.

Mr Beard's face, a face enlarged by baldness, with a fierce bony nose and a veined forehead, took on an incredulous, sharp look.

2

'With an issue to get ready?' he said.

'It's a family emergency,' said Leventhal.

'Can't it wait a few hours?'

'I wouldn't go if I thought it could.'

Mr Beard made a short, unpleasant answer to this. He slapped his metal ruler on the pages of the type-book. 'Use your own judgment,' he said. There was nothing further to be said, but Leventhal lingered beside the desk hoping for something more. Mr Beard covered his blemished forehead with a trembling hand and studied an article silently.

'Goddammed fish!' said Leventhal to himself.

A thundershower began when he approached the outside door. He watched it for a while. The air was suddenly as blue as siphon glass. The blind side wall of the warehouse on the corner was streaked black, and the washed paving stones and tar seams shone in the curved street. Leventhal returned to the office to get his raincoat, and as he was going down the hall he heard Mr Beard saying in that nagging, prosecuting voice of his, 'Walks out right in the middle of everything. Right in a pinch. With everybody else swamped.'

Another voice which he identified as that of Mr Fay, the business manager, answered, 'It's funny that he should just pick up and go. There must be something up.'

'Takes unfair advantage,' Mr Beard continued. 'Like the rest of his brethren. I've never known one who wouldn't. Always please themselves first. Why didn't he offer to come back later, at least?'

Mr Fay said nothing.

Expressionless, Leventhal put on his raincoat. His arm caught in the sleeve, and he pushed it through violently. He walked out of the office with his rather hulking stride, halting in the anteroom to draw a drink from the glass cooler. While waiting for the elevator, he discovered that he was still holding the paper cup. Crumpling it, he threw it with an energetic swing between the bars into the shaft.

The trip to the ferry was short, and Leventhal did not take

off his rubber coat in the subway. The air was muggy; his face grew damp. The blades of the fan turned so slowly in the gloomy yellow light that he could count the revolutions. The shower was over by the time he reached the street, and when the boat rode out of the slip over the slight swell, the sun came out again. Leventhal stood in the open, his coat slung over his shoulder, the folds gathered in his hand. There was a slow heave about the painted and rusted hulls in the harbor. The rain had gone out to the horizon, a dark band far overreaching the faint marks of the shore. On the water the air was cooler, but on the Staten Island side the great tarnished green sheds were sweltering, the acres of cement widely spattered with sunlight. The disembarking crowd spread through them, going toward the line of busses that waited at the curb with threshing motors, in a shimmer of fumes.

Max lived in a large apartment building. His flat, like Leventhal's own on Irving Place, was a high walk-up. Children were running noisily through the foyer; the walls were covered with childish writing. A Negro janitor in a garrison cap was washing the stairs and looked angry at Leventhal's tracks. In the court, the wash swung stiff and yellow in the strong sun; the pulleys were creaking. Elena had not answered Leventhal's ring. The elder of his nephews came to the door when he knocked. The boy did not know him. Of course, Leventhal reflected, how should he? He glanced up at the stranger, raising his arm to his eyes to screen them in the sunny, dusty, desolate white corridor. Behind him the flat was dark; the shades were drawn and a lamp was burning amid the clutter of the dining-room table.

'Where's your mother?'

'She's in here. Who are you?'

'Your uncle,' said Leventhal. Coming into the hall he unavoidably pushed against the boy.

His sister-in-law hurried toward him from the kitchen. She had changed; she was heavier than when he had last seen her.

4

'Well, Elena?' he said.

'Oh, Asa, you're here?' She reached for his hand.

'Sure I'm here. You asked me to come, didn't you?'

'I tried to call you again, but they told me you were gone.'

'Why again?'

'Phillie, take Uncle's coat,' said Elena.

'Doesn't the bell work?'

'We disconnected it because of the baby.'

Leventhal dropped his raincoat into the boy's arms and followed her into the dining-room where she busied herself with clearing a chair for him.

'Oh, look at the house,' she said. 'I haven't had time to clean up. My mind is just miles away. It's already three weeks that I took down the curtains and I haven't got them back yet. And look at me.' She put down the clothes she had lifted from the chair and showed herself to him with outspread arms. Her black hair was in disorder, she was wearing a nightgown under her cotton dress, her feet were bare. She smiled mournfully. Leventhal, impassive as usual, merely nodded. He observed that her eyes were anxious, altogether too bright and too liquid; there was a superfluous energy in her movements, a suggestion of distraction or even of madness not very securely held in check. But he was too susceptible to such suggestions. He was aware of that, and he warned himself not to be hasty. He looked at her again. Her face, once florid and dark, was softer, fuller, and more pale, a little yellow. He was able to picture her as she had once been when he glanced at his nephew. He resembled her strongly. Only his slightly outcurving nose belonged to the Leventhals.

'Now, tell me, what's the matter, Elena?'

'Oh, Mickey is sick, he's terribly sick,' said Elena.

'What's he got?'

'The doctor says he doesn't know what it is. He can't do anything with him. He runs high fevers all the time. It started a couple of weeks ago. I give him to eat and he doesn't keep it down. I try everything. I don't know what I should do with

5

him. And today I got such a scare. I went into the room and I couldn't hear him breathe.'

'No, what do you mean?' said Leventhal.

'Just what I'm telling you. I couldn't hear him breathe,' she said with intensity. 'He wasn't breathing. I put my head on the pillow by his. I couldn't hear a thing. I put my hand over his nose. I couldn't feel anything. I got cold all over. I thought I was going to die myself. I ran out to call the doctor. I couldn't get him. I called his office and everywhere. I couldn't find him. So then I called you. When I got back he was breathing. He was all right. Then I tried to phone you.'

Elena's hand was resting on her bosom; the long, pointed fingers were dirty; beneath them her skin was white and very smooth.

So that was the crisis. He might have guessed it was something like that.

'He was breathing all the time,' he said somewhat roughly. 'How could he stop and start again?'

'No, no,' she insisted. 'He wasn't.'

Leventhal's composure was not perfect; it was tinged with fear. He thought, looking away from her toward a corner of the ceiling, 'What superstition! Just like in the old country. The dead can come back to life, too, I suppose, and all the rest of it.'

'Why didn't you feel his heart?' he said to her.

'I should have, probably . . .'

'You certainly should.'

'You were busy, weren't you?'

'Well, sure, I had work. . . .'

She expressed such contrition at this that he told himself to be kinder. He might as well be; he was here, the harm was done. He assured her that he had an afternoon coming. He had been with the firm six years, and if he couldn't take a few hours off on a personal matter after six years, he might as well give up. He could go away every afternoon for a month without coming close to the number of hours of overtime without

6

pay that he had put in. After he stopped talking his mind ran on in the same strain. In the civil service it was different. There you had your sick leave and you went home with a headache. And you had tenure. . . . But he did not want to dwell on this. He got up and turned his chair, as if to change the subject of his thoughts by changing his position.

'You should raise the shades,' he said to Elena. 'Why do you keep them down?'

'It makes the room cooler.'

'It cuts off the air . . . And you have to keep the lamp on. That gives off heat.'

She had moved the clothing from his chair to the table, pushing back dishes, bread, milk cartons, magazines. He guessed that she kept the shades down for no other reason than to hide her slovenliness from the neighbors across the court. He looked at the room with displeasure. And Max drifted around from Norfolk to Galveston to God knows where. Perhaps he preferred living in rooming houses and hotels.

Elena gave Philip a dollar and sent him down for beer. She took the money from her dress pocket, which was filled with change. When he had gone, Leventhal asked to see Mickey.

He was lying in Elena's hot, shadowy, close room, dozing in the large bed that stood against the wall, the sheet pulled down to his waist. His short black hair seemed damp; his mouth was open. He was wearing a sleeveless undershirt. Leventhal carefully put the back of his hand to his cheek; it was burning. In withdrawing he knocked his ring against the bedpost. The look Elena shot him startled him. He found himself raising the same hand apologetically and felt his face flush. She, however, was no longer looking at him; she was drawing the sheet over the child's shoulder. Leventhal withdrew to the hall and waited for her. She shut the door slowly, with such care that it seemed to him whole minutes passed. He gazed into the room; it grew darker about the figure on the bed partly hidden from him by the bulge of the chiffonier.

7

At last she released the knob and they returned to the dining-room.

He sat down, depressed and gloomy. He began at once to argue that Mickey should be taken to a hospital. 'Who is this doctor of yours?' he said. 'What's wrong with him that he lets you keep the boy at home? The hospital is the place for him.' But he soon realized that Elena, not the doctor, was to blame. She said, with great obstinacy, that he was better off at home, where she could take care of him herself. She showed such a dread of hospitals that at last he exclaimed, 'Don't be such a peasant, Elena!' She was silent, though she appeared more distressed than offended and probably did not under-stand him. He was annoyed with himself for being so vehement, but everything here oppressed him – the house, his sister-in-law, the sick child. How could the boy get well in such a place, in that room? 'Well, for goodness sake, Elena,' he argued in a different tone, 'a hospital is nothing to be afraid of.' She shut her eyes and shook her head; he began to shape another sentence but stopped and lay back in the mohair armchair.

Suddenly she said brightly, almost happily, 'Here's Philip and the beer.' She rose to bring glasses. There was a hunt for the bottle-opener; it was not found, and Philip pried off the caps on the handle of a metal cabinet in the kitchen. Elena wanted to make sandwiches, but Leventhal said he was not hungry. 'Oh, it'll be dinnertime soon. Your missis won't like it if your appetite is spoiled. How is she? She's such a pretty girl.' Elena smiled warmly. She did not even know his wife's name. They had met only once or twice. He hesitated to tell her that Mary had gone South for a few weeks to be with her mother. Elena would have insisted that he stay.

To change the subject, he asked about his brother. Max had been in Galveston since February. He wanted the family to join him, but the city was so crowded it was impossible to find a flat. He looked for one whenever he had time to spare.

'Why doesn't he come back to New York where he's got a flat?' said Leventhal.

'Oh, he makes good money down there; he works fifty, sixty hours a week. He sends me plenty.' She did not appear to feel abandoned or even greatly concerned about Max's absence.

Hurriedly drinking down his beer, Leventhal rose, saying that he might still go back to the office for an hour to clear up some things. Elena gave him a neighbor's phone number; he copied it into his book and told her to ring in a day or two if Mickey did not get better. At the door, he called Philip and gave him a quarter for a soda. The boy took it, muttering 'Thanks,' but with a look that refused obligation. Probably a quarter did not mean much to Philip. Elena's pocket was full of change; she must be free with it. Leventhal drew his finger along the boy's cheek. Philip dropped his head, and, somewhat disappointed and dissatisfied with himself, Leventhal left the house.

He had to wait long for a bus, and it was dusk when he reached Manhattan. Too late to be useful at the office, he nevertheless debated at South Ferry, in the tenebrous brown heat, whether to return. 'Ah, they'll get along without me today,' he finally decided. Beard would interpret his coming in now as an admission that he was in the wrong. Moreover, it might seem that he was trying to establish himself as one of the 'brethren' who was different. No, not even a hint of that, thought Leventhal. He would have an early dinner and go home. He felt dry, rather than hungry, but he must eat. He made an abrupt start and walked toward the train.

2

LEVENTHAL'S figure was burly, his head large; his nose, too, was large. He had black hair, coarse waves of it, and his eyes under their intergrown brows were intensely black and of a size unusual in adult faces. But though childishly large they were not childlike in expression. They seemed to disclose an intelligence not greatly interested in its own powers, as if preferring not to be bothered by them, indifferent; and this indifference appeared to be extended to others. He did not look sullen but rather unaccommodating, impassive. Tonight, because of the heat, he was disheveled, and he was even ordinarily not neat. His tie was pulled to the side and did not close with the collar; his shirt cuffs came out beyond his coat-sleeves and covered his thick brown wrists; his trousers sagged loose at the knees.

Leventhal came originally from Hartford. He had gone through high school there and after that had left home. His father, who had owned a small drygoods store, was a turbulent man, harsh and selfish toward his sons. Their mother had died in an insane asylum when Leventhal was eight and his brother six. At the time of her disappearance from the house, the elder Leventhal had answered their questions about her with an embittered 'gone away,' suggestive of desertion. They were nearly full grown before they learned what had happened to her.

Max did not finish high school; he left in his second year. Leventhal graduated and then went to New York, where for a time he worked for an auctioneer named Harkavy, a friend of his Uncle Schacter. Harkavy took Leventhal under his protection; he encouraged him to go to college at night and even lent him money. Leventhal took a prelegal course, but he did not do well. Perhaps the consciousness that he was attempting to do something difficult overweighed him. And the school itself – its atmosphere, especially on blue winter nights, the grimness of some of the students, many of them over fifty, world-beaten but persistent – that disturbed him. He could not study; he had never learned how, in the room behind his father's store. He finished the course, but without distinguishing himself, and he was not encouraged to go on to law school. He would have been satisfied to remain Harkavy's assistant, but the old man caught pneumonia and died. His son Daniel, then a junior at Cornell, left school to take over the business. Leventhal still remembered how he had come into the shop after the funeral in a bearskin coat, tall, blond, serious, saying emotionally to each of the clerks, 'Let's dig in and hold the line!' Leventhal, virtually the old man's ward, was too dispirited by his death and trusted himself far too little to be of much use to Daniel. The shop was soon shut down. Going back to Hartford was out of the question (his father had remarried), and Leventhal, beginning to drift, was in a short time, a few months after Harkavy's death, living in a dirty hall bedroom on the East Side, starved and thin. For a while he sold shoes on Saturdays in the basement of a department store. Later he found steady work as a fur dyer, and after that, for about a year, he clerked in a hotel for transients on lower Broadway. Then his turn came on a civil-service list and he put himself down for 'assignment anywhere in the United States.' He was sent to the Baltimore customhouse.

The life he led in Baltimore was considerably different; it was not so solitary. It came to him slowly that in New York he had taken being alone so much for granted that he was scarcely aware how miserable it made him. During his first winter in the customhouse he was invited to join a party that went to the opera in Washington on Saturdays. He sat through five or six performances with a kind of alien, skeptical interest. But he began to go out regularly. He learned to like seafood. He bought himself two suits and a topcoat – he who from October to April had sweated in a heavy camel's-hair coat old Harkavy had given him.

At a picnic on the Chesapeake shore one Fourth of July, he fell in love with a sister of one of his friends. She was a tall, heavy-moving, handsome girl. With his eyes, he followed her in the steady, fiery sparkle of the bay when she climbed to the dock from the excursion boat and started arm in arm with her brother toward the grove and the spicy smoke of the barbecue clouding in the trees. Later he saw her running in the women's race, her arms close to her sides. She was among the stragglers and stopped and walked off the field, laughing and wiping her face and throat with a handkerchief of the same material as her silk summer dress. Leventhal was standing near her brother. She came up to them and said, 'Well, I *used* to be able to run when I was smaller.' That she was still not accustomed to thinking of herself as a woman, and a beautiful woman, made Leventhal feel very tender toward her. She was in his mind when he watched the contestants in the three-legged race hobbling over the meadow. He noticed one in particular, a man with red hair who struggled forward, angry with his partner, as though the race were a pain and a humiliation which he could wipe out only by winning. 'What a difference,' Leventhal said to himself. 'What a difference in people.'

He ran in the egg race, he swam, he felt his spirits thawed out that day. He was with Mary most of the afternoon. They took their sandwiches to the beach, walking half-shoe over in the white sand to find a place to themselves. From sundown, when they started back, till they came into the heat of the sluggish harbor among the heels of tankers, and through the yellow film spread over the water and in the air by the mills and piers, they sat together on the fantail of the little steamer. Her brother was waiting for her in the crowd at the gangplank, and they said good night in the noise of the steam plunging loosely skyward.

By autumn they were engaged, and Leventhal's success amazed him. He felt that the harshness of his life had disfigured him, and that this disfigurement would be apparent to a girl like Mary and would repel her. He was not entirely sure of her, and, in fact, something terrible did happen a month after the engagement. Mary confessed that she found herself unable to break off an old attachment to another man, a married man. In the pain of the moment, Leventhal almost lost his power to speak. He looked at her – they were in a restaurant. Then he asked if she had gone on seeing this man during the engagement. She said that she had and only at that moment seemed to realize how serious the matter was. He started to leave, and when she tried to hold him back, he pushed her, and she lost her footing in the booth and fell. He helped her rise; her mouth had gone white, and she averted her eyes from him. They left the restaurant together – she even waited while he paid the check – but outside they instantly separated without speaking.

About two years later she sent him a friendly letter. He did not know how to reply. It stood on his dresser for more than a month, confronting him nightly and overriding all his other concerns. He was still deliberating when he received a second letter from her. In it she asked him directly to consider how harassed she had been; she admitted that she had tried to end her infatuation by becoming engaged to him but that that was not the only reason; she had not chosen him indiscriminately. Leventhal found this letter easier to answer. They began to correspond. At Christmas he went down to visit her, and they were married by a justice of the peace in Wilmington.

He had meanwhile moved back to New York, having left Baltimore a few weeks after the engagement was broken. Daniel Harkavy had somehow landed on a trade paper. Leventhal, who had been editing a book of departmental regulations, thought that he, too, could handle that kind of job. He got in touch with Harkavy, and Harkavy wrote back that he was sure he could place him on a paper if he wanted to come to New York. Harkavy had many connections. Leventhal packed his trunk one week end and sent it to Harkavy's rooming house. He could not bear to stay in Baltimore; he was too wretched. He could not think of it later without flushing and wincing. A man brought up on hardships should have known better than to cut himself adrift. Even then he had realized that it was foolhardy to throw up his job and worse than that to put faith in Harkavy, and he told his chief that he was resigning to take another position. He was ashamed to tell him the truth.

He found Harkavy looking a little different. He was losing his hair and he had grown a red mustache. There was a certain swagger about him; he had taken to wearing large bow ties and black suede shoes. But he was essentially the same. He had written about his connections, but he could think of only one man to call on. This was a middle-aged Kentuckian by the name of Williston, short and ruddy, with a broad head across which his brown hair was brushed with a sort of backwoodsman's Sunday care. He was one of those people who keep their regional traits after twenty years in New York. It was a cold fall day, and he had an electric heater beside his desk. He sat back in his swivel chair, occasionally raising a foot to warm it over the coils.

No, he said, there was no vacancy in his office. An experienced man might find something even now, in bad times. An inexperienced one didn't have a chance. Unless by a freak — his shoe shone over the burnished heater — unless he knew someone very influential.

'We don't,' Harkavy said. 'We have no pull. And how will he get experience?'

He wouldn't suggest, said Williston, that Leventhal try to get a job running copy with a pack of boys at six bucks a week. Even such jobs were scarce. He would suggest that he stick to his trade. Leventhal's face grew dark, more with self-condemnation than with resentment. He might have asked for a transfer instead of quitting the civil service outright and waited it out, no matter how long it took. He imagined that Williston partly divined what had happened. It stupefied him, what he had done. But, Harkavy was saying, speaking of himself, he had gotten his job by luck, without experience. Oh, no, Williston answered, his father's name counted for something in the antiques field – Harkavy worked on a paper for auctioneers and antique dealers. 'Leventhal was with my father and me for a long time,' Harkavy told him. And Williston lifted his shoulders and gazed into the face of the heater as if to say, 'In that case, nothing's too good for him.' He seemed to regret this when he saw Leventhal's pained, lowering look. Of course he would do what he could, he said, but he didn't want them to believe that much could be done. He would phone some people, and meanwhile Leventhal could begin making the rounds.

He began in a spirit of utter hopelessness. The smaller trade papers simply turned him away. The larger gave him applications to fill out; occasionally he spent a few minutes with a personnel manager and had the opportunity to shake someone's hand. Gradually he became peculiarly aggressive and, avoiding the receptionists, he would make his way into an inner office, stop anyone who appeared to have authority, and introduce himself. He was met with astonishment, with coldness, and with anger. He often grew angry himself. They were frightened, he observed to Harkavy, when you got out of line, out of the proper channel. But the channel led out of the door. How could they expect you to stay in it? He discussed it reasonably enough with Harkavy, but the provocations and near-quarrels continued, and in the heat of these provocations he frequently lost sight of his real object. He might remind himself while shaving or when he entered the bank to draw on his savings that he was after all defeating his own purpose, that anyone who, on an outside chance, had a job to give would not give it to him. But he did not change.

This queer condition lasted for about two months. Then, since Harkavy was becoming increasingly difficult to live with (several nights a week he entertained a woman friend and Leventhal, turned out of the room, went to a movie or sat in a cafeteria), and since his money was running low, Leventhal decided to take any job at all, the next that came his way – he was thinking of trying his old hotel on lower Broadway – when he received a note from Williston asking him to come in. One of his men was sick and had to go to Arizona for the winter, and Leventhal could fill his place till he came back.

So it was through Williston that Leventhal got his start in the profession. He was grateful and worked hard for him, and he discovered he had a knack for the job. From June until the end of summer he was idle again – that, too, was a difficult period. But now he had a season's experience and he found a place at last with Burke-Beard and Company. Apart from his occasional trouble with Beard, he was satisfied. He was really better off than in the civil service.

He said occasionally to Mary, revealing his deepest feelings, 'I was lucky. I got away with it.' He meant that his bad start, his mistakes, the things that might have wrecked him, had somehow combined to establish him. He had almost fallen in with that part of humanity of which he was frequently mindful (he never forgot the hotel on lower Broadway), the part that did not get away with it – the lost, the outcast, the overcome, the effaced, the ruined.

3

Leventhal's father-in-law had recently died, and his mother-in-law had been persuaded by the family to give up her house in Baltimore and to live in Charleston with her son. Mary had gone to help her move.

In her absence Leventhal had been eating in an Italian restaurant in the neighborhood. It was in the basement of an old tenement. The stucco walls were almost black. It had a damp, woody smell from the sawdust sprinkled over the plank floor. But it suited him; the meals were cheap, and he generally did not have to wait for a table. Tonight, however, there was only one available. The waiter led him to it. It was in the corner behind a projecting wall which cut off the breeze of the fan. He was about to protest and opened his mouth impatiently, but the waiter, a dark man with thin hair curved over his perspiring forehead, anticipated him with a tired and rather insincere shrug, indicating with a motion of his toweled arm that the place was filled. Leventhal tossed his hat down, moved aside the dishes, and leaned forward on his elbows. Near the kitchen step, the proprietor and his wife were finishing their dinner. She gave Leventhal a look of recognition which he acknowledged, making a stir in his chair. The waiter brought his meal, an omelet in a chipped, blackened enamel dish with tomato sauce hardened on the rim, a salad, and some canned apricots. He ate, and his mood gradually improved. The coffee was sweet and thick; he swallowed even the sediment and put the cup down with a sigh. He lit a cigar. There was no one waiting for the table and he sat awhile, bent backward and puffing, clasping his hands on the densely growing hair on the back of his neck. From the tavern across the way came the slow notes of a guitar, the lighter carried away, the deeper repeated tranquilly.

Presently he shoved a tip under the saucer and went out.

There was still a redness in the sky, like the flame at the back of a vast baker's oven; the day hung on, gaping fierily over the black of the Jersey shore. The Hudson had a low luster, and the sea was probably no more numbing in its cold, Leventhal imagined, than the subway under his feet was in its heat; the trains rushing by under the gratings and along the slanting brown rock walls seemed to set off charges of metal dust. He passed through a small park where the double circle of benches were jammed. There were lines before each drinking fountain, the warm water limping and jetting into the stone basins. On all sides of the green square, the traffic of cars and cabs whipped endlessly, and the cumbersome busses crawled groaning, steering down from the tall blue oblong of light at the summit of the street through a bluish pallor. In the bushy, tree-grown corners, children played and screamed, and a revivalist band sang and drummed and trumpeted on one of the sidewalks. Leventhal did not stay long in the park. He strolled homeward. He thought he would mix a cold drink and lie down beside an open window.

Leventhal's apartment was spacious. In a better neighborhood, or three stories lower, it would have rented for twice the amount he paid. But the staircase was narrow and stifling and full of turns. Though he went up slowly, he was out of breath when he reached the fourth floor, and his heart beat thickly. He rested before unlocking the door. Entering, he threw down his raincoat and flung himself on the tapestry-covered low bed in the front room. Mary had moved some of the chairs into the corners and covered them with sheets. She could not depend on him to keep the windows shut and the shades and curtains drawn during the day. This afternoon the cleaning woman had been in and there was a pervasive odor of soap powder. He got up and opened a window. The curtains waved once and then were as motionless as before. There was a movie house strung with lights across the street; on its roof a water tank sat heavily uneven on its timbers; the cowls of the chimneys, which rattled in the slightest stir of air, were still.

The motor of the refrigerator began to run. The ice trays were empty and rattled. Wilma, the cleaning woman, had defrosted the machine and forgotten to refill them. He looked for a bottle of beer he had noticed yesterday; it was gone. There was nothing inside except a few lemons and some milk. He drank a glass of milk and it refreshed him. He had already taken off his shirt and was sitting on the bed unlacing his shoes when there was a short ring of the bell. Eagerly he pulled open the door and shouted, 'Who is it?' The flat was unbearably empty. He hoped someone had remembered that Mary was away and had come to keep him company. There was no response below. He called out again, impatiently. It was very probable that someone had pushed the wrong button, but he heard no other doors opening. Could it be a prank? This was not the season for it. Nothing moved in the stair well, and it only added to his depression to discover how he longed for a visitor. He stretched out on the bed, pulling a pillow from beneath the spread and doubling it up. He thought he would doze off. But a little later he found himself standing at the window, holding the curtains with both hands. He was under the impression that he had slept. It was only eight-thirty by the whirring electric clock on the night table, however. Only five minutes had passed.

'No, I shouldn't have gone,' he said to himself. He was suddenly full of misgivings. It was a mistake to run out of the office like that. If he had considered the thing sensibly, he would have waited till evening. Five minutes more and Elena would have called him again. Then why hadn't he waited? Did he actually want to stand Beard up for once, was that why he had left the office? No, and Beard's remark was disgusting, besides. It did not come as a surprise. He had known

19

all along that he was capable of making it. If a man disliked you, he would dislike you for all the reasons he could think of. It was not important, merely disgusting. All the same, he shouldn't have gone. He washed his face, put on his shirt, and left the apartment. His difficulty, he reflected, was that when he didn't have time to consider, when pressure was put on him, he behaved like a fool. That, mainly, was what troubled him. For instance, last week at the press Dunhill, the lino-typer, sold him a ticket he didn't want. He protested that he didn't care for shows and had no use for one ticket – this was before Mary left. But because Dunhill had insisted, he bought the ticket. He gave it to one of the girls at the office. Now if only he had been able to say at the outset, 'I will not buy your ticket . . .' He muttered, 'Well, what do I do it for?' frown-ing. One of his neighbors appeared, bare-chested and in tennis shorts, and deposited a clinking bag of bottles to be removed by the janitor.

The Porto Rican superintendent, Mr Nunez, in a straw hat, his dark feet in Chinese straw slippers, was sitting on the stoop. Leventhal asked him whether he had noticed anyone ringing his bell, and he answered that he had been on the stoop for half an hour and that no one had gone out in the last fifteen minutes or come in. 'Maybe you heard the radio,' he suggested. 'Sometimes I think somebody is in the house talking to me, but it's the radio somewhere.'

'No, the bell rang,' Leventhal said positively; he looked seriously at the superintendent. 'Was it the dumb-waiter bell, you think?'

'If somebody was fooling around the basement. I didn't touch it tonight.'

Leventhal set out for the park. Perhaps it was a radio, though he did not think so. Perhaps something in the wiring, affected by the heat – he did not know much about electricity – or the dumb-waiter. What really concerned him was that perhaps his nerves were to blame and that he had imagined the ring just as he had imagined that he had slept. Since

20

Mary's departure his nerves had been unsteady. He kept the bathroom light burning all night. Somewhat ashamed of himself, he had yesterday closed the bathroom door before getting into bed, but he had left the light on. This was absurd, this feeling that he was threatened by something while he slept. And that was not all. He imagined that he saw mice darting along the walls. There actually were mice in the apartment. The building was old; there were bound to be some nesting under the floors. He had no dread of them, and yet he had begun to jerk his head around at the suspicion of a movement. And now he had been unable to fall asleep. Heat had never hitherto interfered with his sleep. He was sure he was unwell.

The park was even more crowded than before, and noisy. There was another revivalist band on the corner, and the blare of the two joined confusingly above the other sounds. The lamps were yellowed, covered with flies and moths. On one of the paths an old man, sunburned, sinewy, in a linen cap, was shining shoes. The fountain ran with a green, leaden glint. Children in their underclothing waded and rolled in the spray, the parents looking on. Eyes seemed softer than by day, and larger, and gazed at one longer, as though in the dark heat some interspace of reserve had been crossed and strangers might approach one another with a kind of recognition. You looked and thought, at least, that you knew whom you had seen.

Some such vague thing was in Leventhal's mind while he waited his turn at the drinking spout, when suddenly he had a feeling that he was not merely looked at but watched. Unless he was greatly mistaken a man was scrutinizing him, pacing slowly with him as the line moved. 'He seems to know me,' he thought. Or was the man merely lounging there, was he only a bystander? Instantly Leventhal became reserved, partly as a rebuff to his nerves, his busy imagination. But it was not imagination. When he stepped forward, the man moved, too, lowering his head as if to hide a grin at the thin-lipped formality of Leventhal's expression. There was no hint of

21

amusement, however, in his eyes – he was now very close; they were derisive and harsh.

'Who's this customer?' Leventhal said to himself. 'An actor if I ever saw one. My God, my God, what kind of a fish is this? One of those guys who want you to think they can see to the bottom of your soul.' He tried to stare him down, only now realizing how insolent he was. But the man did not go. He was taller than Leventhal but not nearly so burly; large-framed but not robust. 'If he starts something,' Leventhal thought, 'I'll grab his right arm and pull him off balance . . . No, his left arm and pull towards my left; that's my stronger side. And when he's going down I'll give him a rabbit punch. But why should he start anything? There's no reason.'

He was squared and resolute; nevertheless there was a tremor in his arms, and during all of it he felt that he himself was the cause of his agitation and suspicion, with his unreliable nerves. Then in astonishment he heard the stranger utter his name.

'What, do you know me?' he asked loudly.

'Do I? You're Leventhal, aren't you? Why shouldn't I know you? I thought you might not recognize me, though. We met only a few times, and I suppose I look a little different than I used to.'

'Oh, Allbee, isn't it? Allbee?' Leventhal said slowly, with gradual recognition.

'Kirby Allbee. So you do recognize me?'

'Well, I'll be damned,' said Leventhal, but he said it rather indifferently. What if it were Kirby Allbee? And he certainly looked changed, but what of that?

Just then several people in the line pushed against him. It was his turn at the spout and, as he took a swallow of the warm water, he looked sidewise at Allbee. The woman who had preceded him – she was painted heavily and looked like a chorus girl who had slipped out of the theater for a breath of air – was in Allbee's way, and while he was trying to step aside, caught in the circle around the spout, Leventhal walked off.

He had never liked this Allbee, but he had never really thought much about him. How was it, then, that his name came to him so readily? He had a poor memory for names; still he saw the man and recognized him in a moment. 'What a box, the mind,' Leventhal thought with something approaching a smile. 'You'd just as soon expect hair to grow in your hand as some of the things that come out of it.'

'Hey, wait!'

Allbee was dodging through the crowd after him. 'What does he want?' Leventhal irritably asked himself.

'Wait, where are you going?'

Leventhal did not answer. What business was it of his?

'Are you going home?'

'Yes, by and by,' he said distantly.

'Well, now you've found out that I still exist and you're going home, is that it?' He had a curious smile.

'Why should I doubt that you exist?' Leventhal was smiling also, but without much mirth. 'Is there any reason why you shouldn't? I'm afraid I don't get it.'

'I mean that you just wanted to have a look at me.'

'Pardon?' said Leventhal. He drew up his brows. 'To have a look?'

'Yes, I think you did want to, to see how I've made out. The results.'

'I came out to cool off a little.' He was beginning to be really annoyed. 'What makes you think you've got anything to do with it?'

'Well, I didn't expect this,' Allbee said. 'Of course, I didn't know what to expect. I wondered what line you were going to take with me.' He brought his lips together as if to hold back laughter, slightly jeering, presumptuous, and drew his hand down his cheek over the blond bristles, and all the while his deeply ringed eyes looked angrily into Leventhal's. He appeared to be saying that he knew perfectly well what he was saying and that it was effrontery and bad acting to deny it. 'Just like a bad actor to accuse everyone of bad acting,' thought Leventhal, but he was troubled nevertheless. What was he after? He studied Allbee more closely; until now he had not noticed how seedy he looked, like one of those men you saw sleeping off their whisky on Third Avenue, lying in the doorways or on the cellar hatches, dead to the cold or the racket or the straight blaze of the sun in their faces. He drank, too; that was certain. His voice was thick. He had fair hair parted in the center over his large forehead, moist in the lamp-light. He wore a flimsy shirt of material that must have been imitation silk; it opened on the chest on the dirty hem of an undershirt; his light cotton suit was soiled.

'The fact remains that you wanted to see me,' he resumed.

'You're mistaken.'

'Well, you got my letter, didn't you? And I asked you to meet me here tonight. . . ?'

'You wrote me a letter? What in the world for? I never got a letter from you. I don't understand this.'

'Neither do I; if you didn't get it, this would be quite a coincidence. But,' he went on, smiling, 'of course you're pretending you didn't get the letter.'

'Why should I pretend?' said Leventhal excitedly. 'What reason have I got to pretend? I don't know what letter you're talking about. You haven't got anything to write me for. I haven't thought about you in years, frankly, and I don't know why you think I care whether you exist or not. What, are we related?'

'By blood? No, no . . . heavens!' Allbee laughed.

Leventhal stared into his laughing face and then began to walk away, whereupon Allbee thrust his arm straight before him and held him back. Leventhal grasped it, but he did not jerk according to his plan. He felt no resistance to his grip. It was he rather than Allbee who was off balance, and he removed his hand; he appeared to scowl – in reality he was clearing his throat – and he said, not at all loudly, 'What do you want?'

'Oh, that's more sensible.' Allbee straightened his shoulders

24

and pulled down his cuffs. 'I don't want to wrestle. I'm probably no match for you. I wanted to talk. I didn't think there would be any physical violence. That's not how you people go about things. Not with violence.'

'What people are you talking about?' asked Leventhal.

Allbee did not reply to this. 'I wanted to take up a few things with you, which is why I wrote,' he said.

'I tell you again, I never got a letter from you.'

'So you're sticking to that.' Allbee smiled deprecatingly as though wondering why Leventhal refused every opportunity to get rid of this clumsy pretense. 'Then why are you here? You wanted to see but not be seen, and you're mad because you got caught.'

'I'm here because I live down the street a way. Why don't you own up instead that you wanted to catch me. God only knows what for and what you've got to say.'

Allbee moved his large face from side to side in denial. 'It's the other way around. You knew I was here ... well, it's immaterial. As for what I have to say to you, I've got plenty to say. But you know that.'

'That's news to me, too.'

Allbee grinned at him with an intimation of a shared secret that aroused and vexed Leventhal, and sickened him.

'Let's sit down,' Allbee proposed.

'Damn him, he's got me, he's got hold of me,' Leventhal thought. 'He's become some kind of a crank. I shouldn't have gone out. I should have tried to sleep, after the day I've had.'

They found a place on a bench.

'I haven't got much time. I get up early. What do you want?'

Allbee regarded him. 'You've become stouter,' he said. 'Darker, too. How much do you weigh?'

'About two hundred and ten.'

'That's too much. It's bad for your heart to carry so much weight. Don't you feel it in this weather? I'll bet your heart takes a beating from it. You have a lot of stairs to climb.'

'How do you know that?'

'Oh, I happen to know that you live on the fourth floor.'

'*How* do you know?' Leventhal insisted.

'I just happen to. Is it some kind of a secret? Isn't anybody allowed to know that you live on the fourth floor?'

'What else do you know about me?'

'You work for the Burke-Beard people. You put out one of their sheets.'

'Any more?'

'Your wife is away. She is . . .' he glanced over as though to see if he was entirely right, 'down South. Went a few days ago. These things aren't hard to find out.'

'Did you ring my bell before?'

'Did I ring it? No, why should I?'

Leventhal grimly looked at him in the light that came through the leaves. He had been spying on him, and the mystery was why! How long had he been keeping watch on him and for what reason – what grotesque reason? Allbee returned his look, examining him as he was examined, in concentration and seriousness, his lower jaw slipped to one side, his glum, contemplative eyes filled with a green and leaden color. And in the loom of these eyes and with the warmth of the man's breath on his face, for they were crowded together on the bench, Leventhal suddenly felt that he had been singled out to be the object of some freakish, insane process, and for an instant he was filled with dread. Then he recovered and told himself there was nothing to be afraid of. The man was a crank and irritating, and certainly it was creepy to think of being observed secretly. But there was nothing so alarming about this Allbee. He had become a bum and a drunk and he seemed to have an idea or a twist about him, a delusion; perhaps it was even invented. How could you tell about these drunks? There must be reasons, but they were beyond anybody's ability to find out – smoky, cloudy, alcoholic. Allbee had taken him by surprise. It was surprising. And in his present state of mind he was, moreover, easily

26

carried away by things. He felt unwell, and that didn't help. He gave a steadying, wary pull to his shoulders.

Still looking at him, Allbee said, 'It's hard to know what kind of a man you are, personally.'

'Oh, it's me you want to talk about?'

'Now, you see? There's an example. You're outspoken, but are you leading away from the main thing? You are. It's a maneuver. I don't know whether you're smart or crude. Maybe you don't even care much about the main thing.'

'What don't I care about?'

'Ah, come on, drop it, Leventhal, drop it! You know what it is.'

'I don't.'

There was a pause; then Allbee said with an effort at patience, 'Well, if that's the way it's got to be – I guess you want me to go over the whole business. I thought it wouldn't be necessary, but all right. *Dill's Weekly*. You remember *Dill's Weekly?* Mr Rudiger?'

'Of course I do. Sure. Rudiger. I have it written down in an old appointment book I've been hoping to run across; his name keeps getting away from me. Oh, Rudiger,' he said reminiscently and began to smile, but with a line of constraint about his mouth.

'So you do remember?'

'Naturally.'

'Now what about the rest of it? No, you won't go on to the rest of it. You'll make me do it. Okay, I will. It was through Rudiger that you got at me.'

'Got at you?' said Leventhal, astonished. He turned his hot face to Allbee, and his scalp seemed to descend toward his brows.

'Got back at me. Got even with me,' Allbee said with great distinctness. His lower lip came forward, it was dry and cracked; his nose looked swollen, all at once. His eyes were open to the full.

'No, no,' Leventhal muttered. 'You're mistaken. I never did.'

Allbee passed his hand before him in a movement of denial and shook his head slowly. 'I couldn't be mistaken about this.'

'No? Well, you are.'

'Did I get you an appointment with Rudiger? I fixed you up with an interview, didn't I?'

'Yes, you did. Yes . . .'

'Then you went in and deliberately insulted Rudiger, put on some act with him, called him filthy names, deliberately insulted him to get me in bad. Rudiger is hot blooded and he turned on me for it. You knew he would. It was calculated. It worked out just as you thought it would. You were clever as hell. He didn't even give me a week's notice. He turned me out.'

'That's all wrong. I heard you weren't with Dill's any more. Harkavy told me. But it couldn't have been my fault. I'm sure you're mistaken. Rudiger wouldn't blame you for the run-in we had. It was his fault, too.'

'Rudiger did,' said Allbee. 'He was plenty clear about it. He almost killed himself blowing his top at me. And that was what you wanted.'

'All I wanted was a job,' Leventhal declared, 'and Rudiger was tough and nasty. There's something wrong with that man. Hot blood isn't the word for it. He's vicious. I didn't exactly keep my temper down. I admit that. Well, if that's the reason I may be to blame in a way, indirectly. But you say . . .'

'I say you're entirely to blame, Leventhal.' He opened his mouth and appeared to hold his breath an instant as he smiled. Leventhal's attempt to keep a clear head came to nothing; he felt himself slipping into confusion.

'And why did I do it, do you say?'

'For revenge. Damn! You want to go over the whole thing to make sure that I'm really on. I really am on, Leventhal. Jesus, do you think I still haven't figured it out? Give me a little more credit than that; I was on a long time ago. But if you want me to pull it all out, I'm willing. I'll start farther back: Williston's house. There was a party.'

'Yes, that's where we met, at Williston's.'

'Ah, well, you recall it. I thought you'd balk all along the line and refuse to remember. Fine. Your friend was there too, another Jewish fellow – you mentioned his name before.'

'Harkavy.'

'That's the one, Harkavy. We're making headway.' He laughed aloud. 'Well, that's the key. A Jewish fellow. Lord, you want to draw the whole business out. Does it have to be drawn out? I suppose it has to. You were sore at something I said about Jews. Does that come back to you?'

'No. Yes, it does. It does, too,' he corrected himself, frowning. 'I also remember that you were drunk.'

'Wrong. I was liquored up but not drunk. Positively not. You Jews have funny ideas about drinking. Especially the one that all Gentiles are born drunkards. You have a song about it – "Drunk he is, drink he must, because he is a Goy ... *Schicker*."' He had ceased laughing; he looked morose.

'Bah!' Leventhal said contemptuously. He pushed at the bar of the bench and got to his feet.

'Where are you going?'

'I had nothing to do with your losing that job. It was probably your own fault. You must have given Rudiger a plenty good reason to fire you, and I can imagine what it was. I'm not the sort of man who carries grudges. It's all in your mind. I remember all about that night at Williston's, but you were drunk and I didn't hold it against you. Besides it was a long time ago, and I don't see your object in looking me up just to remind me of it. Good night!'

He walked away. Allbee stood up and shouted after him, 'You wanted to get even. You did plan it. You did it on purpose!' People turned to look at them, and Leventhal increased his pace.

'If he follows me now I'll punch him in the jaw. I'll knock

29

him down,' he thought. 'I swear, I'll throw him down and smash his ribs for him!'

He opened the mailbox when he got home and found the note. It was signed 'Sincerely, Kirby A.' and said that he would be in the park at nine. Why the park? Well, why such an accusation? What an idea! The one made about as much sense as the other. There was no stamp on the envelope; Allbee must have delivered it himself. Chances were it was he who had rung the bell.

'Some judge of time, that Nunez,' Leventhal growled, starting up the stairs.

4

HE fell asleep without difficulty and slept deeply. The alarm clock on the night table awoke him, and he seized it and clapped down the catch. Then he crouched down at the window – he was naked – and looked over the sill. Already, at half-past seven, the street looked deadened with heat and light. The clouds were heavily suspended and slow. To the south and east, the air was brassy, the factories were beginning to smolder and faced massively, India red, brown, into the sun and across the hot green netting of the bridges. There was a hard encircling rumble of trucks and subterranean trains. Nunez was out in front, cleaning the sidewalk with a bucket of water and the stub of a broom. His wife was busy at the window boxes. New white strings stretched up to the lintel; she was leaning out, training vines on them.

Leventhal washed and shaved. Allbee's note was lying on the kitchen table. He reread it and threw it into the pail beside the sink. He was about to slam down the lid but checked himself – he was behaving as he would have yesterday when he was at the end of his patience – and, almost smiling at himself, he set it in place lightly and pushed the pail toward the wall with his foot. Well, he could have been forgiven yesterday for losing his patience or even his head. What a day! With all that he had weighing on him already, this Allbee shows up to add his little bit. He must have brooded over the affair for years, until he convinced himself that Rudiger had fired him because of that interview. Of course, it was true enough that Rudiger had a rotten bad temper, probably was born bad-tempered, but not even he would fire an employee, not for what the man himself had done but because of someone he had recommended. 'How could he?' Leventhal asked himself. 'Not a good worker; never.' It was absurd. Allbee must have been fired for drunkenness. When could you get a drinking man to acknowledge that he had gotten into trouble through drinking? Especially when he was far gone? And this Allbee was far gone.

He put on the wrinkled brown summer flannels he had thrown over the foot of the bed last night, and a pair of white shoes. He remembered to shut the windows and draw the drapes. The room was darkened. He took a handkerchief from the dresser and came across a statement on tax deductions for the year, a gloomy reminder of Mr Beard and the office. Instead of keeping such things in the desk where they belonged, Mary had the habit of putting them under the linens. Irritated, he buried the paper deeper and roughly shoved the drawer shut. He went out with a frown. Beard would probably send for him and call him down, ostensibly for some mistake which he would dig up. Or he would delegate someone – he had done that before; perhaps that pinch-nosed, knob-faced little Millikan, his son-in-law. 'If he sicks him on me . . .' he thought. But he did not know what threat to make. And now it seemed to him that he had rested badly. His legs were tired, his head ached, and his eyes – he examined them in the long mirror in the pillar before the coffeeshop – were bloodshot; he looked drawn. He shook his head in concern. The corners of the glass were flaming with the blue and red of the spectrum.

For a while he was so preoccupied with what awaited him at the office that he forgot about Allbee. He did not think of him again until he was on the subway. He was even less amused than before. From a sober person – that is, from a normal person, someone you would have to reckon with – such an accusation would be no trifle. With Allbee it came out like a stunt: the note, the bell ringing, the acting. And not quite a stunt, for a stunt was done deliberately, whereas it was questionable whether this queer, beaten, probably suffering Allbee was in control of his actions. Suffering? Of course, suffering, Leventhal told himself gravely: down and out, living in a moldy hotel somewhere, hanging out in bars, sleeping whole days, picked up off the streets by the paddywagon or the ambulance, haunted in his mind by wrongs or faults of his own which he turned into wrongs against himself; and that stirring around of the thoughts and feelings, that churning – everybody experienced it, but for a man like that it must be ugly, terrible, those thoughts wheeling around. It was something like this that Leventhal was thinking of when he occasionally said that he had gotten away with it. But (without taking credit for it; he might have fallen in another way) his character was different. Some men behaved as though they had a horse under them and went through life at a gallop. Or thought they could, at any rate. He was not that way.

He had met Allbee several times at Williston's house. In those unsettled days when he was jobhunting, the Willistons used to give parties frequently. Perhaps they still did; he had not seen them in several years. Because they were room-mates, he and Harkavy were usually invited together. Allbee had shown an antipathy toward Harkavy, and Leventhal recalled that he, as a matter of fact, had been offended by several of Allbee's remarks and by his attitude generally. Mrs Allbee was a quiet blonde. He wondered what had become of her; had she left him, divorced him? He found that he retained a distinct image of her, of the firmness of her face and the form of her eyes, gray eyes. He had thought her much too good for the husband lounging beside her with a glass, staring at the other guests and smiling. He might have been asked by Williston to classify them, he eyed them so, spread out there on the sofa, large-limbed, his face swelling with smiles. From time to time he made a comment to his wife, fixing his look on someone so that it was uncomfortably evident whom he was talking about. He frequently picked out Harkavy, which Leventhal resented, Harkavy himself seemingly unaware that he was being stared at.

It had to be admitted that Harkavy attracted stares. He

liked to talk and at these parties he was easily kindled, for some reason. Any trifle made him enthusiastic, and when he spoke his hands flew and his brows slanted up, sharpening the line of his nose. His eyes were light, round, and depthless, his fair hair was fading back, the curls thinning. Allbee studied him, grinning and curious; Harkavy appeared to delight him. He must have had some witty things to say about him for he sometimes made his wife smile, and as a rule she did not respond to his remarks. Harkavy may have noticed this. Leventhal had never asked him about it, but perhaps it did light on his consciousness, for all his traits, the Jewish especially, became accentuated. He carried on, giving imitations of auctioneers, in reality burlesquing his father. Leventhal watched, unsmiling and even forbidding. The laughter and the somewhat ambiguous applause, sometimes led by Allbee, seemed to excite Harkavy, and he would start again, working up the bid. The Willistons laughed with the guests, though more moderately and with a trace of anxiety about Allbee. Leventhal himself, at times, could not help joining in. But he was annoyed.

The incident Allbee had referred to occurred one night when Harkavy and a girl he had brought to the party were singing spirituals and old ballads. It was late, and everyone else was silent, rather tired. That evening Harkavy had been a little more restrained than usual. He sang poorly, but at least he did not provoke laughter and was not trying to. Nor did the girl sing well; she hesitated over words. It was pleasant, however. Halfway through a ballad Allbee interrupted; regardless of his denial, he was drunk.

'Why do you sing such songs?' he said. '*You* can't sing them.'

'Why not, I'd like to know?' said the girl.

'Oh, you, too,' said Allbee with his one-cornered smile. 'It isn't right for you to sing them. You have to be born to them. If you're not born to them, it's no use trying to sing them.'

His wife spoke up. 'Don't pay any attention to him,' she said. 'You sing it very nicely.'

'Aaah, yes he does,' he said contemptuously.

'Why, thank you, Mrs Allbee,' said Harkavy. 'It's a lovely song.'

'Go on, Dan, go on with it,' Phoebe Williston urged him. And Leventhal said, 'Sing the rest of it.'

'I'm going to,' Harkavy replied, and began over.

'No, no, no!' Allbee broke in again. 'You shouldn't sing those old songs. You have to be bred to them.'

His wife colored and said, 'Kirby, don't be like that.'

'Oh, I don't mind, ma'am.' Harkavy drew in his chin and crossed his arms, his round eyes glimmering.

'Sing, Dan,' said Leventhal.

'Sing a psalm. I don't object to your singing. Sing one of the psalms. I'd love to hear it. Go ahead. I would,' said Allbee.

'I don't know any psalms.'

'Then any Jewish song. Something you've really got feeling for. Sing us the one about the mother.' And with a drunken look of expectancy he bent forward, leaning on his knees, and pretended to prepare to listen. It was apparent to everyone that he was deeply pleased; he smiled at Harkavy and the girl, and he had a glance for Leventhal, too. His wife seemed quietly to dissociate herself from him. The Willistons were embarrassed. Allbee was not merely an acquaintance but a friend, and Williston later tried to make excuses for him and explain away the insult.

That was what had happened. Leventhal had naturally been angry, but not for long. He had shrugged it off. Did Allbee think something like that would make him go to such lengths for revenge? He was an idiot if he did. He overestimated the magnitude of the insult and his power to be insulting. Or did he think that on that night he had revealed something that was not plain before? Then he was twice as idiotic. 'And if I were mad, is that what I would do?' thought

Leventhal. 'He gives himself an awful lot of credit for nothing. Who does he think he is?'

That he had afterwards asked Allbee for an introduction to Rudiger should have shown how much importance he attached to the incident. At that time, Williston's man had returned from Arizona and Leventhal was looking for another place. Williston gave him a very good reference letter which made it easier to get interviews. However, several months went by before Leventhal was hired by Burke-Beard and Company, and during those months he was despondent and became quarrelsome once again, difficult, touchy, exaggerating, illogical, overly familiar. Reports of this reached Williston, who called him in and lectured him. Leventhal was bitter and suspicious of him and he offered to return the letter – foolishly, he now realized. But he thought that Williston regretted writing it.

It was his own idea to approach Allbee about a job at *Dill's*. Williston endorsed it and may have been instrumental in getting Allbee to introduce him to Rudiger. Or perhaps Allbee agreed in order to make up for his unpleasantness. Williston tried continually to explain it away. You had to know Allbee when he was sober, he said; he was intelligent and decent. His New England upbringing was behind his drinking; there were ministers in his family, influences to throw off, and once he threw them off he would be another man. Leventhal indifferently acknowledged that that might be so; he had no particular grudge against him. 'I'll be much obliged to him if he gets me the introduction. What a break if I could land a job with an outfit like that.'

The interview at *Dill's* still troubled him.

Rudiger kept him waiting for nearly an hour in the reception room and for a few minutes more in his office. He was watching several tugs shouldering a huge liner up the river and his back was turned. But as soon as he faced about, Leventhal knew at once that he had nothing to hope for; he saw even before Rudiger uttered his first word that he did not want him. He was a short man, broad featured and red; his hair was intensely red. He had a mustache of short golden hairs overspread by a powerful nose with the cartilages widely separated at the tip. He spoke energetically, peremptorily, quickly, in a husky tone. At the outset Leventhal thought, 'I've hit him at a bad time.' Later he could not decide whether he had come upon him in an unusual mood of great stress and aroused cruelty or whether Rudiger had only treated him as he generally did people whom he didn't want to hire and who were wasting his time. In telling Harkavy about it that same afternoon, Leventhal said, 'He was burning like a boiler. I never saw anything like it.'

'Well?' Rudiger said, putting his hands on the desk. He might have been arresting momentarily a swing back to the window. Leventhal began to speak, and he cut him off with, 'No vacancies, no vacancies here. We're filled. Go somewhere else.'

Leventhal said stumblingly, 'I thought there might be an opening here. I didn't know . . . Didn't Mr Allbee say what I wanted?'

Rudiger looked at him awhile. They were on the sixtieth floor of the Dill Building. The sun was far behind the dull, black, tarnished spikes and pinnacles of the skyscrapers below.

'What's your experience?' he said.

Leventhal told him.

'No, never mind that stuff. What newspapers have you been on?'

'No papers,' Leventhal said rather nervously.

Rudiger burst out, inflamed, 'Then what in the name of hell are you taking up my time for? What are you doing here? Get out. By Jesus, you come pestering around here when I'm busy without a goddam thing to offer.'

'I'm sorry to bother you.' Leventhal spoke stiffly, not to reveal his alarm.

'This is a news magazine. If you have no news experience,

you've got no business here. Do you think we run a vocational school?'

'I thought I could do the work. I've read your magazine, and I thought I could.' He labored at the words, stalling, and bent his head.

'Oh, did you? Did you?'

'Yes . . .' He was beginning to recover his presence of mind. 'I didn't know my experience wasn't the right kind for you. I have a letter from Mr Williston. He says he knows you.' Leventhal reached into his pocket.

But Rudiger exclaimed, 'I don't want to see it.'

'Well, Mr Williston said he didn't see why I shouldn't be able to handle a job here . . .'

'Nobody asked him. I don't care what he said.'

'I think he knows what he's talking about. I respect his opinion.'

'I know my own business. Never mind about Williston. I ought to know what I need here. You're not it.'

'You probably know your business,' Leventhal said stolidly, evenly, hunching his head forward. 'I'm not saying you don't. But there's nothing so special about your magazine. I've read it, as I said.' He put a cigarette in his mouth and, without asking Rudiger's permission, reached for a packet of matches on his desk, tore out one, struck it, and threw it into a tray. Angry and tense, he managed to present a surface of dry, uncaring calm. 'Anybody who can write English can write for it. If you gave a man a try and then thought he couldn't make the grade, I'd say you knew your business a lot better. That's a prejudice, Mr Rudiger, about newspaper experience.'

Rudiger shouted, 'Oh, is it?' Leventhal saw that he was not invulnerable, and by now a spell had been created, an atmosphere of infliction and injury from which neither could withdraw.

'Sure it is,' said Leventhal rather easily. 'It's a guild. Any outsider hasn't got a chance. But as a matter of fact you

38

ought to think of your paper first and hire people because they can do the work. It wouldn't hurt.'

'You think you could improve the paper?'

Leventhal replied that not his only but any fresh point of view wouldn't hurt. His confidence was enormous, so radically unusual that, despite his calm, it was like a seizure or possession, and he said things which his memory, limited by what was habitual, could not retain. So he did not know now exactly what followed. He recalled something like, 'Well, you buy an article in the grocery and you know what you're getting when you buy a standard brand. You open up the can and the product is inside. You're not disappointed and you're not overjoyed. It's standard.' He shrank from the recollection as from a moment of insanity and he flushed roughly; he surmised that he might be making it worse than it had been, but even one tenth of the reality was calamitous.

Then, glaring at him crazily, Rudiger said, 'What did you want to be here for if it's so bad!'

And he answered, 'I need a job, it so happens.'

The air between them must have shaken, it was so charged with insult and rage. Under no circumstances could he imagine doing now what he had done then. But he had determined not to let his nose be pulled. That was what he told himself. 'He thinks everybody who comes to him will let his nose be pulled.' Too many people looking for work were ready to allow anything. The habit of agreement was strong, terribly strong. Say anything you like to them, call them fools and they smiled, turn their beliefs inside out and they smiled, despise them and they might grow red, but they went on smiling because they could not let themselves disagree. And that was what Rudiger was used to.

'Get out!' Rudiger cried. His face was aflame. He rose with a thrust of his stocky arm while Leventhal, evincing neither anger nor satisfaction, though he felt both, rose, smoothed the groove of his green velours hat, and said, 'I guess you can't take it when people stand up to you, Mr Rudiger.'

'Out, out, out!' Rudiger repeated, pushing over his desk with both arms. 'Out, you case, you nut, you belong in the asylum! Out! You ought to be committed!'

And Leventhal, sauntering toward the door, turned and retorted, made a remark about two-bit big shots and empty wagons. He didn't believe he had said more than that – notwithstanding Allbee's charge that he swore. He had said something about empty wagons being noisy. His present mortification would not be greater if he had sworn. He did remember, and very clearly, too, that he was elated. He congratulated himself. Rudiger had not pulled his nose.

He went at once to see Harkavy and, over a cup of coffee in a corner cafeteria, told him the whole story. It delighted him.

'You said that to Rudiger? Oh, golly, that must have been something. Really something, Asa my boy. He's a bull, that man. I've heard stories about him. A regular bull!'

'Yes. Well, you've got to remember one thing, Dan.' Leventhal's spirits dropped suddenly. 'Someone like that can make trouble for me. He can have me black-listed. You've got to realize . . . Eh, can he?'

'Never, Asa,' Harkavy said.

'You don't think so?'

'Never. Who do you think he is?' Harkavy looked at him severely with his round, clear eyes.

'He's a big shot.'

'There isn't a thing he can do to you. Whatever you do, don't get ideas like that into your head. He can't persecute you. Now be careful. You have that tendency, boy, do you know that? He got what was coming to him and he can't do anything. Maybe that Allabee, what-do-you-call-him, put him up to it, wanted to play you a dirty trick. You know how it goes: "There's a fellow bothering me. Do me a favor and give him the works when he comes around." So he does it.

Well, he fouled his own nest. You follow me, boy? He fouled his own nest. So by now he realizes it was his own fault and he had it coming. How do you know it wasn't rimmed?'

'You really think they did? I don't know. And I didn't bother that Allbee. I only asked him once.'

'Maybe he didn't put him up to it. But he might have. It's a possibility. Something like that happened to another friend of mine – Fabin. You know him. They gave him the works, and it was a put-up job. Only he didn't talk back the way you did. He just let them fling it at him. No, you did right and you haven't got a thing to worry about.'

Nevertheless, Leventhal was not reassured. And on afterthought he had misgivings about Harkavy's reference to persecution. Harkavy used such words whether they fitted or not. Rudiger's anger was not imaginary, and he was a man to fear. There were black lists; that was well known. Of course, he had not actually worked for Rudiger and Rudiger could not black-list him as a former employee. In the nature of it, it must be a secret process, passing through many connections, private and professional. After all, Rudiger was influential, powerful. And who knew how these things were done, through what channels? It was downright silly of Harkavy to speak of imaginary persecution.

Leventhal suspected, in the days that followed, that the black list was real enough, for firm after firm turned him down. It was only when he found his present job that his suspicions faded and he ceased to fear Rudiger.

Beard did not send for him; Leventhal's apprehensions were unfounded. The old man, when they met in the lavatory in the afternoon, was not affable, but he was not so disagreeable as Leventhal had anticipated. He even asked about the family troubles. It was Leventhal himself that was distant.

'Was it as urgent as you thought?' said Beard.

'Oh, absolutely,' Leventhal replied. 'And my brother is away. I have to look out for his family.'

41

'Yes, I see. Naturally. Your brother is a family man, is he?'

'He has two children. He's married to an Italian woman.'

Mr Beard said with a look of mild inquiry, 'Oh, a mixed marriage.'

Leventhal nodded slightly. Mr Beard shook his dripping hands and dried them on the towel he carried over his shoulder. He did not use the paper towels in the tin box. In words hardly above a whisper, he made some comment about the heat, wiped his wan forehead, and went out, tightening his belt, pulling down his white vest, a round-shouldered figure with bald head and large elbows. The old man's mildness made him feel easier. They had met the deadline without him. It hadn't been so catastrophic; Fay and Millikan stayed an hour overtime. He would have done the same in a similar emergency. Had done it. And what if he himself had been sick? A man wasn't made of metal parts. Damn him, old Beard might have let him off a little more pleasantly. It gratified Leventhal, however, to have made that remark about Elena. Mixed marriage! It had come out instantaneously. He wondered how to hint to the old man that he had heard him yesterday, or that he was under no illusions, at any rate. He wanted him to know.

On the way to his desk he met Millikan, nervous, narrow-faced, sallow, with his scrap of mustache. He carried a towel, too, and approached, signaling with it. How he aped his father-in-law!

'Telephone, Leventhal. Miss Ashmun's been looking for you. Some party on your line.'

'Who?' Leventhal was filled with anxiety, suddenly. He went rapidly to his desk.

'Asa?' It was Elena.

'Yes, what's the matter? Anything wrong?'

'The baby is worse. Mickey ...' he heard her say. Her voice shot up and she became incoherent.

'Slower, slower Elena, please. I can't follow you. What's happening over there?' He guessed, his heart sinking, that she, too, was growing worse. 'Now tell me slowly what's the matter.'

'I want to get a specialist.'

'Why don't you send the boy to the hospital?'

'I want a specialist to come to the house.'

'What does your doctor say?'

'He didn't come today. Let him stay away. What good does he do him anyway? He doesn't do any good. He doesn't come even when he knows Mickey is so sick. Asa, do you hear me? I want a big man.'

'All right. But if you took my advice about the hospital...'

Again she cried out incoherently, piercingly. He made out phrases of exclamation and question but scarcely any words except the persistent 'No! No, no, no!' He attempted to interrupt. It was the operator, depositing the coin with a mechanical whirr, who put a stop to it. Elena, in fear, shrieked, 'Asa!'

'Here. We haven't been cut off yet. I'm still on the wire. Listen, I'll get another doctor and be out myself after work.'

'A specialist ... I don't want anybody else.'

Twice the operator demanded another coin. 'Shut up!' Leventhal at last said, exasperated. 'Can't you wait another second.' But he was already talking on a dead line. He banged the instrument and jolted it aside with his elbow. Miss Ashmun seemed astonished. He gazed at her gloomily and presently picked up the phone again. He called the Harkavys. Harkavy's sister Julia had a child and should be able to recommend a good doctor. Harkavy's mother answered the phone. She was extremely fond of Leventhal and spoke to him cordially, asking about his wife. 'But I guess it's Dan'l you want to talk to. "Dan'l!"' she called. 'He's home today.'

Leventhal at once explained it was Julia he wanted. Afterward he regretted that he had not taken the opportunity to ask Harkavy about Kirby Allbee. But what a time it was to have thought of him!

43

5

AFTER a hurried supper of a sandwich and a bottle of soda
at a stand near the ferry, Leventhal crossed to Staten Island.
He walked onto the deck with his hands in the pockets of his
fully buttoned, wrinkled jacket. His white shoes were soiled.
Posted beside a life ring, his dark forehead shining faintly
under his ill-combed, thick hair, he gazed out on the water
with an appearance of composure; he did not look as burdened as he felt. The formless, working, yellowish-green
water was dull, the gulls steered back and forth, the boat
crept forward into the glare. A barge was spraying orange
paint over the hull of a freighter, which pointed high, lifting
its bow out of the slow, thick cloud. Surely the sun was no
hotter in any Singapore or Surabaya, on the chains, plates,
and rails of ships anchored there. A tanker, seabound, went
across the ferry's course, and Leventhal stared after it, picturing the engine room; it was terrible, he imagined, on a
day like this, the men nearly naked in the shaft alley as the
huge thing rolled in a sweat of oil, the engines laboring. Each
turn must be like a repeated strain on the hearts and ribs of
the wipers, there near the keel, beneath the water. The
towers on the shore rose up in huge blocks, scorched, smoky,
gray, and bare white where the sun was direct upon them.
The notion brushed Leventhal's mind that the light over
them and over the water was akin to the yellow revealed in
the slit of the eye of a wild animal, say a lion, something in-
human that didn't care about anything human and yet was
implanted in every human being too, one speck of it, and
formed a part of him that responded to the heat and the

glare, exhausting as these were, or even to freezing, salty things, harsh things, all things difficult to stand. The Jersey shore, yellow, tawny, and flat, appeared on the right. The Statue of Liberty rose and traveled backwards again; in the trembling air, it was black, a twist of black that stood up like smoke. Stray planks and waterlogged, foundering crates washed back in the boat's swell.

The specialist was coming. But what he could do depended on Elena. Contagious cases were hospitalized; the health authorities were called in. But the first doctor seemed to have given up the struggle with Elena, and presumably he knew the law. With unconscious grimness, Leventhal prepared himself to struggle with her. As long as she held out, all the specialists in the world were futile. The prospect of interfering, rushing in to rescue the boy, was repugnant to him; it made him feel, more than ever, that he was an outsider. But what could you do with Elena? To begin with, ordinary good care might have kept the child from falling sick, and judging from what he had seen . . . well, her fear of the hospital was an indication of her fitness to bring up children. Some people would say that she loved them and that her love made up for her shortcomings – not to look too closely at those shortcomings. Love, by all means. But because the mother and the child were tied together in that way, if the child died through her ignorance, was she still a good mother? Should someone else – he thought of it seriously – have the right to take the child away? Or should the fate of the two of them be considered one and the same, and the child's death said to be the mother's affair only because she would suffer most by its death? In that case the child was not regarded as a person, and was that fair? Well, that was the meaning of helplessness; that was what they meant when they said it. Now with that in mind you could understand why little children sometimes cried the way they did. It was as if it were in them to know. Unfair, thought Leventhal, not to say tragic.

He began to consider his own unfortunate mother whose large features and black hair he could summon up very faintly. Invariably he saw her wearing an abstracted look, but he was not in fact sure that her look was abstracted. Perhaps he attributed it to her. And when he examined his idea of her more closely he realized that what he really meant by abstracted was mad-looking; a familiar face and yet without anything in it directed toward him. He dreaded it; he dreaded the manifestation of anything resembling it in himself. A period of coolness toward Harkavy had followed the latter's remark about persecution. Knowing his history, how could Harkavy say that to him? But eventually he satisfied himself that Harkavy was merely thoughtless and didn't sufficiently understand what he was saying. Until he spoke, he himself didn't know what was coming. So he had forgiven Harkavy, but he was left more conscious of his susceptibility to remarks of that kind. He was afraid the truth about him was so apparent that even Harkavy might see it.

He had spoken of his fears to Mary late one night in bed. She laughed at him. Why did he accept his father's explanation of his mother's illness? And he had never really learned the facts about it, it was true. He had only his father's word for it that she died insane. Many of the things that terrified people lost their horror when a doctor explained them. Years ago everyone spoke of brain fever; now it was known that there was no such sickness. 'For my own peace of mind,' Mary said. 'I would try to find out what she had.' But, although Leventhal then promised that he would go into the matter soon, make a real inquiry, so far he had done nothing about it. As for his fears, he was too ready, Mary told him, to believe anything and everything about himself. 'That's because you're not sure of yourself. If you were a little more sure you wouldn't let yourself be bothered,' she said with all the firmness of her own confident strength. And she was probably right. But, my God, how could anyone say that he was sure? How could he know all that he needed to know in order to say it? It wasn't right. Leventhal felt the presumption of it without, however, blaming Mary; he knew she expressed truthfully what she felt.

'The only proof there is of anything wrong with your mother is that she married that father of yours,' Mary had ended. This remark brought tears into Leventhal's eyes as he sat in the dark, cross-legged, bending away from the pillow at his back. Nevertheless Mary's words were beneficial on the whole. Till he had better evidence, his fears were the fears of hypochondria. The word was helpful; it gave them an amusing aspect. Still the fact remained that when he called up his mother's face at some moment it was, for all of that, abstracted.

He gazed down at the dented deck brass. For the present he preferred to be cautious about Elena and assume that her nerves were overworked. She gave way without control to what any parent with a sick child was liable to feel. But when he allowed himself to go further, to think of more than overworked nerves and Italian emotions, he saw the parallel between her and his mother and, for that matter, between himself and Max and the two children. The last was not so important. But it gave him a clearer view of each of the women to consider that they were perhaps alike. At least you could say of them that they were both extraordinary when they were disturbed (he had not forgotten his mother's screaming) – whatever the right word for it was.

The winches began to rattle, a gate dropped resoundingly in the green wooden cove of the slip. The water turned yellow and white under the bows like stale city snow. The boat started back and then, with shut engines, glided in, bumping the weedy timbers. On the long hill beyond the arches of the sheds, the house fronts were suddenly present, and Leventhal, moving ashore in the crowd, heard the busses throbbing before the station.

Philip again let him in. Recognizing his uncle he stood aside for him.

47

'Where's Elena. Is she here?' Leventhal said, striding into the dining-room. 'How's the boy?'

'He's sleeping. Ma's downstairs using Villani's telephone. She said she'd be up right away.' He turned to the kitchen, explaining from the doorway, 'I was eating supper.'

'Go ahead, finish,' said Leventhal. He walked restlessly round the room. Mickey was asleep; the second alarm seemed to be like the first. Touching the hall door, he debated whether to go into the child's room alone. No, it would be wiser not to; there was no telling how Elena would take it.

It was shortly before sundown, and there were lights in the flats giving on the airshaft where the walls, for a short distance below the black cornice, were reddened by the sky. Leventhal went into the kitchen where Philip sat beside the table on a high stepstool. He had a bowl of dry cereal before him and he poured milk over it, digging up the flap of the milk carton with his thumbnail; he peeled and sliced a banana, sprinkled sugar over it, and flipped the skin into the sink with its pans and dishes. The paper frills along the shelves of the cupboard crackled in the current of the fan. It ran on the cabinet, sooty, with insectlike swiftness and a thrumming of its soft rubber blades; it suggested a fly hovering below the tarnish and heat of the ceiling and beside the scaling, many-jointed, curved pipes on which Elena hung rags to dry. The boy's knees were level with the tabletop, and he bent almost double as he ate, spreading his legs. Leventhal reflected that he had taken the stool instead of a chair because he felt the need to do something extreme in his presence. 'I used to do stunts, too, when there was a visitor,' he reminded himself. 'And that is what I am here, a visitor.'

'Is this your whole supper?' he asked.

'When it's hot like this, I never eat a lot.' The boy had a rather precise way of speaking.

'You ought to have bread and butter, and so on, and greens,' said Leventhal.

Philip interrupted his eating to look at his uncle briefly.

48

'We don't cook much during the heat wave,' he said. He set his feet on a higher rung and bent even lower. His hair had been newly cut, roughly clipped on top and shaved high up the back of his neck to a line above his large but delicately white ears.

'What kind of a barber do you have?'

Philip looked up again. 'Oh, Jack McCaul on the block. We all go to him; Dad too, when he's home. I told him to cut it this way. I asked for a summer haircut.'

'They ought to take away the man's license for giving you one like that.' He said this too forcefully and overshot his intended joke, and he paused and made an effort to find the right tone.

'Oh, McCaul's all right,' said Philip. 'He takes care of us. I was waiting for the kid to get better so's we could go together. But Ma said I should go and have a trim before she had to buy me a fiddle to go with my hair. This haircut is all right for the weather. Last summer I got a baldie – all off.'

'Well, it's really okay.' Leventhal watched him eat, penetrated with sympathy for him. 'An independent little boy,' he thought. 'But how they treat him.'

He sat down by the window, unbuttoning his creased jacket, and glanced at the sky through the airshaft's black square. In one of the other flats, a girl in a parlor chair was brushing a dog that yawned and tried to lick her hand. She pushed its muzzle down. A woman in a chemise passed through the room, back and forth from kitchen to hall. Mickey's window gave on the shaft; it was on the corner, and if he were awake now he might be able to see his brother and his uncle.

'The doctor's going to be here any minute.' Leventhal was suddenly impatient. 'I thought Elena was in such a hurry for him to come. What's keeping her?'

'I'll go and see.' Philip sprang from the stool.

'Don't leave your supper. Tell me where she is and I'll

49

find her.' But Philip was already in the corridor. Leventhal, however, instead of footsteps, heard voices through the open doors. Had he met Elena coming up the stairs? The light went on in the dining-room, under the green glass panes of the shade, and Leventhal had a glimpse of a woman in a black dress moving beside the table.

'Boy?' he called out. 'Say, Phil?'

'Here. Come on in.'

'Who is it?' he inquired in a low voice. He tried to see beyond the lamp to the other end of the room.

'My grandmother.'

'The old woman?' said Leventhal in surprise. He had heard something about her from Max but had never seen her. He started from the doorway and, looking confused, went toward her around the dining-room table, changing his direction when she turned and sat down in the mohair arm-chair.

'This is Dad's brother,' Philip said to her. Leventhal was conscious of prolonging his nod almost into a bow; he wanted to be prepossessing. The old lady gave him only a brief sharp glance. Taller than Elena, she was gaunt and straight-backed, and the carriage of her head was tense. She wore large gold earrings. The hair came out short and white at her temples; toward the back of her head it was black and tightly knotted. Her dress also was black, a black silk, and despite the heat she wore a shawl on her shoulders.

Since she remained silent, Leventhal stood undecided; it seemed inadvisable to say more; to sit down without being answered would embarrass him. But, also, it might be impolite to return to the kitchen. Maybe he misunderstood her taciturnity. However, she seemed to avert her head from him, and he had to struggle with an angry urge to compel her to face him. Nevertheless she had not spoken, and he could not be sure. It was possible that he was mistaken.

'I thought you were going to fetch your mother,' he said to Philip somewhat impatiently. And when Philip started to leave, he said hastily, 'I'll go with you.' He had decided that the grandmother's look was unfriendly, though in the dusty green-tinged light that came through the lampshade it was difficult to get a definite impression. But he felt her antagonism. In a shambling gait – the heat made him heavy – he followed Philip down several turns of the stairs to the neighbor's flat. Philip knocked, and in a few seconds Elena came hurrying out to them, eager and fearful.

'Oh, Asa, you,' she said. 'And the specialist? Did you bring him?'

'He said between seven and eight. He ought to be here soon.'

The neighbor, Mr Villani, smoking a twisted stogie, appeared in the hallway and cried out to her, 'You let us know right away what he says about the boy up there.' He looked at Leventhal, perfectly unconstrained in his curiosity. 'How do?' he said to him.

'This is my husband's brother,' said Elena.

'Yes, sure,' said Villani taking the cigar out of his mouth. Leventhal impassively looked back at him, his eyes solemn and uncommunicative, only a little formally inquiring. A drop of sweat ran down his cheek. Villani, one hand in his pocket, spread his trousers wide. 'You look like Mr Leventhal, all right,' he said. He turned to Elena. 'And what the doctor tells you, you do it, missis, you hear? We're gonna pull that boy through, so don't worry. What I think is he's only got summer fever,' he said to Leventhal. 'It ain't serious. My kids had it. But this missis is the worrying kind.'

'It's plenty serious,' said Elena. She spoke quietly, but Leventhal, watching her closely and paying particular attention to the expression of her eyes, felt a pang of his peculiar dread at their sudden widening.

'Ah, ah, how do you know? Are you a doctor? Wait a while.'

'The man is right, I think, Elena,' said Leventhal.

'Sure I am. You got to have confidence in the doctor.' An

impassioned, sharp sound caught in his throat and he flung his arm out in a short, stiff, eloquent curve. 'What's the matter! Sure! You listen to me. That boy is all right.' The cigar glowed in his fingers.

'She'll have confidence,' Leventhal assured him.

They started upstairs. On the fourth floor Elena stopped and with an excited escape of breath, 'Phillie, what did you tell me – Grandma's here?'

'She just came.'

'Oh my!' She turned with anxious abruptness to Leventhal. 'What did she say to you, anything?'

'Not a single word.'

'Oh, Asa, if she does . . . Oh, I hope to God she doesn't. Let her say what she wants. Just let it pass.'

'Oh, sure,' he said.

'She's a very peculiar type of person, my mother. She acted terrible when Max and I got married. She wanted to throw me out of the house because I was going with him. I couldn't bring him in. I had to meet him outside.'

'Max mentioned once or twice . . .'

'She's an awfully strict Catholic. She said if I married anybody but a Catholic she wouldn't have any more to do with me. She would curse me. So when I left the house she did. I didn't even see her until Phillie was born. I still don't see her much, but since Mickey is sick she's here pretty often. If Max is home she won't even come in. She's very superstitious, my mother. She has all the old-country ways. She thinks she's still in Sicily.' Elena spoke in a near-whisper, covering the side of her face with her hand.

'Don't worry, I'll know how to take her.'

'She just is that way,' Elena explained, smiling helplessly.

'You can stop worrying.'

The old woman met them in the hallway and she began immediately to speak to her daughter, her eyes occasionally moving to Leventhal's face. Her voice had what to him was a characteristic Italian hoarseness. Her long head was drawn

52

back rigidly on her black shoulders. He observed how she turned down her underlip, exposing her teeth as she lingered on a syllable. Elena, dejected, shook her head and answered in short phrases. Leventhal tried to seize a word here and there. He understood nothing. Suddenly Elena interrupted her mother, crying out, 'Where? Why didn't you say so right away, Mamma? Where is he? The man is here!' she exclaimed to Leventhal. 'The specialist!' She ran in. Leventhal, walking behind the grandmother in the hall leading to the bedroom, contorted his face in an unusual release of feeling. Ugly old witch! To make her daughter wait and listen to her complaints before telling her the doctor had arrived. 'Parents!' he muttered. 'Oh, yes, parents! My eye, parents!' He was tempted to jostle her.

They entered the bedroom. The doctor had pulled up Mickey's shirt and was listening to his heart. The child seemed scarcely awake; he was dull and submitted to the examination, listless with the fever, lifting his eyes only to his mother, identifying rather than appealing to her. Philip leaned on the bedpost to see him.

'Phil, don't shake, stay off it,' Elena said.

The doctor turned a glance over his shoulder. He was a young man with a long, rosy face and thin, gold-rimmed lenses over his close-set eyes. While he pressed the stethoscope on the child's chest and shoulders, he looked steadily at Leventhal, evidently taking him for the father. At first Leventhal was bothered by this error. Soon, however, he grasped the fact that the doctor was trying to tell him the illness was serious. Unobserved by Elena, who was folding back the counterpane, he gave him a gloomy nod to show that he understood. The doctor let the earpieces of the instrument fall around his neck and felt the boy's arms with his clean red fingers. In the yellowish, stiff web over the blackness of the window, the ferns and the immense moths were shot with holes and gaps. The kitchen air and the noises of the court entered the room. The boy was raised and his pillow turned over.

53

'You should sponge him every few hours,' said the doctor.
'I did it this afternoon. I'll do it again soon,' said Elena.

She had been whispering to him from time to time and now she spoke up eagerly, almost joyfully. She seemed to feel there was nothing to fear any longer. 'I trust him so much,' she said to Leventhal, gazing at the doctor. Leventhal's hands were damp and chill. He was beginning to feel ill from the sudden doubling of his tension. He wiped his face, passing the handkerchief over the bristles on his cheek and leaving a piece of lint on them. He was sure he had interpreted the doctor's silent communication correctly. Elena's hopefulness stunned him. He turned, careworn, looking at her and at the children, and a few moments passed before it came to him that this burden after all belonged to his brother. At once he was furious with Max for being away. He had no right to go in the first place. Leventhal felt for his wallet; he had put Max's card in it. He would wire him tonight. Or no, a night letter was better, he could put more into it. He began to form the message in his mind. 'Dear Max, if you can tear yourself away from what you're doing . . . if you can manage to get away for a while . . .' He would not spare him. The harsher the better. Just look at what he left behind him: this house, a tenement; Elena, who might herself need taking care of; the children they had brought into the world. Leventhal returned to the composition of the night letter. 'You are needed here. Imperative.' That it was he, almost a stranger to the family, who was sending the message, should show Max how serious the matter was. Ah, what a business! And the grandmother? If anything happened to the boy she would consider it in the nature of a judgment on the marriage. The marriage was impure to her. Yes, he understood how she felt about it. A Jew, a man of wrong blood, of bad blood, had given her daughter two children, and that was why this was happening. No one could have persuaded Leventhal that he was wrong. Hardly hearing what was being said in the room, he contemplated her grimly, her grizzled temples, the thin straight line of her nose, the severity of her head pressed back on her shoulders, the baring of her teeth as she opened her lips to make a remark to her daughter. No, he was not wrong. From her standpoint it was inevitable punishment – that was how she would see it, a punishment. Whatever else she might feel – and after all the boy was her grandson – she would feel this first.

He just then observed great agitation in Elena and began to pay attention to the conversation. He heard the doctor speaking of the hospital and he thought, 'She can't keep the kid here any more. She'll have to give in.'

'I told her yesterday she ought to send him to the hospital,' he said.

Elena still resisted. 'But why isn't it just as good for him at home? Better. I can look after him better than a nurse.'

'He's got to go if you want me to take the case.'

'But what's the matter here?' she pleaded.

'Has to be done,' said the doctor knocking up the clips of his bag.

'Should I go for a cab?' Philip softly asked his uncle.

Leventhal nodded. Philip ran from the room.

6

THE doctor told Leventhal on the way back to Manhattan
that he thought – though he needed more evidence to confirm
the diagnosis – Mickey had a bronchial infection of a rare
kind. He named it two or three times, and Leventhal tried to
fix it in his mind but failed. Such cases were serious; not
necessarily fatal, however. 'You think you'll be able to help
him, doctor?' he asked in great eagerness, and the doctor's
word of hope raised his spirits. The boat moved out; the
immense golden crowns of light above the sheds now had
space to play on the water between the stern and the shore.
'I was going to wire my brother to come,' said Leventhal – he
had already explained that he was not the father. The doctor
answered that he didn't think it was necessary at present. It
was enough to tell him to stand by. Leventhal accepted this as
sensible advice. Why create a scare now? It wasn't so critical
after all. He would send Max a night letter and let him
decide for himself whether to come or wait. The ferry
crawled in the heat and blackness of the harbor. The mass of
passengers on the open deck was still, like a crowd of souls,
each concentrating on its destination. The thin discs of the
doctor's spectacles were turned to the sky, both illumined in
the same degree by the bulb over his head. Leventhal wanted
to ask him more about the disease. It was rare. Well, did
medicine have any idea how a thing like that singled out a
child in Staten Island rather than, say, St Louis or Denver?
One child in thousands. How did they account for it? Did
everyone have it dormant? Could it be hereditary? Or, on
the other hand, was it even more strange that people, so

different, no two with the same fingerprints, did not have more individual diseases? Freed from his depression by the doctor's encouragement, he had a great desire to talk. He would have liked to discuss this but he had already asked the name of the disease several times and failed to retain it, and so the doctor must have a poor opinion of him. And maybe he would be condescending to a layman. Accordingly, Leventhal was silent and thought, 'Well, let it ride.' But he continued to wonder about it. They said that God was no respecter of persons, meaning that there were the same rules for everybody. Where was that? He tried to remember.

They were in the middle of the harbor when the heat was suddenly lifted by a breeze. High and low between the shores, the lights of ships, signals, and bridges drifted and ran, curved, and stood riding on the swell, and the sonorous, rather desolate bells rang from the water when the buoys were stirred. The breeze blew a spray to the deck, and the boat now and then seemed to tremble to the pull of the ocean beyond the islands. As they neared the Manhattan side, people began to get up from the benches in the salon; there was a great press when the chains were dropped. Leventhal was separated from the doctor.

He went home on the subway, pushing through the revolving steel gate at his station and breathing the cooler air of the street with deep relief.

He was expecting a letter from Mary – one was about due – and he opened the mailbox swiftly while Nunez' dog sniffed at his legs. Instead of a letter, Mary had sent two post cards closely covered with writing. She and her mother were starting for Charleston on Friday. The house was sold. They were both well and she hoped he was, too, in spite of the heat. It was fine old Baltimore summer weather – it simply drugged you. The second card was different; there were intimate references on it. Only Mary could write such things on cards for everybody in the world to read. Amused, proud, pleased with her, pleased rather than embarrassed at the possibility that postal clerks had read the cards, he put them in his pocket. 'Do I pass inspection?' he demanded of Nunez' dog. 'Blow now.' Stooping he caught the dog's head and rubbed it. He started up stairs and the animal came after him. 'Blow now, I say.' He barred the way with his leg, then whirled inside and slammed the hall-door. 'Go home!' he yelled, and laughed uproariously. 'Go on home!' He pounded the glass, and the dog barked raucously and leaped at the pane. Leventhal told one of the neighbors, whom he hardly knew, 'The super's dog is having a fit. Hear him?' An elderly, guarded, pale face gave him an uncertain smile and seemed to listen in awe to the racket in the foyer. Leventhal hurried up with thumping steps, whipping his hat on the banister and entering his flat with a commotion. Dear Mary! If she were only here now to put his arms around and kiss. He flung away his hat and his jacket, pulled off his shoes, and went to open the windows and push aside the curtains. It had turned into a beautiful night. The air was trembling and splendid. The moon had come out; there were wide-spaced stars, and small clouds pausing and then spinning as the cool gusts broke through the heat.

He lit the lamp on the secretary and began to write to his wife. Gnats fell and rose again from the illuminated green blotter. He gave her an account of himself, forgetting that he had felt nervous, restive, and unwell. He said nothing about what had happened at the office. It did not seem worth saying. He wrote swiftly and exuberantly; he discussed the weather, he mentioned that Wilma had drunk the beer, that the parks were terribly crowded. Then he found himself telling her about his nephew, writing with sudden emotion, the words beginning to sprawl as his hand raced. In a changed tone he described Elena. He had been afraid to look at her, he confessed, when she got into the cab and he laid the bundled-up child – she had him in two blankets although the temperature must have been over ninety – on her lap. All the impressions of the moment returned to him – the boy's

eyes with the light of the meter on them, the leathery closeness of the back seat, the driver's undershot jaw and the long
peak of his black cap, Philip's crying, Villani keeping back
the children on the sidewalk. The beating of Leventhal's
heart rose and his tongue became dry. As for his brother . . .
But when he had written Max's name he stood up and leaned
over the paper. He had meant to send the night letter before
coming up. The pen was staining his fingers. He dropped it
and began looking for his shoes outside the circle of lamplight.
He had just found them and was forcing his feet into them
without bothering about the laces when his bell rang, piercingly and long. Leventhal straightened up with a grunt of
annoyance and surprise. 'Now who in the name of hell would
ring like that?' he said. But he already knew who it was. It
was Allbee. It must be. He opened the door and listened to
the regular sibilance and knocking of the footsteps in the
hollow stair well. It occurred to him that he could escape
Allbee by going to the roof. If he went out stealthily he could
still get away. And if he were followed, the next rooftop was
only a matter of six inches away, an easy step over. Then he
could get into the street and good-by. He could go even now.
Even *now*. Yet he stood firm and strangely enough he felt
that he had proved something by doing so. 'I won't give
ground,' he thought. 'Let him. Why should I?' He promptly
went back to his letter, leaving the door open. He finished it
abruptly with a few perfunctory sentences and read it over.
He wrote 'All my love,' signed his name, addressed the envelope, and by that time Allbee was in the room. He knew that
he had come in; nevertheless he controlled his desire to turn.
He stamped the envelope first, sealed it, momentarily guessed
at its weight, and only then did he appear to take notice of
his visitor, who smiled at him without parting his lips. To
enter without a knock or invitation was an intrusion. Of
course the door was open, but it was taking too much for
granted all the same not to knock. Leventhal thought there
was a trace of delight in the defiance of Allbee's look. 'I *owe*

him hospitality, that's how he behaves,' passed through his mind.

'Yes,' he said tonelessly, indifferently polite.

'You're well fixed up here,' said Allbee taking in the room. He might have been comparing it with his own place. Leventhal could imagine what that was like.

'As long as you're here, sit down,' Leventhal said. 'What's the use of standing?' He would not get rid of him without hearing him out, and it might as well be now as another time.

'Much obliged,' said Allbee. His head came forward courteously and he seemed to read Leventhal's face. 'It's a long pull up those stairs. I'm not used to these high walkups.' He drew a chair close to the desk, crossed his legs, and clasped his knee with somewhat rigid fingers. His cuffs were frayed, the threads raveled on the blond hairs of his wrist. His hands were dirty. His fair hair, unevenly divided on his scalp, was damp. It was apparently true that the climb had been hard for him. 'It's quite a height, this,' he smiled. 'And for me, well . . .' he caught his breath, 'I'm used to low places.' He pointed his finger at the floor and worked it as though pulling a trigger.

'Are you here to give me the same song and dance as the last time? Because if you are let me tell you once and for all . . .'

'Oh, hold on,' said Allbee. 'Let's be sensible and open. I didn't come to complain to you. Why should I? I only said what's obvious. Nothing to wrangle about. I'm on the bottom. You don't want to deny that, do you?' He extended his arms as if to offer himself for examination, and although he did it wryly Leventhal saw that he was really in earnest. 'Whereas you . . .'

He indicated the flat. Leventhal said, 'Oh, please,' and shook his head. 'Don't give me that stuff.'

'It's a fact, a hard fact,' said Allbee. 'I'm the best judge of the facts. I know them intimately. This isn't just theoretical with me. The distance between you and me is greater than between you and the greatest millionaire in America. When I compare myself with you, why you're in the empyrean, as they used to say at school, and I'm in the pit. And I have been in your position but you have never been in mine.'

'What do you mean? I've been down and out.'

Allbee gave him a tolerant smile.

'Stony broke, without a nickel for the automat,' Leventhal said.

'Ah, go on. You don't know anything about it, I can tell by your talk. You've never been in my place. Nickels for the automat ... temporary embarrassment. That ...' and he ended with his head to one side nearly touching his shoulder, and with his outstretched arm and open hand he made a gesture of passing the comparison away. There rose immediately to Leventhal's mind the most horrible images of men wearily sitting on mission benches waiting for their coffee in a smeared and bleary winter sun; of flophouse sheets and filthy pillows; hideous cardboard cubicles painted to resemble wood, even the tungsten in the bulb like little burning worms that seemed to eat up rather than give light. Better to be in the dark. He had seen such places. He could still smell the carbolic disinfectant. And if it were *his* flesh on those sheets, *his* lips drinking that coffee, *his* back and thighs in that winter sun, *his* eyes looking at the boards of the floor ... ? Allbee was right to smile at him; he had never been in such a plight. 'So I'm mistaken,' he reflected. 'Why do I have to match him in that? Is it necessary? Anyway, what does he want?' For a time he forgot about the night letter. He waited for Allbee to reveal what he had come for. He did not know just what to expect, but he considered it very likely that he would repeat his charge despite his saying that he was not here to complain.

'Well,' he said, prefacing his remark with a short laugh. 'It's a peculiar statement to begin a visit with.'

'Why, no. What could be better. It's the height of politeness

61

to admire your host's house. And the contrast between us should please you very much. It should give you a lot of satisfaction to have done it all yourself.'

'Done what myself?' said Leventhal suspiciously.

'Raised yourself up, I mean,' said Allbee quickly. 'You were just telling me you were once broke, which is to say that you're a self-made man. There's a lot of satisfaction in that, isn't there? And when you see somebody that hasn't made out so well it adds something to your satisfaction. It's only human. Even if you know better.'

'I didn't say I was a self-made man or any such thing. That's a lot of nonsense.'

'I'm glad to be corrected then,' Allbee replied. 'I must have had the wrong impression. Because, you know, the more I think about it the more I feel it's bunk, this self-made business. The day of succeeding by your own efforts is past. Now it's all blind movement, vast movement, and the individual is shuttled back and forth. He only thinks he's the works. But that isn't the way it is. Groups, organizations succeed or fail, but not individuals any longer. Don't you agree?'

'Oh, it's not that way, exactly,' Leventhal said. 'No, I don't.'

'You don't agree that people have a destiny forced on them? Well, that's ridiculous, because they do. And that's all the destiny they get, so they'd better not assume they're running their own show. That's the kind of mistake I wouldn't care to make. There's nothing worse than being confused, too, in addition to being unlucky. But you find people who have their luck and take the credit for it, too – all brains and personality, when all that happened was that they were handed a bucket when it rained.'

'Let's have this cleared up right now, if you please,' said Leventhal coldly. 'We might as well be open and aboveboard. What does all this lead up to?'

'Oh, it doesn't lead to anything. It's just discussion, talk. Talk, talk, talk, talk, talk!' he exclaimed grinning, flinging up his hands. His eyes began to shine.

Leventhal impassively looked at him. 'And what's that for?' he asked.

Allbee now appeared to be very depressed, perhaps at his own unsteadiness, and Leventhal was a little sorry for him. His alternation of moods, however, affected him unpleasantly. It was clear that the man was no fool. But what was the use of not being a fool if you acted like this? For instance, there was his language, did he have to speak like that, make himself sound so grand? Because he needed something to brace himself on? Oh, there was a smashup somewhere, certainly, a smashup and a tragic one, you could be sure of that. Something crushing, a real smash. But the question that remained uppermost with Leventhal was, 'What does he want?' And notwithstanding his insistence on being above-board, he was unable to ask it.

'Is that your wife?' Allbee looked over Leventhal's head at a framed photograph on the secretary.

'Yes, that's Mary.'

'Oh, say, she's charming. Ah, you're lucky, you know?' He stood up and bent over him, turning the photograph to the light. 'She is charming.'

'It's a good picture of her,' said Leventhal, not liking his enthusiasm.

'She has that proud look that's proud without being hard. You know what I mean. It's a serious look. You see it in Asiatic sculpture.'

'Oh – Asiatic!' said Leventhal scoffing.

'Certainly, Asiatic. Look at the eyes, and those cheekbones. You're married to a woman and don't know she has slant eyes?' He made a descriptive turn of his thumb. 'She's positively Asiatic.'

'She comes from Baltimore.'

'First generation?'

'Her mother is native-born, too. Further back than that I don't know.'

'I'm willing to bet they came from Eastern Europe, originally,' said Allbee.

'Why, that's not so stupendous. You wouldn't get any takers.'

'I know I wouldn't get any takers in your case.'

'No? Maybe since you investigated me and found out so much about me, you took the trouble to find out what part of Europe my parents came from.'

'It's apparent enough; it doesn't need any investigating. Russia, Poland . . . I can see at a glance.'

'You can, ah?'

'Well, of course. I've lived in New York for a long time. It's a very Jewish city, and a person would have to be a pretty sloppy observer not to learn a lot about Jews here. You know yourself how many Jewish dishes there are in the cafeterias, how much of the stage – how many Jewish comedians and jokes, and stores, and so on, and Jews in public life, and so on. You know that. It's no revelation.'

Leventhal refrained from answering. It was, after all, no revelation.

Allbee once more turned his attention to Mary's picture. As he studied it and nodded, his eyes, to Leventhal's amazement, filled with tears, and he took on an expression of suppressed grief and injury.

'*Your* wife . . . ?' Leventhal ventured in a low voice.

'She's dead,' replied Allbee.

Leventhal's tone fell even lower as he said, with a resonance of horror, 'Dead? Oh, too bad. I'm sorry . . .'

'So you should be. So you should.' The words seemed to have been brought up from Allbee's chest as if they had been stored there and were now dislodged and uttered irregularly before he could hold them back.

Leventhal concentrated on them, averting his face – a characteristic of his when he was puzzling something out. He did not understand what Allbee meant.

'Of course I should be,' he murmured, not quite aware that he was acknowledging a charge. The things that had happened to him in the last two days had made him acutely

64

responsive, quick to feel. 'What a shame!' he said in deep
emotion, recalling the woman's face. 'She was much too good
for him, much too good,' he thought. 'But why should I say
that? He was her husband, so that doesn't enter in now. He
has to be considered. She's dead, but he's alive and feels.
That's what brought him down. He wouldn't be like this
otherwise.'

'So you're alone, now,' he said.

'Yes, I'm a widower, have been for over four years. Four
years and about three weeks.'

'And how did it happen?'

'I don't know exactly. I wasn't with her. Her family wrote
the news. She was hurt in an automobile accident. They
thought she would recover, but she died suddenly. That's all
I know. She was buried before I had a chance to get to
Louisville.'

'They didn't wait till you came?'

'Well, to tell you the truth I didn't want to be there. It
would have been a terrible business. The family would have
relieved itself by being angry with me. I would have tried to
relieve myself by sneaking out to a bar, probably sat in the
bar and missed the whole thing. That would have made it ten
times worse for everybody. I was in that condition. And it
was hot then. Louisville in hot weather. For *that!* Oh no,
brother, I holed up where I was. It would have been brutal.
She was dead. I wouldn't have been going to see *her* but
them, her people. Dead is dead. Finished. No more. You long
for your wife when she goes, if you love her. And maybe
sometimes if you don't love her so much. I wouldn't know.
But you're together, she bends to you and you bend to her in
everything, and when she dies there you stand, bent, and look
senseless, fit nothing. That's my personal feeling. Of course,
I'm the first kind. I loved her. Well, I say, you long for her . . .
but everything inanimate is the same to me. I'm not sentimental.'

He was acting, lying, Leventhal decided. His moment of

65

genuineness had passed and once more he had taken up his poise, mystifyingly off center and precarious. When he had announced his wife's death, he had sounded wrathful, but Leventhal had felt himself come nearer to him or to something clear, familiar, and truthful in him. Now he was repelled again. He wondered whether Allbee was not actually a little drunk.

'But,' said Allbee, 'that's not all there is to it.'

'No? There's more, eh?'

'Somewhat. We were separated before she died. That's why my relations with her family weren't good. Naturally, from their standpoint . . .' He paused to rub his eyelid and when he stopped it was red and appeared to have gone lower than the other. 'They were prejudiced against me, wanted to shove the whole blame on me. I could blame them, if I wanted to. Her brother was driving the car; got off with scratches and a few bangs. The way those Southerners drive. Pickett's charge over and over again. Well . . . we were separated. Do you know why?'

'Why?'

'Because after Rudiger fired me, I couldn't get a job.'

'What do you mean? You couldn't find any jobs? No jobs at all?'

'Not in my line. What could I have earned at any job? Not enough to keep going. After a man spends years in one line he doesn't want to change. He isn't in a position to do much. In something else he has to start at the bottom. What was I going to do, become a peddler? Salesman? Besides, I'd have to stop looking for what I wanted by taking any job.'

'I would have taken anything before I let my wife go.'

'We're made of different stuff, you and I.' Allbee grinned. 'And I didn't let her go. She left me. I didn't want her to go. She was the one.'

'You're not telling me all there is to tell.'

'No, no,' he said, almost delightedly. 'I'm not. And what's the rest? You tell me.'

'Didn't your boozing have something to do with it?'

'Oh, there you go, there you go,' said Allbee, smiling at the floor and swaying his large frame slightly. 'My vice, my terrible vice. She left me because of my drinking. That's the ticket.'

'A woman doesn't leave her husband for anything – just for a trifle.'

'That's perfectly true, she doesn't. You're a true Jew, Leventhal. You have the true horror of drink. We're the sons of Belial to you, we smell of whisky worse than of sulphur. When Noah lies drunk – you remember that story? – his gentile-minded sons have a laugh at the old man, but his Jewish son is horrified. There's truth in that story. It's a true story.'

'Watch your talk,' said Leventhal stiffly. 'You sound like a fool. I don't know what you're after, but you're not doing yourself any good with talk like that. I tell you that straight.'

'Well...' he began; but he arrested himself. 'All right, never mind. But it's unfair to try to put the blame for my wife's death on me. It's worse than unfair; it's cruel when you consider what she was to me and what I've been through. I don't know how you look at it, but I take it for granted that we're not gods, we're only creatures, and the things we sometimes think are permanent, they aren't permanent. So one day we're like full bundles and the next we're wrapping-paper, blowing around the streets.'

'But I warn you I won't stand for such talk. Get that!' Leventhal spoke curtly, and Allbee seemed to lose his presence of mind and lowered his head, grieved and incapable of answering. It was hard to tell whether he was looking for the strength to continue, conniving something new, or disclosing his true state without pretense. Leventhal saw the side of his face, deeply indented at the lid and mouth, his cheek and chin covered with golden bristles, the blue of his eye fixed in brooding. The skin of his forehead, even-grained by the light of the lamp, was wet, and that of his jaw and throat was creased in a way that made Leventhal think of gills. Allbee's remark about creatures had touched his imagination in a singular way, and for an instant he was no more human to him than a fish or crab or any fleshy thing in the water. But only for an instant, fleetingly, until Allbee moved and looked at him. He appeared discouraged and tired.

'You'll excuse me,' said Leventhal with somewhat provocative politeness, 'but I have a wire to send. I was about to go send it when you came.' Did that sound like an invention? Allbee might think so and interpret it as a maneuver to get rid of him. However, he had seen him writing when he entered, so why shouldn't it be true? He might have been drafting the message. Anyhow, why should he care? And besides, it was absolutely a fact that he was going to wire Max. Allbee could come along and check up on him if he wanted to. He studied his face to see how he was taking it. Allbee had risen. Suddenly Leventhal twisted about and his heart sprang. He thought he had seen a mouse dart into the corner and he hurried after it, lit a match, and examined the molding. There was no hole. 'Ran away!' he thought. Or was it his fancy? 'We have mice here,' he explained to Allbee, who was at the door in the dark vestibule. He seemed to turn his head away, unresponding.

When they reached the lower hall, Allbee stopped and said, 'You try to put all the blame on me, but you know it's true that you're to blame. You and you only. For everything. You ruined me. Ruined! Because that's what I am, ruined! You're the one that's responsible. You did it to me deliberately, out of hate. Out of pure hate!'

He had clutched Leventhal's shirt and he twisted it as he spoke.

'You're crazy!' Leventhal shouted in his face. 'You're a crazy stumblebum, that's what you are. The booze is eating your brain up. Take your hands off me. Off, I say!' He pushed Allbee with all the force of his powerful arms. He fell

68

against the wall with an impact that sickened Leventhal. Allbee stood up, wiped his mouth, and stared at his hand.

'No blood. Too bad. Then you could say I spilled your blood, too,' Leventhal cried.

Allbee answered nothing. He dusted his clothes unskillfully, stiff-handedly, as though beating his arms. Then he went. Leventhal watched his hasty, unsteady progress down the street.

Mr Nunez, who had seen the incident, started up astride the striped canvas of his beach chair, and his wife, who lay on the bed near the window in a white slip, whispered, '*Que pasa?*' Leventhal looked at her in bewilderment.

7

'THE nerve of him, that damned clown!' said Leventhal fiercely. His high, thick chest felt intolerably bound and compressed, and he lifted his shoulders in an effort to ease his breathing. 'Ruined! I'll ruin him if he comes near me. What a gall!'

The letter to Mary was crumpled in his hand. It was impossible to send it like this. He would have to get another envelope and stamp, and for a moment this inconvenience grew overwhelmingly into the worst consequence of the scuffle. He tore the letter open, crushed the envelope, and threw it over the balustrade. Nunez had gone into the house and he was alone on the stoop. His glance seemed to cover the street; in reality he saw almost nothing but was only aware of the featureless darkness and the equally featureless shine of bulbs the length of the block.

Then his anger began to sink. He drew in his cheeks, somberly enlarging his eyes. The skin about them felt dry and tight. To think up such a thing! The senselessness of it perturbed him most of all. 'Why me?' he thought, frowning. 'Of course, he has to have someone to blame; that's how it starts. But when he goes over everybody he knows, in that brain of his, how does he wind up with me?' That was what was puzzling. No doubt the Rudiger business had a bearing on it; for some reason it caught on, and worked on a deeper cause. But that alone, out of hundreds of alternatives, had snagged.

In a general way, anyone could see that there was great unfairness in one man's having all the comforts of life while another had nothing. But between man and man, how was this to be dealt with? Any derelict panhandler or bum might buttonhole you on the street and say, 'The world wasn't made for you any more than it was for me, was it?' The error in this was to forget that neither man had made the arrangements, and so it was perfectly right to say, 'Why pick on me? I didn't set this up any more than you did.' Admittedly there was a wrong, a general wrong. Allbee, on the other hand, came along and said '*You!*' and that was what was so meaningless. For you might feel that something was owing to the panhandler, but to be directly blamed was entirely different.

People met you once or twice and they hated you. What was the reason; what inspired it? This Allbee illustrated it well because he was too degenerate a drunk to hide his feelings. You had only to be yourself to provoke them. Why? A sigh of helplessness escaped Leventhal. If they still believed it would work, they would make little dolls of wax and stick pins into them. And why do they pick out this, that, or the other person to hate – Tom, Dick or Harry? No one can say. They hate your smile or the way you blow your nose or use a napkin. Anything will do for an excuse. And meanwhile this Harry, the object of it, doesn't even suspect. How should he know someone is carrying around an image of him (just as a woman may paste a lover's picture on the mirror of her vanity case or a man his wife's snapshot in his wallet), carrying it around to look at and hate? It doesn't even have to be a reproduction of poor Harry. It might as well be the king of diamonds with his embroidery, his whiskers, his sword, and all. It doesn't make a bit of difference. Leventhal had to confess that he himself had occasionally sinned in this respect, and he was not ordinarily a malicious person. But certain people did call out this feeling. He saw Cohen, let us say, once or twice, and then, when his name was mentioned in company, let fall an uncomplimentary remark about him. Not that this Cohen had ever offended him. But what were all the codes and rules, Leventhal reflected, except an answer to our own nature. Would we have to be told 'Love!' if we loved as we breathed? No, obviously. Which was not to say that we didn't love but had to be assisted whenever the motor started missing. The peculiar thing struck him that everything else in nature was bounded; trees, dogs, and ants didn't grow beyond a certain size. 'But we,' he thought, 'we go in all directions without any limit.'

He had put the letter in his pocket and he now took it out and debated whether to climb up to the flat for a stamp and envelope, or to try to buy them in a drugstore. He might not be able to obtain a single envelope. He did not want to buy a box of stationery.

Then he heard his name called and recognized Harkavy's voice.

'Is that you, Dan?' he said looking down the stairs at the dim, tall figure on the sidewalk. The shifting of the theater lights across the way made his vision uncertain. It was Harkavy. There were two women with him, one holding a child by the hand.

'Come down out of the clouds,' said Harkavy. 'Are you asleep, or something, on your feet?'

Nunez returned to his deck chair. His wife was in the window, resting her head on the sash.

'Do you go into a trance when the little woman is away?'

Harkavy's companions laughed.

'Dan, how are you?' said Leventhal, descending. 'Oh, Mrs Harkavy, so that's you?'

'Julia, Julia, too.' Harkavy pointed at his sister with his cigarette holder.

'Julia, Mrs Harkavy, glad to see you both.'

'And my granddaughter Libbie,' said Mrs Harkavy.

'Oh, this is your girl, Julia?'

'Yes.'

Leventhal tried to make out the child's features; he saw

only the vivid pallor of her face and the reddish darkness of her hair.

'Very active, Libbie,' said Harkavy. 'A little too energetic, at times.'

'Oh, she runs me ragged,' Julia said. 'I can't keep up with her.'

'It's the food you give her. No child should have so much protein,' said Mrs Harkavy.

'Mother, she doesn't get more than others do. It's just her nature.'

'We came to call on you,' Harkavy said to Leventhal. 'But it looks as if you're stepping out.'

'I have a couple of errands,' said Leventhal. 'I was going to send a wire.'

'We'll walk you to Western Union, then. Are you wiring Mary? I suppose you want her back already.' Harkavy smiled.

'Daniel, it's not a thing to joke about, if a couple is devoted,' his mother said. 'It's nothing to ridicule. These days when marriages are so flimsy it's a real pleasure to see devotion. Couples go to City Hall like I might go to the five-and-dime to buy a hinge. Two boards on a hinge, and clap, clap, clap, that's a marriage. Wire your wife, Asa, it's the right thing and it's sweet. Never mind.'

'It's my brother I've got to send the wire to, not Mary.'

'Libbie, come here to me, here!' Julia furiously exclaimed, pulling the child's arm. 'I'll tie you in the middle with strings!'

'Oh, your brother?' said Mrs Harkavy.

Leventhal flushed, inexplicably. 'Yes, it was his boy I called Julia about. My nephew.'

'Did you get hold of the doctor?' Julia asked. 'Doctor Denisart, mother.'

'Oh, he's a fine doctor, Asa; his mother is a lodge sister of mine and I've known him since he was a boy. You can have confidence in him. They gave him the very best education. He studied in Holland.'

'Austria, mother.'

'Abroad, anyway. His uncle put him through. He was in jail afterwards, the uncle, for income taxes, but that wasn't the Denisarts' fault. They used to send him pheasant to Sing Sing and they say he was allowed to have card parties in his cell. But they really learn in Europe, you know. That's because their slums are worse; they get complicated cases in their clinics. Our standard of living is so high, it's bad for the education of our doctors.'

'Why, who says so?' said Harkavy, looking at his mother with interest.

'Everybody. Why, all the medical books Papa used to bring home from the salesroom were full of European cases – Fräulein J. and Fräulein K. and Mademoiselle so and so. The best medical education is foreign.'

'And how is your nephew?' Harkavy said.

'They took him to the hospital today.'

'Oh, very sick, does that mean? I'm sorry to hear it,' said Julia.

'Very.'

'But you can depend on Doctor Denisart. He's a fine young man – brilliant. I'll talk to his mother tomorrow. He'll take more interest in the case.'

'I'm sure he'd do his best without being spoken to,' said Julia. They were walking, and she pressed her daughter's head to her side.

'Influence is a good thing,' Mrs Harkavy said. 'You mustn't forget it. If you don't use it, you're left behind in the race of the swift. Everything depends on it. Of course, the doctor would do his best because of his ethics and so on, but if I talk to his mother he'll pay special attention to the case and do his very best. People are bound not to take things too much to heart, for their own protection. You've got to use influence on them.'

'Take it up with Mrs Denisart, then. It can't hurt,' said Harkavy.

'I will.'

'Dan,' said Leventhal, drawing his friend behind, 'do you remember a fellow called Allbee?'

'Allbee? Who? What's his last name?'

'Allbee is his last name. Kirby Allbee. We met him at Williston's. A big man. Blond.'

'I suppose I could remember him if I put my mind to it. I have a pretty good memory.'

They had come to the telegraph office, and Leventhal, standing at the yellow pine counter, wrote out a message to his brother entirely forgetting the sharp words he had intended to use. When he came out, he took Harkavy aside.

'Dan, could we have a private conversation for a few minutes?' he said.

'Why, I should say so. What's the matter, old fellow? Wait a minute. Let's ditch the women.'

Mrs Harkavy, Julia, and Libbie were waiting at the corner.

'Ladies, excuse us,' said Harkavy with a pleased smile, fitting a cigarette into his holder. 'Asa wants to talk over something with me.'

'I'll see Mrs Denisart for you tomorrow. Don't you worry,' Mrs Harkavy said.

Leventhal thanked her, and he and Harkavy crossed the street.

'Now what's the trouble, did you get into a scrape?' asked Harkavy. 'You know you can trust me. It's safe to tell me anything. You can bank on it. Anything you confide in me will never come back to you through a third party, not any more than if you whispered it in the confession box. So let's have it.'

'There's no secret to keep. It's nothing like that.' Glancing at his friend, he hesitated, dissatisfied. Would it be worthwhile to explain the whole matter to Harkavy? He was warmhearted and a sincere friend, but he frequently put emphasis on the wrong things. He was already on the wrong track, suspecting a scrape. He probably meant an intrigue, a scrape with a woman. 'It's this Allbee,' Leventhal said. 'He's been giving me a headache. You must remember him. He made fun of your singing one night at Williston's. You and that girl. Sure you can recall him. He worked at Dill's . . .'

'Oh, *him*. That bird.' It seemed to Leventhal that Harkavy listened more gravely, though perhaps it was his own wish to have something so troubling to him taken seriously that was behind this impression. He described his first meeting with Allbee in the park. When he told him how amazed he was at Allbee's spying, Harkavy murmured, 'Well, isn't that the limit? Isn't that disagreeable? Nervy. Disagreeable.'

'I thought you wouldn't forget how he went for you over that song.'

'Oh, no, I have him definitely placed now. So that's the man?' He drew his head back with a restrained rearing motion and, from the stretching of his clear eyes, Leventhal saw that a connection of the utmost importance had been established in his mind.

'Dan, do you know any facts about him that I don't?'

'What do you call facts? It depends. I think so. I mean, I've heard. But was he around again? Let's have the rest of it.'

'What have you heard?'

'You tell me first. Let's see if it's all one piece. Maybe it isn't. It may not be worth bothering about – loony all of it, and we ought to tie a can to it?'

He would not speak, and Leventhal hurriedly set forth all that Allbee had done and said, and, despite his haste and his eagerness to find out what Harkavy knew, he interrupted himself from time to time to make scornful, almost laughing comments which in his heart he recognized to be appeals to Harkavy to confirm the absurdity, the madness of the accusations. Harkavy, however, did not respond to these appeals. He was sober. He continued to say, 'Disagreeable, disagreeable,' but his manner did not give Leventhal much comfort.

'He makes out a whole case that I'm responsible for his

wife and everything . . . !' said Leventhal, his voice rising nearly to a cry.

'His wife? That's far-fetched, far-fetched,' said Harkavy. 'I wouldn't listen to stuff like that.'

'You think I do? I'd have to be crazy too. How could anybody? Could you?'

'No, no, I say it's far-fetched. He's overstraining the imagination. He must have a loose screw.' Harkavy twisted a finger near his head and sighed. 'But the story went round that he was canned, and then I heard that he couldn't get another job. They canned him at quite a few places before.'

'Because of drinking . . .'

Harkavy shrugged. His face was wrinkled and he was half turned away from Leventhal. 'Maybe. He wasn't in good anywhere, as I heard it, and he was just about running out of breaks when he got the job with Dill's.'

'Who told you that?'

'Offhand I don't recollect.'

'Do you think there's a black list, Dan? When I talked over that Rudiger thing with you, you laughed at the idea.'

'Did I? Well, I don't believe in such stuff in general.'

'All right, here's proof. You see? There is a black list.'

'I'm not convinced. This man of yours wasn't steady, and the word got around. It just got to be known he wasn't reliable.'

'Why did he lose the job at Dill's? It was because he boozed, wasn't it?'

'Why, I can't say,' Harkavy replied, and Leventhal thought that he looked at him anxiously. 'I haven't got the inside information on it. As it came to me, the reason was different. In these cases, though, you get all kinds of rumors. Who knows? The truth is hard to get at. If your life depended on getting it, you'd probably hang. I don't have to tell you how it is. This one says this, and that one says that. Y says oats, and Z says hay, and chances are . . . it's buckwheat. Nobody can tell you except the fellow that harvested it. To the rest it's

77

all theory. Why? He was skating on thin ice and he had to skate fast, faster and faster. But he slowed up . . . and he fell through. As I see it . . .' Harkavy himself was discontented with this explanation; it was obviously makeshift. He faltered and his glance wandered. He had, unmistakably, information that he was trying to hold back.

'Why did he lose the job? What do they say?'

'There's no "they".'

'Dan, don't try to give me the runaround. This is something I won't rest easy about till I know. It's no trifle. You must tell me what they say.'

'If you don't mind, Asa, there's one thing I have to point out that you haven't learned. We're not children. We're men of the world. It's almost a sin to be so innocent. Get next to yourself, boy, will you? You want the whole world to like you. There're bound to be some people who don't think well of you. As I do, for instance. Why, isn't it enough for you that some do? Why can't you accept the fact that others never will? Figure it on a percentile basis. Is it a life and death matter? I happen to have found out that a young lady I always liked said I was conceited. Perhaps she didn't think it would get to me, but it did. Too bad people everywhere don't know what I'm really like. Or you. It would be a different universe. Things are too subtle for me; I have to knock along on common sense. What about this girl? I know she has reasons that she doesn't understand herself. All I can say is, "Lady, God bless you, we all have our faults and are what we are. I have to take myself as I am or push off. I am all I have in this world. And with all my shortcomings my life is precious to me." My heart doesn't sink. Experience has taught me to expect this once in a while. But you're so upset when somebody doesn't like you, or says this or that about you. A little independence, boy; it's a weakness, positively.'

'I want you to tell me,' Leventhal persisted. 'I'll stick to you till you do. Considering what I'm being blamed for, it's natural that I should want to find out.'

Harkavy gave in to him. 'Williston thought you made trouble for this fellow when you went to Dill's and you acted up. He kind of hinted that it was intentional.'

'What? Williston says that? Did he say that?'

'Well, something like it.'

'How could he? Is he such an idiot?' Pale, his lips tight, making a great effort to hold back his anger and the unaccountable fear that filled him, Leventhal put his hand to his throat and stared frowningly at Harkavy. He said loudly, 'And did you stand up for me?'

'Naturally I said he was mistaken and did all I could. I told him he was wrong.'

'You ought to have said that I came to you immediately with the whole story about Rudiger. You even thought that it might be rigged up, that Allbee and Rudiger wanted to make a fool of me and it was hatched out by the two of them. Did you bring that up?'

'No, I didn't take the trouble.'

'Why not!' He swiftly clenched his fist as though catching at something in the air. 'Why not!' he demanded. 'It was your duty if you're a friend of mine. Even if you didn't know the facts you should have defended me. And you did know the facts. I told them to you. You should have said it was a slander and a lie. If anybody repeated such a lie to me about you, you'd see how fast I'd take him up on it. It's not only loyalty but fairness. And how did he know what I did at Dill's? Why were you such a stick? Were you afraid to hurt his feelings by contradicting him?'

'I was not,' said Harkavy. His marveling eyes took Leventhal in, but he answered quietly. 'I didn't think it would benefit you if I argued with Williston. I just said that he was wrong.'

'My friend!'

'Yes, if you ever had one. I am your friend.'

'He might have asked me, before he said a thing like that, given me a chance to defend myself. He'd rather take that

79

drunk Allbee's word for it. Where's their Anglo-Saxon fairness . . . fair play?'

'It's hard for me to understand Williston's side of it. I had an idea he was pretty level.'

'Is it so hard?' Leventhal said bitterly. 'I told you why Allbee said I was out for revenge. And if Williston believes that I went to Dill's to make trouble, he must think what Allbee does, all around.'

'Who, Williston? Oh, you're way off, boy, way off.'

'Oh, am I? Well, you don't know what it's all about, I can see that. Williston is too nice a fellow, you mean. Talk about being innocent! Talk about a man of the world! Any child knows more about these things than you do, Dan. If he has it in him to think it was that insult . . . the insult to you, too, Dan, come to think of it. If that's what he believes . . .'

'Williston *is* a nice fellow,' said Harkavy. 'Remember, he was nice to you.'

'I do remember. What makes you think I don't? That's exactly it. That's what makes it so bad, horrible. That's the evil part of it. Of course he helped me. So now if he wants to believe this about me he has the right? Can't you see how it stacks up?' He groped. 'Certainly he helped me.'

'You can be sure he doesn't know what your Mr Allbee is up to and wouldn't like it if he did. Regardless. I mean that he couldn't believe that he says . . . that you ruined him. The man is off his trolley, sleuthing after you like that. He's disturbed in his mind. Haven't you ever seen such a case before? It's very pitiful. It happened in the family. My father's sister got strange during the change of life – said all the clocks were warning her to look out, look out, look out. Oh, she was just off. It was a calamity. She claimed that somebody was stealing out of her mailbox, taking letters. Oh, all kinds of things. I couldn't begin to tell you. Well, obviously that's the kind of case you're up against. It's disagreeable, but it's nothing to be alarmed about. She started telling people that she was Krueger the match king's widow, though my uncle was still living. Sometimes she said Cecil Rhodes, not Krueger. My grandfather fought in the Boer War. Where else could she have gotten that? She went to an institution, poor thing. How those ideas get into their heads only Heaven knows.'

Leventhal nodded inattentively. He could only brood over Williston. How could Williston believe that of him? Was it possible to know him and yet think him capable of deliberately injuring someone? For a reason like that? For any reason, even strict self-defense? He could not have imagined and carried out such a plan. Leventhal was deeply roused. He turned away from Harkavy, wrinkling up his eyes. Williston had helped him. He was indebted to him. Would he deny it? Harkavy had in his way rebuked him for seeming to forget it. He had not forgotten. But it was only natural to ask how much he owed Williston and how far gratitude should be expected to stretch. He had used the word 'evil' a while ago, and what had given rise to it was a feeling that Williston had made the accusation under an influence against which he could not help himself. If he was ready to believe that he was such and such a person – why avoid saying it? – that he would carry out a scheme like that because he was a Jew, then the turn he always feared had come and all good luck was canceled and all favors melted away. He looked hopelessly before him. Williston, like himself, like everybody else, was carried on currents, this way and that. The currents had taken a new twist, and he was being hurried, hurried. His heart shrank and he felt faint for a moment and shut his eyes.

'I'll get it from him straight,' he muttered, recovering himself a little. 'I won't take somebody else's word for it. That would be doing what he did.' He pulled out his handkerchief and mopped his face.

8

But the week passed and Leventhal made no move to get in touch with Williston, though he promised himself every day to clear up the whole business. Allbee did not appear, and Leventhal hoped that he had seen the last of him without really believing that he had. But at least matters in Staten Island were going better. Mickey was by no means out of danger; still he was improving, and Leventhal felt less worried about him. Max had wired back that he was ready to leave as soon as the doctor gave the word, and Leventhal wrote to say that while he thought Max ought to come home where he was needed, the decision was his own to make.

On Friday night Leventhal felt Mary's absence keenly. Before going to bed, he was tempted to put in a call to Charleston. He even went to the telephone, lifted it, and turned it, untangling the cord, but he set it down and went on undressing. He put on a white cotton robe she had given him on his last birthday, smoothing the lapels lightly and glancing down. She would be sure to feel if he called her now, at the beginning of the week-end, that he found being alone unendurable and was appealing to her to come home. And that would be unfair, since she could not come as long as her mother needed her. Also, when he hung up and she was inaccessible again, he would miss her even more than he did now. And she him.

There were several glasses on the sink. He washed them and turned them upside down to dry. Then he went into the dining-room which had been shut since her departure. He left all the doors in the flat standing open; it made him feel easier.

He did not sleep well. Most of the night he could hear the motor of the refrigerator shuddering and rocking as it started and stopped. Several times he opened his eyes because of it. The light was burning in the bathroom. There was a short downpour and mist floated at the window. Toward morning he was aware that someone was speaking loudly in the street and he listened, breathing heavily. There was enough light to see by. He had gone to bed in the cotton robe and he lay, both pillows under his head, his hands joined on his chest; his feet and outspread legs were visible beside the deep shadow of the wall. The air was gray and soft in the long defile of the street.

A woman's voice cried out, and he flung himself up, brushing aside the curtains with a clatter of rings. There was a commotion at the corner. He saw a man start a crazy rush at one of two women; another threw himself in his way, shrieking, and held him off. Across the street two soldiers stood watching. They had been with the women, it was clear enough, and then the man had caught them – perhaps a husband, a brother, probably the former – and they drew off. The man circled with short, sidling steps, and the woman hung back dumbly, with horrible attentiveness, ready to run. Her high heels knocked on the pavement. He had reached her once, her dress was ripped from neck to waist. She shook her head and pulled back her hair. He darted in again, grabbing at her, and the friend, uttering her begging, agonized cries, caught his arms and was swung round by him. The soldiers had an air of being present at an entertainment especially arranged for them, and seemed to laugh to themselves from time to time. The husband's soles scraped on the pavement as he pushed toward his wife, and this time she ran away. She ran up the street awkwardly but swiftly, her soft figure shaking, and the soldiers started off at once in the same direction. The husband did not chase her; he stood still. The other woman with her hands on his arm spoke to him urgently, thrusting forward her face. The rain was rapidly, unevenly drying from the street. Leventhal growled under his breath and wound the robe around himself more tightly. There was a gleam, as if a naked copper cable was lifted from the water and rose quickly, passing over masonry and windows. The sun was forcing its way through a corner of the gray air. The woman was still speaking to the man, imploring, pulling him the other way. She wanted him to go with her. Leventhal drew the shade and dropped into bed.

He was up at ten o'clock with a free week-end before him. The day had changed its look since dawn; it was warm, singularly beautiful. The color of the sky was strong; the clouds were as white as leghorn feathers rolling before a breeze that blew into the curtains and hauled at the strings of Mrs Nunez' flower boxes. Leventhal bathed, dressed, and went down for breakfast. In the restaurant he took a booth instead of sitting at the counter as he did on weekdays. He found a copy of the *Tribune* on the seat and read, propping the paper on the sugar shaker while he drank his coffee. Afterward he took a walk uptown, enjoying the weather and looking into shopwindows.

The scene on the corner remained with him, however, and he returned to it every now and then with the feeling that he really did not know what went on about him, what strange things, savage things. They hung near him all the time in trembling drops, invisible, usually, or seen from a distance. But that did not mean that there was always to be a distance, or that sooner or later one or two of the drops might not fall on him. As a matter of fact he was thinking of Allbee – he was not sure that he had stopped spying on him – and with the thought came a faint sick qualm. Once more he reminded himself that he had to call Williston. But gradually the qualm passed, and his intention slipped to the back of his mind. And later, when he took some nickels out of his pocket to pay for a drink and saw an empty phone booth at the rear of the store, he reconsidered and decided, for the time being, not to make the call. He had not seen Williston for three years or more, and to ask him, out of a clear sky, about something so difficult and obscure, perhaps forgotten, might appear strange. Besides, if Williston was capable of believing he had injured Allbee on purpose, he would be cold to him. And perhaps Harkavy was right. Perhaps he would be trying to get Williston to assure him that he still liked him, to demand that assurance of him more than fairness. He pictured Williston sitting before him in a habitual pose, at ease in his chair, his fingers in the pockets of his vest, red-cheeked, his blue eyes seeming to say, 'So much frankness and no more,' the exact amount remaining in doubt. In all likelihood Williston had made up his mind that he was responsible for what had happened to Allbee and while he would listen – if Leventhal knew him – with an appearance of courtesy and willingness to suspend judgment, he would already be convinced. To imagine himself pleading with him filled Leventhal with shame. Didn't he know, he himself, that he had never consciously wanted to harm Allbee? Of course he did. It was for Williston, even if he was his benefactor, to explain why he was ready to believe such a thing. And when you said that someone was your benefactor, what did it actually mean? You might help a man because he was a bother to you and you wanted to get rid of him. You might do it because you disliked him unfairly and wanted to pay for your prejudice and then, feeling that you had paid, you were free and even entitled to detest him. He did not say that it was so in Williston's case, but in a question like this you couldn't be blamed for examining every possibility, or accused of being cold-blooded or heartless. It was better to think well of people – there was a kind of command that you should. And on the whole it was Leventhal's opinion that he had an unsuspicious character and preferred to be taken advantage of rather than regard everyone with distrust. It was better to be genuinely unsuspicious; it was what they called Christian. But it was foolish and miserable to refuse to acknowledge the suspicions that came into your mind in an affair like this. Because if you had them you should not put on an innocent front with yourself and deny that you did.

At the same time Leventhal was reasonable enough to admit that he might be trying to release himself from a sense of obligation to Williston by finding fault with him. He had never been able to repay him. Was he looking for a chance to cancel the debt? He did not think so. He wished he could be sure. Ah, he told himself, he was sure. He had never felt anything but gratitude. Again and again he had said – Mary could testify – that Williston had saved him.

But then, as he dwelt on it, the whole affair began to lose much of its importance. It was, after all, something he could either take seriously or dismiss as an annoyance. It was up to him. He had only to insist that he wasn't responsible and it disappeared altogether. It was his conviction against an accusation nobody could expect him to take at face value. And what more was there for him to say than that his part in it was accidental? At worst, an accident, unintentional.

The morning, with its brilliance and its simple contrasts, white and blue, shining and darkened, had a balancing effect on him of which he was conscious. He looked up, and a slight smile appeared on his face, swarthy in the sunlight. His clean white shirt was crookedly buttoned and tight at the neck; he put his fingers inside the band and tugged at it, drawing his chin up, and he straightened his shirt front clumsily, his gold wedding ring clicking on the buttons.

At noon he was in the west Forties. He ate a bowl of chili in a place opposite a music shop where a man in shirt sleeves, standing at one of the broad-swung windows on the second floor, blurted out an occasional note, testing a horn, one arm embracing the shining roundness of the brass. He was blowing erratically rich impatient notes and deep snores whose resonance Leventhal felt somehow entering his very blood as he gazed into the sun and dust of the peaceful street. He broke a cigar out of its wrapper, making a ball of the cellophane small enough to squeeze into the band. He felt along his thigh for matches and, when he had blown out his first puff, he walked into a booth and phoned Elena. One of the Villani children was sent to fetch her. Leventhal's eyes remained fixed on the horn player during the conversation.

Elena sounded quieter than usual. She was going to visit Mickey at three o'clock. He asked her about Philip and while Elena, after she had said, 'Oh, Phillie? He's upstairs,' went on talking about the hospital, Leventhal conceived the idea of spending the day with him and interrupted her to propose that Philip come over to Manhattan.

'I'll meet him at South Ferry. If you want me to, I'll come for him.'

'Oh, I'll send him,' said Elena. 'That's fine. He'll like it. No, he can go on the ferry himself. What's there to it?'

Already full of plans, Leventhal hurried into the street. They would take a ride along the Drive on an open bus. The boy might enjoy that. Perhaps he would prefer Times Square, the shooting galleries, the penny arcades and pinball games. He congratulated himself on having thought of Philip; he was delighted. He would have passed the time tolerably well, he reflected, until some time toward evening when he realized he had not spoken three words to a living soul and the blues descended on him. And Philip, too, would have been left alone when his mother went to the hospital. Leventhal took the train downtown and sat in the small square on a bench commanding the ferry gates.

He kept his swarthy, unimpassioned face turned to the exit. The strain of waiting made him almost tremble, yet it was pleasurable, a pleasurable excitement. He wondered why it was that lately he was more susceptible than he had ever been before to certain kinds of feeling. With everybody except Mary he was inclined to be short and neutral, outwardly a little like his father, and this shortness of his was, when you came right down to it, merely neglectfulness. When you didn't want to take trouble with people, you found the means to turn them aside. Well, the world was a busy place – he

87

scanned the buildings, the banks and offices in their Saturday stillness, the pillars ribbed with soot, and the changeable color of the windows in which the more absolute color of the sky was darkened, dilated, and darkened again. You couldn't find a place in your feelings for everything, or give at every touch like a swinging door, the same for everyone, with people going in and out as they pleased. On the other hand, if you shut yourself up, not wanting to be bothered, then you were like a bear in a winter hole, or like a mirror wrapped in a piece of flannel. And like such a mirror you were in less danger of being broken, but you didn't flash, either. But you had to flash. That was the peculiar thing. Everybody wanted to be what he was to the limit. When you looked around, that was what you saw most distinctly. In great achievements as well as in crimes and vices. When that woman faced her husband this morning after he had most likely tracked her all night from joint to joint and finally caught her catting, too red-handed to defend herself; when she faced him, wasn't she saying, silently, 'I'm being up to the limit just what I am'? In this case, a whore. She may have been mistaken in herself. You couldn't expect people to be right, but only try to do what they must. Therefore hideous things were done, cannibalistic things. Good things as well, of course. But even there, nothing really good was safe.

There was something in people against sleep and dullness, together with the caution that led to sleep and dullness. Both were there, Leventhal thought. We were all the time taking care of ourselves, laying up, storing up, watching out on this side and on that side, and at the same time running, running desperately, running as if in an egg race with the egg in a spoon. And sometimes we were fed up with the egg, sick of it, and at such a time would rather sign on with the devil and what they called the powers of darkness that run with the spoon, watching the egg, fearing for the egg. Man is weak and breakable, has to have just the right amounts of everything – water, air, food; can't eat twigs and stones; has to keep his bones from breaking and his fat from melting. This and that. Hoards sugar and potatoes, hides money in his mattress, spares his feelings whenever he can, and takes pains and precautions. That, you might say, was for the sake of the egg. Dying is spoiling, then? Addling? And the last judgment, candling? Leventhal chuckled and rubbed his cheek. There was also the opposite, playing catch with the egg, threatening the egg.

Boats from the island were arriving every few minutes, and, after the crowds had several times poured out and dispersed, Leventhal saw Philip standing at the gates. He got up and beckoned him, grunting, 'Here, this way,' and, waving his arm, advanced to the curb. The noise of the busses made shouting useless. 'Here, here!' He motioned, and at last the boy saw him and came over.

'Well, was it nice crossing?' were Leventhal's first words. 'It's a swell day. You can smell the sea here.' He breathed deeply. 'Fish and clams.'

He observed approvingly that Philip's short hair was wetted and brushed, and that his shirt collar, which lay over the collar of his coat, was fresh and clean. He himself was wearing a seersucker suit that had just come back from the laundry; it made him feel set for the holiday.

'Now, how will we go uptown? On the bus?' He touched the boy on the shoulder. 'There isn't much to look at on a Saturday from the Broadway bus.'

'Oh, I get over to Manhattan,' said Philip. 'I know what it looks like. Let's take the subway.'

They walked down, Leventhal guiding him through the turnstile and the gloom of the curved platform. A distant, rapid concussion of cars, like hammer blows, came to them in the tunnel.

It was fortunate that Philip was talkative, for, if he had been shy, Leventhal would have thought he was being reproached for his past neglect, not to be made up for in a single afternoon. He had read such a reproach into his silence last week, when he gave him the quarter. But there was no cause for misgiving. Philip talked on fluently, and Leventhal, though his mind sometimes appeared to be elsewhere, was secretly minutely attentive. The emotions Philip raised in him deepened his ordinary stolidity. But he glanced frequently at the slope of his cropped, handsome long head and into his face, and he thought that Elena's blood might show in his features but not in his nature. There they had something in common. The boy seemed to see it, too, Leventhal told himself.

Philip put his hand on a chocolate slot machine on one of the pillars, and Leventhal hastily went through his pockets for pennies and put in five or six, turning the knobs. The train rolled in while he was getting the chocolate out of the metal trough, and they abandoned the machine and ran.

'What do you say we walk a little?' Leventhal suggested at Pennsylvania Station. They got out and started up toward Times Square.

The air was stiller here in midtown, and they walked, Leventhal listening to Philip's chatter, often a little puzzled by it. Philip was curious about the foundations of the skyscrapers. Was it true that they had to have shock absorbers? They must have something to ride out the vibrations of the subway and to take in the play at the top, the swaying. They all swayed. Max had told him that in a ship the plates were arranged in parts of the deck to give when there was bad weather to ride out.

'It sounds reasonable,' said Leventhal. 'Of course, I'm no engineer.'

Philip went on, speculating about what there was under the street in addition to foundations: the pipes, water pipes and sewage, gas mains, the electrical system for the subway, telephone and telegraph wires, and the cable for the Broadway trolley.

'I suppose they have maps and charts at City Hall.' Leventhal stopped. 'What about a drink?'

They had a glass of orangeade at a bamboo stand where the paper grass bristled on the walls. The woman at the tank clapped down the pull with her wrist, holding her fingers with their cameo rings rigid. The drink was slightly bitter with ground rinds.

Coming out of the stand they walked into a crowd that had formed around a man selling toy dogs that skittered and barked. The peddler, in a flecked sweat shirt and broken shoes, a band with Indian figures on his forehead, pushed them with his wide toe whenever they slowed down. 'Run three minutes, guarantee,' he said. To wind them he clasped them by the head; his fingers were too big to get at the key easily. 'Three minutes. Two bits. They cost me eighteen. That's the con.' He made his joke sullenly. His cheeks were heavy, his gaze unconciliating. 'Three minutes. Don't pester, don't *shtup*. Buy or beat it.'

There was laughter among the bystanders. 'What's he saying?' Philip wanted to know.

'He's telling them in Yiddish not to push,' Leventhal replied. He was reminded of what Allbee had said about Jews and New York. 'Come on, Phil,' he said.

On Forty-second Street the boy stopped often to look at the stills outside theaters, and Leventhal reluctantly – he did not care for movies – asked whether he wanted to take in a show. 'I'd certainly like to,' Philip said. Leventhal surmised that Mickey's illness had probably interfered with his Saturday movie-going.

'Any one you want,' he said.

Philip chose a horror picture, and they bought tickets and passed over the brown rugs of the sunless lobby, between the nebulous lamps in their shattered, dust-eaten silk shades, and the long brocaded chairs, into the stifling darkness. They sat down in the leather seats.

On the screen an old scientist was seen haunting the dressing room of a theater where he had murdered his mistress many years ago. He had hallucinations about a young star who resembled her and he attempted to strangle the girl. The flaring lights hurt Leventhal's eyes, the music was strident, and, after half an hour of it, his nerves jarred, he went down to the lavatory. He found an old man there, leaning against a yellow sink, picking clean the end of a rolled cigarette.

'The stuff they put Karloff in,' he said. 'A man of his ability.'

'You like him?' said Leventhal.

'In his line, he's a genius.' He offered Leventhal a light, holding the match vertically pinched between limy white nails; his fingers were raw; he must be a dishwasher. 'Here he's horsing around. It's an inferior vehicle. Even so, he shines. He really understands what a mastermind is, a law unto himself. That's what he's got my admiration for.'

Leventhal threw away his cigarette; the smell of disinfectants interfered with the taste of it. He rejoined Philip, sliding into the seat. He shortly fell asleep. The efforts of the man next to him to push out of the row woke him up. He rose suddenly and heard the music of the newsreel.

'Phil, let's go. There's no air in the place,' said Leventhal. 'It's a wonder anybody stays awake.'

The street was glaring when they emerged. The lights in the marquee were wan. There was a hot, overrich smell of roasting peanuts and caramel corn. A metallic clapping sound came to them from a shooting gallery. And for a time Leventhal felt empty and unstable. The sun was too strong, the swirling traffic too loud, too swift.

'Well, where next?' he asked. 'What about the park? We can take in the zoo. A little fresh air wouldn't be bad, would it? Out in the open? We'll have a sandwich first and then walk down.'

Philip agreed, and Leventhal could only guess whether the idea pleased him, or whether, having had his way about the movies, he felt obliged to acquiesce. 'I'm out of touch with kids,' he thought. 'Maybe he's too sophisticated for the zoo.

But I don't know why he should be.' His earlier confidence in the understanding between them was fading.

'Is there anything you'd rather do instead?' he said to the boy. 'You don't have to be afraid to speak up.'

'The only thing I can think of is the Dodgers against Boston. But it must be about the fifth inning by now. I'm not afraid to speak up.'

'Good. We'll get the ball game another time. When you've got something on your mind, I want you to tell me. Meanwhile let's have a bite.'

The restaurant they went into was an immense place, choked with people. There were several lines before each counter. Leventhal sent Philip to buy soft drinks; he himself went for sandwiches. They found a table and Leventhal began to eat, but Philip went in search of a mustard jar. Leventhal sat sipping out of his bottle. Suddenly there was a stir in the crowd at the front of the restaurant; voices rose sharply. Several people stood up on chairs to see what was happening. Leventhal, too, lifted himself up and looked around for Philip, frowning, beginning to feel troubled. He entered the crowd and pushed forward.

'Here's my uncle. Uncle!' shouted Philip, catching sight of him. His arm was held by a man whose back was turned but whose blond head and cotton jacket Leventhal immediately recognized.

'What are you doing?' he said. In his astonishment he spoke neither to Philip nor to Allbee, but, as it were, to them both.

'I took the mustard from the table and this man grabbed me,' Philip cried.

'That's right, I did. You put it back.'

Leventhal flushed and pulled Philip away from Allbee.

'Oh, so this is your uncle?' Allbee smiled, but his eyes did not rest long on Leventhal. He was playing to the crowd and, standing there, his head hung awkwardly forward, he could hardly keep from laughing at the sensation he was making.

And yet there was the usual false note, the note of impersonation in what he did.

'I asked if I could have the mustard. I asked a lady and she said it was all right,' said Philip. 'Where is she?'

'That's right, mister.' Leventhal met the distressed eyes of a young girl. White-faced, she pressed her pocketbook to her breast.

'What did I tell you?'

'You sneaked the mustard jar away. It doesn't belong to this young woman. It belongs to the table.'

'I didn't see you at the table,' she cried.

'You keep on following me around,' said Leventhal in a low voice, tensely, 'you keep it up and see what happens. I'll get out a warrant. I'm not joking.'

'Oh, I could get a warrant out for you on a battery charge. Very easily. There was a witness.'

'I should have broken your neck,' Leventhal muttered. His large head twitched. Because of the boy he dissembled his anger.

'Oh, you should have. I wish it was broken.' Allbee moistened his lips and stared at him.

'Come on, Phil.' Leventhal led him out of the crowd.

'Who is he?' asked Philip.

'He's a nuisance. I used to know him years ago. Don't pay any attention to him. He's just a nuisance.'

They sat down. Philip smeared mustard on his sandwich and looked silently at his uncle.

'It didn't upset you, did it?'

'Well, I jumped when he grabbed me, but I wasn't afraid of him.'

'He's nothing to be afraid of.' He pushed his plate across the table. 'Here, eat this half of mine, Phil.' His heart was pounding. He gazed at the entrance. Allbee was out of sight for the moment.

'I won't stand it,' he thought. 'He'd better stay away from me.'

9

In the thronged zoo, Leventhal kept an eye out for Allbee. Defiant and alert at first, he soon became depressed. For if Allbee wanted to trail him how could he prevent it? Among so many people he could come close without being seen. Frequently Leventhal felt that he was watched and he endured it passively. Half out of fear of being mistaken, he made no effort to catch Allbee. He tried to put him out of his thoughts and give all his attention to Philip, forcing himself to behave naturally. But now and then, moving from cage to cage, gazing at the animals, Leventhal, in speaking to Philip, or smoking, or smiling, was so conscious of Allbee, so certain he was being scrutinized, that he was able to see himself as if through a strange pair of eyes: the side of his face, the palpitation in his throat, the seams of his skin, the shape of his body and of his feet in their white shoes. Changed in this way into his own observer, he was able to see Allbee, too, and imagined himself standing so near behind him that he could see the weave of his coat, his raggedly overgrown neck, the bulge of his cheek, the color of the blood in his ear; he could even evoke the odor of his hair and skin. The acuteness and intimacy of it astounded him, oppressed and intoxicated him. The heat was climbing again, and the pungency of the animals and the dry hay, dust, and manure filled his head; the sun, overflowing above the topmost twigs and bent back from bars and cages, white and glowing in long shapes, deprived him for a moment of his sense of the usual look of things, and he was afraid, too, that his strength was leaving him. But he felt normal again when he forced himself to walk on.

Leaving the zoo, he and Philip went into the park. Philip wanted to rest and went toward a bench. But Leventhal said, 'We'll find a place with more shade,' because this was at a crossing of two paths and exposed to all directions. They sat down on a slope where no one could approach unseen. At the crossing, about fifty yards distant, there was a knot of people, one of whom might have been Allbee. Evening was coming on, and a new tide of heat with it, thickening the air, sinking grass and bushes under its weight. Leventhal watched. He even thought of turning the tables on Allbee, lying in wait for him somewhere. But what if he did trap him, what use was it? Would he embarrass him? He was beyond being embarrassed. Beat him? With pleasure. But he felt that he ought to beware, for his own sake, of countering absurdity with absurdity and madness with madness. And of course he did not want to make another scene while Philip was with him. He did not know what effect Allbee had had on him in the restaurant. He believed that Philip realized how much the incident had disconcerted him and therefore tactfully hid his feelings. He had a mind to talk to him about it. But he did not want to betray his anxiety; furthermore, he was afraid to begin a conversation without knowing in advance where it would lead. And maybe he was giving the boy credit for too much discernment. But the mood of the outing had changed. Philip looked pensive; he had nothing to say; and it would have been natural for him to mention the incident once, at least. Certainly he hadn't forgotten it.

'What's up, Phil,' he said.

'Nothing. My feet are tired,' he answered, and Leventhal remained in the dark as to what Philip really felt.

He decided to take a taxi to the ferry and he stood up, saying, 'Let's go, Phil. Time to get you back.' He set a rapid pace toward Fifth Avenue. Philip appeared to be somewhat puzzled by his haste but he enjoyed the ride in the open-roofed cab. Leventhal accompanied him to Staten Island and put him on the bus. Then he returned to Manhattan.

About nine o'clock, after a seafood dinner he barely tasted, he was on his way home without a thought of going elsewhere. He wandered into a cigar store, glanced round at the shelves beyond the flame on the counter, and bought a package of cigarettes. He took the change absent-mindedly, but, instead of putting it in his pocket, he began to look through it to find a nickel with which to phone Williston. For all at once he had a consuming need to get an explanation from him, tonight, immediately. He could not understand why he had put it off all week. He leafed through the directory quickly, copied the number out, and went into the booth.

Phoebe Williston answered, and the sound of her voice gave him an unexpected stab; he was reminded of the many times he had called to ask a favor of Williston, to get advice from him, or an introduction. The Willistons had been patient with him, usually, and he had often rather helplessly and dumbly put his difficulties in their hands and waited, sat in their parlor or hung on the telephone, waiting while his problems were weighed, conscious that he was contributing nothing to their solution, wishing he could withdraw them but powerless to do so. Inevitably there had been times when his calls were unwelcome and the Willistons' patience overdrawn. Whenever he rang their bell, or dropped a nickel in the slot and heard the dial tone, the question in his heart was, 'How will it be this time?' And now, too, it was present, despite the fact that the circumstances were altogether different.

'This is Leventhal,' he said. 'How are you?'

'Leventhal? Oh, Asa Leventhal. How are you, Asa?' He thought she didn't sound unfriendly. It was too much to ask that she should be positively cordial, considering that this was his first call in three or four years.

'I'm good enough.'

'You want to talk to Stan, I suppose.'

'Yes.'

He heard the instrument being laid on the table with a

97

knock and then, for several minutes, the sound of a conversation carried on at a distance. 'He doesn't want to talk to me,' thought Leventhal. 'He must be telling her that she should have said he was out.' Presently the phone was picked up.

'Hello, there.'

'Yes, hello. Is that you, Asa?'

Leventhal said without preliminaries, 'Say, Stan, I want to see you. Can you give me a little time tonight?'

'Oh, tonight? That's pretty short notice.'

'Yes, I know it is. I should have asked if you were going out.'

'Well, we were planning to later, as a matter of fact.'

'I won't stay. About fifteen minutes is all I want.'

'Where are you now?'

'Not far. I'll grab a taxi.'

It seemed to him that Williston did not conceal his reluctance. But when he said, 'All right,' Leventhal did not even bother to say good-by. He did not care how Williston consented to see him, just so he consented. He went into the middle of the street and flagged a cab. Of course, he observed to himself getting in, Williston was displeased by his phoning and blurting out his request, dispensing with the usual formalities. But there was much more than that to be concerned about, assuming that Williston really did side with Allbee. There was fairness, a man's reputation, honor. And there were other considerations as well.

The cab raced uptown, and Leventhal suddenly felt his face burning, for he had just recalled a verse his father had liked to repeat:

> *Ruf mir Yoshke, ruf mir Moshke,*
> *Aber gib mir die groschke.*

'Call me Ikey, call me Moe, but give me the dough. What's it to me if you despise me? What do you think equality with you means to me? What do you have that I care about except the *groschen*?' That was his father's view. But not his. He rejected it and recoiled from it. Anyway, his father had lived poor and died poor, that stern, proud old fool with his savage looks, to whom nothing mattered save his advantage and to be freed by money from the power of his enemies. And who were the enemies? The world, everyone. They were imaginary. There was no advantage. He carried on like a merchant prince among his bolts and remnants, and was willing to be a pack rat in order to become a lion. There was no advantage; he never became a lion. It gave Leventhal pain to think about his father's sense of these things. He roused himself to tell the driver to hurry. But the cab was already in Williston's block, and he grasped the handle of the door.

He recognized the elderly Negro who took him up in the elevator. Short, broad-shouldered, and slow, he stooped over the lever, handling it with the utmost deliberateness. They rose and stopped smoothly on the fourth floor. The knocker on Williston's door was also familiar – a woman's head cast in copper that surprised you by its heaviness.

Phoebe Williston let him in. Leventhal shook hands with her and she preceded him along the high-walled gray corridor into the living-room. Williston stood up from his chair in the bay window, a newspaper falling from his lap and spreading around the base of the lamp. He was in his shirt sleeves, the cuffs turned back on his smooth, reddish forearms. He hadn't lost any of his ruddy color. His brown hair was brushed sideways and his dark green satin tie hung unknotted from his buttoned collar.

'Pretty much the same, eh?' he said in his pleasant, deep voice.

'Yes, just about. You, too, I see.'

'A couple of years older all around,' Phoebe remarked.

'Well, it goes without saying.'

Williston brought another chair forward in the bay window and the two men sat down. Phoebe remained standing, resting her weight on one foot, her arms folded, and Leventhal thought that her look was fixed on him longer than it

99

need have been. He submitted to this prolonged look with an air of allowing her the right, under the circumstances, to inspect him.

'You seem to be all right, filled out,' she said. 'How's your wife?'

'Oh, she's out of town for a while, down South with her mother and family. She's fine.'

'Lord! South in this weather? And are you still in the same place?'

'Address or job? Both the same. The same job, Burke and Beard; same people. I guess Stan knows.'

The maid came in to ask Phoebe a question. She was a pale, slow-spoken girl. Phoebe listened, inclining her head and twisting her necklace in her fingers. She went back with her to the kitchen. Williston explained, 'That's a new girl learning her way around.' Leventhal, as in the past, felt conscious of a household that had more of the atmosphere of established habit than any he had ever known. Williston lay loosely in his chair, crossing his feet, his fingers pushed under his belt. Within the metal guard of the semicircular window were several flowerpots with blossoms coarse as bits of red ore. Looking at them, Leventhal considered how he should begin. He was unprepared. It had seemed simple enough; he came with a grievance and he wanted an explanation. Perhaps he had counted on finding Williston roused against him; he certainly had not expected him to sit back and wait while minute after minute of the time he had requested ran out. He had not foreseen the effect Williston was having on him; he had forgotten what he was like. More than once, in the old days, he had mistrusted him. He had been full of rancor toward him when he thought Williston was uneasy about the reference letter. But on that occasion and others he had changed his opinion; he invariably did when he was face to face with Williston. He came to him complaining, but soon, without quite knowing how it happened, he began to feel unsure of his ground. So it was now, and he was unable to start.

He sat in the bay window looking down, over the heads of the flowers, at the sprinting headlights in the depth of the park below the net of trees, as they turned on a curve and illuminated the boulders and trailing bushes of a steep hillside, one beam after another passing through an immobility of black and green.

'I wanted to talk to you about your friend Allbee,' he said at last. 'Maybe you understand what he's up to.'

Williston was immediately interested; he lifted himself up in his chair. 'Allbee? Have you seen him?'

'I sure have.'

'I lost track of him years ago. What's he doing? Where did you see him?'

But Leventhal would answer no questions till he knew where he stood with Williston. 'What was he doing last time you saw him?' he said.

'Nothing. He was living on insurance money. His wife was killed, you know.'

'I heard.'

'It hit him hard. He loved her.'

'All right, he loved her. He didn't go to her funeral. And why did she leave him?'

Williston raised his eyes to him curiously. 'Why,' he said with a certain reserve, 'I can't say for sure. That was something between them.'

Leventhal was quick to feel the rebuke in this and he changed his tone somewhat. 'Yes, I guess a third party never really gets the true story. I thought maybe you knew.' He sensed that he ought to explain himself further. 'I'm not trying to find out something that's none of my business. I have a good reason. Maybe you have an idea what it is . . . ?'

'Well, I think I do,' Williston replied.

Leventhal's heart ran hot. 'I understand that you take his side,' he said. 'You know what about. You think I'm responsible for everything, just as he does.'

'Everything takes in a lot of territory,' said Williston.

'What are you driving at? I'd be more specific about something I was going to land on a man for.' He was not quite so composed and genial, now; his voice was beginning to sound taut, and Leventhal thought, 'Better, much better. Maybe we'll get somewhere.' He bent his heavy, dark face forward.

'I didn't come to accuse you of anything, Stan. I'm not landing on you. I came to ask why you said certain things about me without hearing my side of the case?'

'Unless you tell me exactly what you're talking about, I can't answer.'

'You want me to believe that you don't know? You know . . .' he made an ill-defined pushing gesture. 'I want you to tell me right out if you think it's my fault that Allbee was fired from *Dill's Weekly*.'

'You do? You want to?' Williston asked this grimly, as if offering him the opportunity to reconsider or withdraw the question.

'Yes.'

'Well, I think it is.'

A hard stroke of disappointment and anger went through Leventhal and drove the breath from his body. His limbs were empty; his thighs felt hollow and rigid as brass, and he could not stir his hands from them. He hardly knew what expressions were crossing his face.

'It is . . . It is?' he said, struggling. 'I don't see why.'

'For definite reasons.'

Leventhal, his glance bitter and uncertain, said stumblingly, 'I wanted to know . . .'

Williston did not treat this as needing an answer.

Leventhal continued more surely, 'I asked you, so you were bound to give me your opinion. If it's right, fair enough. But what if it's wrong? It might be wrong.'

'I'm not infallible.'

'No. When you say it's my fault, you're as good as telling me that I set out to make trouble for Allbee because of the way he acted toward Harkavy that night at your house, here.

It must mean that I wanted to get even with him because of what he said about Jews.' Williston's frown told him that this was something he didn't want to hear. Ah, but he would hear it, Leventhal said to himself fiercely. 'That's what Allbee claims, that I wasn't going to let him get away with it and I made a plan to get him kicked out of his job. So, now, do you think that too?'

'I didn't say so.'

'But if you blame me you must have the same idea. I don't see any difference. And what if it is wrong? Isn't it awful if you're wrong? Doesn't it make me out to be terrible without giving me a chance to tell my side of it? Is that fair? You may think you have a different slant on it than Allbee has, but it comes out the same. If you believe I did it on purpose, to get even, then it's not only because I'm terrible personally but because I'm a Jew.'

Williston's face had flamed up harshly. At either corner of his mouth there was a white spot of compression. He looked at Leventhal as though to warn him of the dangerous strain on his self-control. 'I shouldn't have to tell you, Asa, that that wouldn't enter into it with me,' he said. 'You misunderstand me. I hope Allbee didn't tell you that I agree with him about that. I don't.'

'That sounds fine, Stan. But it adds up to the same thing, as far as I'm concerned. You think that he burned me up and I wanted to get him in bad. Why? Because I'm a Jew; Jews are touchy, and if you hurt them they won't forgive you. That's the pound of flesh. Oh, I know you think there isn't any room in you for that; it's superstition. But you don't change anything by calling it superstition. Every once in a while you'll hear people say, "That's from the Middle Ages." My God! We have a name for everything except what we really think and feel.'

'Looks like you're pretty sure of what I feel and think,' Williston said stingingly, and then he shut his teeth and seemed to fight off his exasperation. 'The Jewish part of it is your own invention. You take it for granted that I think you got Allbee in trouble purposely. I didn't say that. Maybe you aimed to hurt him and maybe you didn't. My opinion is that you didn't. But the effect was the same. You lost him his job. He might have lost it anyway, eventually. He was shaky at *Dill's*; they had him on probation.'

'How do you know?'

'I knew it then and I had a talk with Rudiger about it later. He told me so himself.'

Leventhal's black eyes went vacant. 'Go on!' he said.

'That's the story. I would have told you right away but you wanted to jump all over me first. Rudiger claimed that Allbee brought you up to Dill's on purpose and that he either gave you instructions or knew you would act as you did. They had it in for each other. I guess Rudiger isn't an easy person to please. He was giving Allbee a last chance but he was more than likely hankering for him to make a false step so that he could land on him. He must have been on his tail all the time and he knew best whether Allbee had reasons for wanting to get a lick in at him.'

'The whole thing is crazy. You can't answer for everybody you recommend. You know that . . . But that's what Rudiger told you?'

Williston nodded.

'And didn't Allbee's boozing have anything to do with it?'

'He lost quite a few jobs because he drank. I won't deny it. His reputation wasn't good.'

'Was he on a black list?' Leventhal said, intensely curious.

Williston was not looking at him. His face was directed reflectively toward the flowers, rough and crumbling in the warm night air.

'Well, as I say, he was on probation at *Dill's*. I asked Rudiger about the drinking. He had to admit Allbee had stayed on the wagon. He wasn't fired because he drank.'

'So . . .' Leventhal said blankly. 'In a way it really seems to be my fault, doesn't it?' He paused and gazed abstractedly at Williston, his hands still motionless on his knees. 'In one way. Of course I didn't mean to get him in trouble. I didn't know what this man Rudiger was like . . .'

'No, you didn't.'

There was something more than agreement in this reply. Leventhal waited for Williston to make it explicit but he waited in vain.

'How was I supposed to know what I was walking into?' he said. 'This Rudiger . . . I don't see how anybody works for him. He's vicious. He started right away to tear at me like a dog.'

'Rudiger said that never in all his experience had he had such an interview.'

'Nobody ever talked back to him. He's used to doing whatever he likes. He . . .'

Williston whose color had deepened again to a hard red interrupted. 'Don't let yourself off so easily. You were fighting everybody, those days. You were worst with Rudiger, but I heard of others. You came to ask him for a job and he wouldn't give you one. He didn't have to, did he? You should have had better judgment than to blow up.'

'What, wipe the spit off my face and leave like a gentleman? I wouldn't think much of myself if I did.'

'That's just it.'

'What is? What I think of myself? Well . . .' He checked himself, sighed, and gave a slightly submissive shrug. 'I don't know. You go to see a man about work. It isn't only the job but your right to live. Say it isn't his lookout; he's got his own interests. But you think you've got something he can use. You're there to sell yourself to him. Well, he tells you you haven't got a goddam thing. Not only what he wants, but nothing. Christ, nobody wants to be cut down like that.' He suddenly felt weak-headed and confused; his face was wet. He changed the position of his feet uneasily on the soft circle of the carpet.

'You were wrong.'

'Maybe,' Leventhal said, drooping. 'My nerves were shot. And I never was any good at rubbing people the right way. I don't know how to please them.'

'You're not long on tact, that's perfectly true,' said Williston. He seemed somewhat appeased.

'I never intended to hurt Allbee. That's my word of honor.'

'I believe you.'

'Do you? Thanks. You'd do me a favor if you'd tell Allbee that.'

'I don't see him. I told you before that I haven't seen him for years.'

Allbee was ashamed to show himself to his old friends, Leventhal thought. Of course it was only natural.

'He thinks I'm his worst enemy.'

'Where did you run into him? What's he doing? I didn't even know he was still in New York. He sank out of sight.'

'He's been following me around,' Leventhal said. And he told Williston about his three encounters with Allbee. Williston listened with a gravely examining expression and a modified but noticeable disapproving tightness at the corners of his mouth. Leventhal concluded, 'I don't see what he's after. I can't find out what he wants.'

'You ought to,' said Williston. 'You certainly ought.'

'Does he mean that I ought to do something for him?' said Leventhal to himself. That, unmistakably, was what he implied. But what and how? It was not at all clear. He felt that he had not said everything he had come to say. The really important things, the deepest issues, had not been touched. But he saw that it was necessary for him to accept some of the blame for Allbee's comedown. He had contributed to it, though he had yet to decide to what extent he was to blame. Allbee had been making a last great effort to hold on to his job . . . However, it was time to go. He had taken up much more than his fifteen minutes. He stood up.

Williston said at the door that he expected to hear from

him about the matter; he was very much interested in what was happening to Allbee.

Leventhal pressed the button for the elevator. It started up with a subdued meshing and locking of the metal doors and rose with measured slowness.

In bed later, lying near the wall, his knees pulled up and his face resting on the striped ticking of the mattress, Leventhal went over his mistakes. Some of them made him wince; others caught at his heart too savagely for wincing, and he stifled his emotion altogether and all expression, merely moving his lids downward. He did not try to spare himself; he recalled them all, from his attack on Williston tonight to the original scene in Rudiger's office. When he came to this, he turned on his back and crossed his bare arms over his eyes.

But even as he did so, he recognized one of those deeper issues that he had failed to reach before. He was ready to accept the blame for losing his head at *Dill's*. But why had he lost it? Only because of Rudiger's abuse? No, he, he himself had begun to fear that the lowest price he put on himself was too high and he could scarcely understand why anyone should want to pay for his services. And under Rudiger's influence he had felt this. 'He made me believe what I was afraid of,' Leventhal thought, and he doubted whether Williston could have understood this. For he belonged to the professional world and was loyal to it. There was always a place for someone like him, there or elsewhere. And another man's words and looks could never convert him into his own worst enemy. He did not have to worry about that.

Williston had not tried to justify Rudiger, true, but to Leventhal it was apparent that he himself was considered the greater offender. And looking at the incident from Rudiger's standpoint and taking Allbee's character into account, too, it was, after all, plausible that he, Leventhal, had been sent with instructions to make a scene. Harkavy had suspected Allbee and Rudiger of rigging it up in the first place. It had seemed reasonable to him and it seemed reasonable also to Rudiger. Only to Rudiger the suspicion was instantly true, true because it occurred to him, probably. That was the kind of man he was.

There was still another consideration – he ran his hand down his throat and through the hair of his chest which began with the shaven line above his collarbone. Had he unknowingly, that is, unconsciously, wanted to get back at Allbee? He was sure he hadn't. The night of the party he was angry, of course. But since then, no. Truthfully, no. Williston had said that he believed him; he wondered, however, whether he really did. It was hard to tell where you stood with Williston.

10

LEVENTHAL ran into Harkavy early Sunday afternoon in a cafeteria on Fourteenth Street.

He had come in as much to escape the hot wind as to eat. The glass door shut on the dusty rush behind him, and he advanced a few steps over the green tile floor and paused, opening his mouth a little to take in the coolness of the place. The trays were on a stand nearby, and he picked one up and started toward the counter. The cashier called him back. He had forgotten to pull a check from the machine. She smiled. 'Sunday hangover, or what?' But Leventhal did not respond. He turned from the machine and found Harkavy standing in his path.

'Are you hard of hearing this morning? Man, I called you three, four times.'

'Hello. Oh, the cashier was yelling too. I can't hear everything at once.'

'You're not very alert today, are you? Anyway, come sit with us. I'm here with some people. My brother-in-law – you know Julia's husband, Goldstone – and some of his friends.'

'Do I know them?'

'I think you do,' said Harkavy. 'Shifcart's one of them.'

'That musician? The trumpeter?'

'Not any longer. Give the woman your order or you'll never get waited on. No, he's not in that line any more. He's with a big Hollywood outfit, Persevalli and Company, the impresarios and talent farmers, or whatever you call them. And you remember Schlossberg.'

'Do I?'

'Oh, sure you do. The journalist. He writes for the Jewish papers.'

'What does he write?'

'Whatever comes to hand, I think. Nowadays, theater reminiscences – he used to be a theatrical man. But science, too, I hear. You know, I can't read Yiddish.'

'Let me have a Swiss on rye,' said Leventhal over the counter. 'Elderly man, isn't he? Didn't I meet him at your house with someone else?'

'That's right; his son, whom he still supports at thirty-five.'

'Is he sick?'

'No, just looking around; hasn't made up his mind about a vocation. There are daughters, too. Worse yet.'

'Loose?'

'Here's your sandwich,' said Harkavy. The woman sent the plate across the counter with a spin and a rattle, and Harkavy hurried Leventhal to his table. The three men shifted their chairs to make room.

'This is an old friend of mine, Leventhal.'

'I think I used to know Mr Shifcart,' said Leventhal. '– How are you? – When I roomed with Dan, we met.'

'In the bachelor days,' Harkavy said. 'Goldstone – no introduction needed. And this is Mr Schlossberg.'

Shifcart was bald and high-colored, his neck was thick and his lips small but fleshy. He said amicably, 'Yes, I think I place you,' and with a spanning hand pressed on the round gold rims of his glasses. Schlossberg repeated his name sonorously but obviously did not remember him. He spoke in deep tones, not always distinctly because of his heavy breathing. He was a large old man with a sturdy gray head, hulking shoulders, and a wide, worn face; his eyes were blue and disproportionately small, and even their gaze was rather worn. But he was vigorous and he must once have been (some of his remarks evoked him, for Leventhal, as a younger man) sensual, powerful, flashy, a dandy – as his double-breasted vest and pointed shoes attested. He wore a knitted tie which had lost its shape with pulling and was made up with a bold, broad knot. Leventhal felt himself strongly drawn to him.

'We were just talking about an actress Shifcart sent out West a few years ago,' said Goldstone bringing his long, bony, hairy hand to the back of his head. 'Wanda Waters.'

'Persevalli is the one that makes them,' Shifcart said. 'He's a great showman.'

'But you picked the girl.'

'I didn't know she was your discovery, Jack,' said Harkavy.

'Yes, I saw her singing with a band one night.'

'You don't say.'

'At the shore in New Jersey. I was on vacation.'

'She's very appealing,' said Goldstone.

'You might not like her much, in person.'

'Why, she certainly looks like a gingery piece in the pictures,' said Harkavy.

'Yes, she has magnetic eyes. But you'd pass her on the street any day and not notice her.'

'Oh, I don't know,' Harkavy said. 'You have a professional attitude in this, seeing so many beauties. I'm still unspoiled. I suppose you can do a lot with paint and cameras, but there has to be something to start with. You can't fake those gorgeous sex machines, can you? Or is it the gullible public again? They look genuine to me.'

'Some really are. And if the rest take you in, that's what they're supposed to do.'

'It must be quite a knack to pick them,' Goldstone remarked.

'It isn't all guesswork. You can't go and run a screen test for every girl you see. But I myself, personally, don't care for some of the best successes I sent into Hollywood.'

'Which do you like?' asked Goldstone.

'Oh,' he said slowly, thinking, 'there's Nola Hook.'

'You don't mean it,' said Schlossberg. 'A little cactus plant . . . skinny, dry . . .'

'I think she has a kind of charm. Or what's the matter with Livia Hall?'

'Such a discovery!'

'She is. I'll stand up for her.'

'Oh, a firebrand.' The old man's countenance was too large for fine degrees of irony. Only Shifcart, his lips open to begin his reply, did not join in the laughter.

'What's the matter; hasn't she got anything?'

'She's got!' Schlossberg waved him down. 'God made her a woman, so who are we to say? But she isn't an actress. I saw your firebrand last week in a picture. What is it? She poisons her husband.'

'In *The Tigress*.'

'What a lameness!'

'I don't know what your standards are. A perfect piece of casting. Who else could have done it?'

'Wood, so help me. She poisons her husband and she watches him die. She wants the insurance money. He loses his voice and he tries to appeal to her she should help him. You don't hear any words. What is she supposed to show in her face? Fear, hate, a hard heart, cruelness, fascination.' He shut his eyes tightly and proudly for a moment, and they saw the veins in his lids. Then he slowly raised them, turning his face away, and a tremor went through his cheeks as he posed.

'Oh, say, that's fine!' Harkavy cried, smiling.

'That's the old Russian style,' said Shifcart. 'That doesn't go any more.'

'No? Where's the improvement? What does she do? She sucks in her cheeks and stares. A man is dying at her feet and all she can do is pop out her eyes.'

'I think she was marvelous in that show,' said Shifcart. 'Nobody could have been better.'

'She is not an actress because she is not a woman, and she is not a woman because a man doesn't mean anything to her. I don't know what she is. Don't ask me. I saw once Nazimova in *The Three Sisters*. She's the one whose soldier gets killed in a duel over a nothing, foolishness. They tell her about it. She looks away from the audience and just with her head and neck – what a force! But this girl . . . !'

'Terrible, ah?' Shifcart said sardonically.

'No, isn't it? And this is a success? This is your success, these days. You said you could pass this Waters on the street and not recognize her. Imagine!' the old man said, making them all feel his weighty astonishment. 'Not to recognize an actress, or that a man shouldn't notice a beautiful woman. It used to be an actress was a woman. She had a mouth, she had flesh on her, she carried herself. When she whispered tears came in your eyes, and when she said a word your legs melted. And it didn't make any difference; on the stage or off the stage you knew she was an actress.'

He stopped. They considered his words gravely.

'Say,' began Harkavy. 'My father used to tell a story about Lily Langtry, the English actress, when she was presented at court by Edward the Seventh. Old Victoria was still alive, and he was the Prince of Wales.'

'That's the one they call the Jersey Lily, isn't it?' said Shifcart.

'I've heard this.' Goldstone got up and took Leventhal's tray. 'Does anyone want coffee? I'm going to the counter.'

'Is it good, Monty?'

'My late father-in-law's favorite.' He strode off to the steam table.

'Pop told me this one after I was old enough to vote. He saved up all his best stories till I was of age. Before that . . . But of course you pick up everything yourself and they know it. It's only off the record. Well, you know that Edward was a sport. And when he fell in love with Langtry he wanted to present her at court. They say people in love want to be seen together in public. Proud to have it known. I suppose it has a dangerous outcome, sometimes. Well, he wanted to present her. Everybody was scandalized. What was Lily going to say to the old woman, and wouldn't Victoria be angry at having her son's mistress in St James or Windsor or wherever? All the reporters were waiting after the ceremony. She came out, and they asked her, "Lily, what did you say to Her Majesty?" "I was worried that I would say the wrong thing," said Lily. "But the last moment the right one came to me. I kissed the hem of her dress and said, '*Ich dien*'!"'

A smile went around the table. Goldstone, carrying the tray, pulled his chair aside with his foot.

'The motto of the King of Bohemia in the Hundred Years War,' Harkavy explained, his round eyes shining at them. 'They found it on his helmet after the Battle of Poitiers.'

'I doubt very much if she would kiss the queen's dress,' said Leventhal. 'Is that a part of the ceremony?'

'Curtsy,' Goldstone laughed, pulling his napkin open to demonstrate.'

'All right, I tell it as my father did. I haven't changed a word.'

'The old woman being a German, she figured she'd understand her,' Schlossberg said.

'What? No, that's the Hanoverian motto,' Goldstone said.

'That was a deal. A German queen, a British Empire, and an Italian Jew for prime minister.'

'Disraeli an Italian?' said Goldstone. 'Wasn't he English born?'

'But his father.'

'Not even his father. His grandfather. He was an authentic Englishman, if citizenship stands for anything.'

'He wasn't an Englishman to the English,' Leventhal said.

'Why, they loved him,' said Goldstone.

'Then who said he was the monkey on John Bull's chest?'

'He had enemies, naturally.'

'I understand they never took him in,' Leventhal declared.

'Wrong!' Harkavy cried. 'He was a credit to them and to us.'

'I don't see that,' Leventhal slowly shook his head. 'It didn't make any difference to them that Victoria was a German. But Disraeli . . . ?'

'He showed Europe that a Jew could be a national leader,' said Goldstone.

'That's Leventhal all over for you,' exclaimed Harkavy. 'That shows you where he stands.'

'Jews and empires? Suez and India and so on? It never seemed right to me.'

'To teach the world a lesson with empty hands – I know that stuff by heart.' Harkavy stared at him with shocked, reprimanding eyes. 'The Empire was certainly his business. He was an Englishman and a great one. Bismarck admired him. *Der alter Jude, das ist der Mann!*'

'Is there such a difference between an empire and a department store?' asked Shifcart. 'You're managing a business.'

'And he was managing the firm?' said Goldstone. 'Bull and Company. The sun never sets on our stores. B. Disraeli, chief buyer.'

Leventhal at the outset had been a little reluctant to speak and had a fleeting feeling that it was a mistake to be drawn or lured out of his taciturnity. Nor had he thought, with his first remark, that he had much to say on this subject. But now, to his surprise, he was unable to hold back his opinions – they were his, of course, but he had never before expressed them, and they sounded queer to him.

'You bring up Bismarck,' he said. 'Why did he say *Jude* instead of Englishman? Disraeli was a bargainer, so he was a Jew to him, naturally.'

'Don't misrepresent Bismarck on the Jews,' warned Harkavy. 'Be careful, boy. He lightened their load.'

'Yes, he had something to say about making a great race. What was it, now? "A German stallion and a Jewish mare."'

'A regular Kentucky Derby,' said Schlossberg. 'Hay for everybody.'

'Don't be down on a man for a figure of speech,' said Goldstone. 'He was an old cavalryman. That was just his way of talking about the best qualities of both.'

'Who needs his compliments?' Schlossberg said. 'Who wants them?'

'Does it sound like flattery to you?' Leventhal raised his hand from the top of his head questioningly.

'I see what's on your mind,' Goldstone answered. 'You're blaming him for the Germans of today.'

'I don't,' cried Leventhal. 'But why are you so glad to have one word of praise from Bismarck, and cockeyed praise too?'

'Why do you have it in for Disraeli?' demanded Harkavy.

'I don't have it in for him. But he wanted to lead England. In spite of the fact that he was a Jew, not because he cared about empires so much. People laughed at his nose, so he took up boxing; they laughed at his poetic silk clothes, so he put on black; and they laughed at his books, so he showed them. He got into politics and became the prime minister. He did it all on nerve.'

'Oh, come on,' Harkavy said.

'On nerve,' Leventhal insisted. 'That's great, I'll give you that. But I don't admire it. It's all right to overcome a weakness, but it depends how and it depends what you call a weakness ... Julius Caesar was sick with epilepsy. He learned to ride with his hands behind his back and slept on the bare ground like a common soldier. What was the reason? His disease. Why should we admire people like that? Things that are life and death to others are only a test to them. What's the good of such greatness?'

'Why, you're succumbing yourself to all the things that are said against us,' Harkavy began in an upbraiding tone.

'No, I don't think I am,' said Leventhal. He declined to argue further. He had already said too much and he gave notice by the drop of his voice that he intended to say no more.

A Filipino busboy came to clear the table. He was an old man and frail looking, and his hands and forearms were whitened by immersions in hot water. The cart loaded, he bent his back low over it, receiving the handlebar in his chest, and pushed away slowly. Behind the steam tables, one set of white-lettered menu boards was hauled down and another sent up in the steel frame with a clash.

'I have seen only one actor do Disraeli,' said Goldstone. 'That was George Arliss.'

'Made for the part, that man,' Shifcart asserted.

'Him I liked in that,' said Schlossberg. 'You're right, Jack, he was made for it. He had the right face to play it, with his thin lips and long nose.'

'Somehow I've passed up all the Victorias,' remarked Goldstone. 'I haven't seen a single one.'

'So what have you missed?' said Schlossberg. 'A successful Victoria I have yet to see.'

It was a slow hour in the restaurant. On all sides there were long perspectives of black-topped tables turned on an angle to appear diamond-shaped, each with its symmetrical cluster of sugar, salt, pepper, and napkin box. From end to end their symmetry put a kind of motion into the almost empty place. At the rear, under the scene of groves painted on the wall, some of the employees sat smoking, looking toward the sunlight and the street.

'I have seen good ones,' Shifcart contended. 'Don't you like any of them?'

'No. One thing is why there should be so many Victorias. Maybe it's because she was so plain. An ordinary-looking queen has a lot of appeal these days. Everything has to be pulled down a little. Isn't it so? Why is she so popular?' He held out his hands to them as though soliciting a better answer. 'She loved Albert; she was stubborn; she was a good housekeeper. It goes over.'

'I thought Eunice Sherbarth was a good Victoria,' said Harkavy.

'She's a healthy, beautiful lady; it's a pleasure to look at her,' said Schlossberg.

'So what's the matter?' asked Shifcart. 'She can't act? You only wish you had her contract, Schlossberg.'

'Why not?' Schlossberg admitted. 'As long as I'm wishing,

I'd like to be thirty years old today with death a little farther off than it is. Besides, my pants are shiny. And who can't use money? She must make plenty, I can imagine. And partly she has it coming because she's good to look at. But act? I could play a better Victoria myself.' And indeed he could, thought Leventhal with more respect than amusement, if his voice weren't so deep.

'Yes, in skirts you could be a hit,' said Shifcart.

'Anybody could be a hit today,' Schlossberg replied. 'With the public so crazy to be pleased. It's a regular carnival. Everybody is on the same side with illusion. Tell me, Jack, do you think you have ever discovered a good actress?'

'You mean an artist, I suppose, not a little type like Waters.'

'I mean an actress.'

'Then I say Livia Hall.'

'You mean that?'

'Yes, I do.'

'Impossible,' said Shifcart. 'A pair of chopsticks.'

Shifcart's stout neck grew red in patches and he said, a shade away from anger, 'She is not a cheap success. Not everybody is so hard to satisfy, Schlossberg. It looks like it's a big job to entertain you and maybe nobody does.'

'You are a tough critic, Marcus,' Goldstone said.

'Do I make up the specifications?' said Schlossberg. '*Narischer mensch!* I'm speaking for you, too. This is not the public. Between ourselves we can tell the truth, can't we? What's the matter with the truth? Everything comes in packages. If it's in a package, you can bring the devil in the house. People rely on packages. If you will wrap it up, they will take it.'

'I didn't claim the woman was Ellen Terry. I only said she was a good actress. You have to admit, Schlossberg, she's got some ability.'

'For some things, maybe. Not too much.'

'But some?'

'Yes, some,' Schlossberg carelessly granted.

'*Something* at last pleases him, thank God!' Shifcart said.

'I try to give everybody credit,' declared the old man. 'I am not a knocker. I am not too good for this world.'

No one contradicted him.

'Well,' he said. 'And what am I kicking for?' He checked their smiles, holding them all with his serious, worn, blue gaze. 'I'll tell you. It's bad to be less than human and it's bad to be more than human. What's more than human? Our friend –' he meant Leventhal, 'was talking about it before. Caesar, if you remember, in the play wanted to be like a god. Can a god have diseases? So this is a sick man's idea of God. Does a statue have wax in its ears? Naturally not. It doesn't sweat, either, except maybe blood on holidays. If I can talk myself into it that I never sweat and make everybody else act as if it was true, maybe I can fix it up about dying, too. We only know what it is to die because some people die and, if we make ourselves different from them, maybe we don't have to? Less than human is the other side of it. I'll come to it. So here is the whole thing, then. Good acting is what is exactly human. And if you say I am a tough critic, you mean I have a high opinion of what is human. This is my whole idea. More than human, can you have any use for life? Less than human, you don't either.'

He made a pause – it was not one that invited interruption – and went on.

'This girl Livia in *The Tigress*. What's the matter with her? She commits a murder. What are her feelings? No love, no hate, no fear, no lungs, no heart. I'm ashamed to mention what else is missing. Nothing! The poor husband. Nothing is killing him, less than human. A blank. And it should be so awful the whole audience should be afraid positively to look in her face. But I don't know if she's too pretty or what to have feelings. You see right away she has no idea what is human because her husband's death doesn't mean to her a thing. It's all in packages, and first the package is breathing and then it isn't breathing, and you insured the package so you can marry another package and go to Florida for the winter. Now maybe somebody will answer me, "This sounds very interesting. You say less than human, more than human. Tell me, please, what is human?" And really we study people so much now that after we look and look at human nature – I write science articles myself – after you look at it and weigh it and turn it over and put it under a microscope, you might say, "What is all the shouting about? A man is nothing, his life is nothing. Or it is even lousy and cheap. But this your royal highness doesn't like, so he hokes it up. With what? With greatness and beauty. Beauty and greatness? Black and white I know; I didn't make it up. But greatness and beauty?" But I say, "What do you know? No, tell me, what do you know? You shut one eye and look at a thing, and it is one way to you. You shut the other one and it is different. I am as sure about greatness and beauty as you are about black and white. If a human life is a great thing to me, it *is* a great thing. Do you know better? I'm entitled as much as you. And why be measly? Do you have to be? Is somebody holding you by the neck? Have dignity, you understand me? Choose dignity. Nobody knows enough to turn it down." Now to whom should this mean something if not to an actor? If he isn't for dignity, then I tell you there is a great mistake somewhere.'

'Bravo!' said Harkavy.

'Amen and amen!' Shifcart laughed. He drew a card out of his wallet and threw it toward him. 'Come and see me; I'll fix you up with a test.'

The card fell near Leventhal, who seemed to be the only one to disapprove of the joke. Even Schlossberg himself smiled. The sunlight fell through the large window over their heads. It seemed to Leventhal that Shifcart, though he was laughing, looked at him with peculiar disfavor. Still he did not join in. He picked up the card. The others were rising.

'Don't forget your hats, gentlemen,' called Harkavy.

The musical crash of the check machine filled their ears as they waited their turn at the cashier's dazzling cage.

'I SAW Williston last night,' Leventhal mentioned to Harkavy outside.

'How is Stan? Oh, yes, about that thing you were telling me.' Harkavy would perhaps have said more, but the others were waiting for him. 'Say, one of these days let me know how you're making out with it, will you?'

'Sure,' Leventhal said. And Harkavy loitered off eastward on Fourteenth Street with Goldstone and his friends. He was the tallest among them. His yellow hair drifted flimsily, silkily over his bald spot. Leventhal watched him go. He would not admit to himself that he felt deserted. 'Maybe it's a good thing he isn't interested,' he thought. 'I don't know if I could explain it anyhow. It's getting too complicated. And he'd give me all kinds of useless advice – the usual. Anyhow I'm glad. I don't think I really wanted to talk about it.' He remained aimlessly in the same place for a while and then walked off, pressing the bulky Sunday paper under his arm. He did not have a conscious destination and was distantly under the dread of being the only person in the city without one.

In the next block he remembered that he had neglected to call Elena to make sure Philip had gotten home safely and to ask about Mickey. He stopped at a cigar store and dialed Villani's number. He sat in the booth, one leg stretched out of the door. No one answered. Leaning out, he looked at the clock cut squarely into the patterned tin of the wall. It was half-past two, and Elena had probably left to visit Mickey. He phoned the hospital, though he understood well enough that the information given about patients wasn't reliable. He heard that Mickey was doing nicely, which was what he had expected to hear. There were upward of three thousand beds in the hospital. How could the girls at the switchboard be expected to know anything but the bare facts about each patient – whether he was alive or dead, that is? The word 'dead,' dissociated from what he had thought, accompanied him ominously out of the store, and he made haste to get rid of it, simultaneously realizing, in another part of his mind, how superstitious he was becoming. All he had meant was that the hospital was too vast, and suddenly he had to erase an incidental word. Why, everyone born was sick at one time or another. Nobody grew up without sickness. He had had pneumonia himself and an ear infection, and Max had been down, too – he couldn't recall with what.

He began to wonder how long Max was going to put off coming home. 'Maybe he's afraid of being tricked into returning,' he thought. 'I'll have a thing or two to say to him when I see him. For once in our lives. It's time somebody called him down. Elena won't, so he's used to doing whatever he wants.' And what would Max have to say for himself? Something simple minded and foolish, he was certain. Because he was foolish. Philip already had more common sense than his father. Leventhal visualized his brother's strongly excited face and imagined his incoherencies. 'He sends them money and that makes him a father. That's the end of his responsibilities. That's fatherhood,' he repeated to himself. 'That's his idea of duty.'

From the dark staircase and hall, he entered the brilliantly sunlit front room. He sat on the edge of the bed and pushed off his shoes. The sheets were warm to his touch. The heavy folds of the curtain, the brown door, the fine red flowers in the carpet slowly consumed into a light smoke of dust, gave him a feeling of suspension and quietness. There was a long spider's thread on the screen, quivering red, blue, and deeper blue against the wires like the last pliant, changeable thing in the stiffening, fixative heat. With one stockinged foot set on the other, his shoulders drooping, Leventhal sat watching, his face somnolent, his hands looking as if it would require a great effort to unclasp them.

Presently he went into the kitchen. He absent-mindedly rinsed a few dishes under the rumbling tap and, returning to the front room, unbuckled his belt, drew the curtains, and, with the Sunday paper unheeded under his legs, went to sleep.

A deep rolling noise awakened him. He thought at first that it came from below, out of the subway. But there was no accompanying tremor through the building. He soon placed the sound outside and above him. It was thunder. He looked out. There had been a storm. The screen was still clogged with raindrops. The street was softly darkened by the clouds and the wet brownstone. In one of the rooms across the way a two-branched green lamp was shining. A woman lay on a sofa, one arm bent over her eyes. At the next sound of the retreating thunder she moved her legs.

Leventhal glanced again into the mist and water of the street and then went to the phone and tried Villani's number. There was still no answer. Apparently they were out somewhere, making a day of it. He poised the receiver over the hook, aimed it, and let it fall into place.

He worked his feet into his shoes, treading down the heels, and went down to the restaurant for an early dinner. The waiter, the same bald, lean man who last week had anticipated his protest about the bad table with a gesture of insincere helplessness, appeared to be occupied with thoughts of his own. His black suit looked damp, and his leather bow tie was not fastened but hung on its elastic from a buttonhole. He brought Leventhal a veal cutlet and a bottle of beer and hurried away with a muscular swing, softly – his soles were padded with sawdust – to wait on a long table of *boccie* players whose game had been rained out and who were drinking wine and coffee. The odor of wet wood was very noticeable. Leventhal did not linger over his meal. He was soon outside again. The air was dimmer than before, and hotter. He turned west on Eighteenth Street and saw Allbee waiting for him on the corner. He had to look twice in the wavering, longitudinal grays and shadows of the watery street to identify him.

Leventhal did not halt until Allbee detained him, stepping in his way. He dropped his head diffidently and clumsily, as though asking Leventhal to understand that he was compelled to do this.

'Well?' Leventhal said after a moment's silence.

'Why didn't you stop? You saw me . . .'

'And if I did? I'm not looking for you. You're the one. You follow me around.'

'You're mad about yesterday, aren't you? That was a coincidence.'

'Oh, it was for sure.'

'I wanted to talk to you yesterday, it so happens. You won't hunt me up. If I want to talk to you, I have to find opportunities.'

'Is that the way you describe it?'

'But when I remembered it was Saturday – you people don't do business on Saturday – I postponed it.' The saying of this appeared to delight him. But then his expression changed. He seemed to recognize and even to be depressed by the poorness of his joke. He looked somberly and earnestly at Leventhal, who understood that Allbee wanted him to know of the feelings that gave rise to it, and to know also that since those feelings were dire and powerful the joke dissembling them was actually a courtesy.

'I don't observe the holiday,' said Leventhal deliberately and dryly.

'Oh, of course not,' said Allbee, and he again began to smile. He added, a second later, 'As far as "following" is concerned, that's not the way to put it. I have a perfect right to see you. You act as if I had some kind of game, whereas you're the one that's playing a game.'

'How do you figure that?'

Allbee raised his hand. 'You pretend that I haven't got a grievance against you. That's playing.' His fingers brushed over his chest, and then he covered his mouth and cleared his throat.

'Say . . . with the kid – stuff like that has got to stop.'

'I didn't know he was with you.'

'Not much! Well, I'm telling you. Besides, I told you the first time, I never wanted to do you any harm.'

'We differ about that. And there was a second time, too.' He gave an illustrative push that stopped short of Leventhal's shoulders. 'That was a little too much game for me. Or were you trying to scare me off?'

'If I was, you mean that I can't, huh?'

'Well,' Allbee suggested, 'you might have sent me to the hospital and gotten rid of me that way for a while.' He grinned. 'You said you should have broken my neck.'

Leventhal said contemptuously, 'But otherwise . . . to scare you? It's impossible to scare you, isn't it?'

'A year ago I couldn't have come to you. But now that I've done it, made up my mind, it is impossible.'

'What was different a year ago?' asked Leventhal.

'Then I was getting by, somehow, and I wouldn't have thought of coming near you,' he said quite seriously.

'And now?'

'My wife left me some money. It wasn't a lot, but I stretched it. As long as it lasted – why, if I were still getting by you'd never hear from me. I'll say it again. But maybe I don't have a real sense of honor or I wouldn't put myself in such a position. I mean real honor. There's no getting away from it, I suppose, honor is honor. Either you've got it up to here,' he drew a line across his throat, 'or you haven't got it. It doesn't make you any happier to tell yourself you ought to have it. It's like anything else that counts. You have to make sacrifices to it. You know, I'm from an old New England family. As far as honor's concerned, I'm not keeping up standards very well, I admit. Still, if I was born with my full share of it, in New York I'd have an even worse handicap. Oh, boy! – New York. Honor sure got started before New York did. You won't see it at night, hereabouts, in letters of fire up in the sky. You'll see other words. Such things just get swallowed up in these conditions – modern life. So I'm lucky I didn't inherit more of a sense of it. I'd be competing with Don Quixote. Now with you it's different, altogether. You're right at home in this, like those what-do-you-call 'ems that live in the flames – salamanders. If somebody hurts you, you hit back in any way and anything goes. That's how it is here. It's rugged. And I can appreciate it. Of course, the kind of honor I'm familiar with doesn't allow that. Mine tells me not to ask for damages, and so on. But I have it in diluted form; that's obvious.'

Allbee said this conversationally, in a factual manner; nevertheless Leventhal heard the spiteful ring in it. But he evinced no feeling and made no comment.

'I have an idea that it's one of those things that's bound to go.'

'You went through the money,' Leventhal said, disregarding the rest. 'Why didn't you get a job?'

'What did I want to work for? What sort of a job could I get anyhow? Nobody would give me what I wanted. And do you think I could take a leg job, like a high-school kid? An errand boy? Besides, I was in no hurry. Why should I be?'

'Were you black-listed?' Leventhal was unable to conceal his concern. 'Is that the reason?'

Allbee did not reply to this directly. 'Why, Rudiger wouldn't have taken me back even to empty his ash trays.'

After this they were both silent for a while. Under its flat rim the ball of the lamp nearby began to shine in the gray and blue depth of the air, revealing suddenly the perspiration on Allbee's face. The rings under his eyes gave him an aspect of suffering anger and hate. Yet he seemed unaware of any exposure and spoke evenly.

'No, I didn't want to work,' he said. 'I had a hell of a time after my wife was killed and I decided to take myself off the market for a while. I lived like a gentleman.'

Leventhal said grimly to himself, 'Oh, gentleman. It looks like it. A marvelous gentleman.'

'Well, what do you want from me?' he asked Allbee. 'You lived like a gentleman. I guess that means getting up at eleven or twelve every day. I get up at seven and go to my job. You've had a long vacation. Still you want me to do something for you. I don't know what you want. What do you want?'

'I could use some help. The vacation's lasted a little too long.'

'What sort of help?'

'I don't know what sort. I wanted to take that up with you. You could help me if you wanted to. You must have connections. I'd like to get away from my old line, something new, a complete change.'

'For example?'

'Do you think you can get something for me in a bank?'

'Oh, you want to go straight where they keep it, where the money is,' said Leventhal.

'Or a brokerage firm?'

'Stop your joking,' Leventhal said somewhat sharply. 'I don't care for the sort of jokes you make. I'm not under an obligation to you. I'll do something for you if I can. And just remember, it doesn't mean I admit anything. I think you're crazy. But Stan Williston thinks I ought to help you, and out of respect for him I'll try.'

'What!' exclaimed Allbee. 'You discussed me with Williston? What did you tell him about me?'

'Oh, you don't like that? No, I see you don't,' said Leventhal. I didn't make anything up.'

'What did you tell him?' he said again, in agitation.

'What do you think I could tell him? Are you afraid I blackened your character? Are you touchy about your reputation? I thought you had lost your sense of honor?'

'You had no business – no damned business!' Allbee cried out in a flash of hatred and with an intensity of shame that disturbed Leventhal in spite of himself.

'Well, you're a crazy, queer bastard,' he said. 'What's the matter with you? You come to me with this hokum about being too down and out to have any pride left – you can even come to me, and this and that. I knew it was all fake. One minute you're on the bottom, couldn't be any lower, and the next you're a regular Lord Byron.'

There was an interval of silence during which Allbee appeared to be struggling for control over himself. Then he said in a low voice, 'Williston is an old friend of mine. I just happen to have special feelings about him and Phoebe. But I guess it really doesn't make much difference.' He gradually recovered his smile and he remarked, withdrawing his eyes from Leventhal and beginning a protracted, glittering study of the street behind him, 'I should have expected you not to miss still another chance to get at me.'

'Are you in your right mind?' Leventhal demanded. 'Are you straight in the head? Is it the booze or what? God almighty! Every day I see new twists.' He looked heavenward and gave way to a short laugh. 'So help me, it's like a menagerie. They say you go to the zoo to see yourself in the animals. There aren't enough animals in the world to see ourselves in. There would have to be a million new feathers and tails. There's no end to the twists.'

Allbee, preoccupied with the dwindling violets and grays of twilight and the swarms of light, seemed also to find this comical.

'Well, you've got nothing on me,' he said.

'You think not?'

'You're just as much of a monster to me.'

'I am?'

'Hell, yes. Well, you look like Caliban in the first place,'
Allbee said, more serious than not. 'But that's not all I mean.
You personally, you're just one out of many. Many kinds.
You wouldn't be able to see that. Sometimes I feel – and I'm
saying this seriously – I feel as if I were in a sort of Egyptian
darkness. You know, Moses punished the Egyptians with
darkness. And that's how I often think of this. When I was
born, when I was a boy, everything was different. We thought
it would be daylight forever. Do you know, one of my ances-
tors was Governor Winthrop. Governor Winthrop!' His voice
vibrated fiercely; there was a repressed laugh in it. 'I'm a fine
one to be talking about tradition, you must be saying. But
still I was born into it. And try to imagine how New York
affects me. Isn't it preposterous? It's really as if the children
of Caliban were running everything. You go down in the subway and Caliban gives you two nickels for your dime. You go
home and he has a candy store in the street where you were
born. The old breeds are out. The streets are named after
them. But what are they themselves? Just remnants.'

'I see how it is; you're actually an aristocrat,' said Leventhal.

'It may not strike you as it struck me,' said Allbee. 'But I
go into the library once in a while, to look around, and last
week I saw a book about Thoreau and Emerson by a man
named Lipschitz . . .'

'What of it?'

'A name like that?' Allbee said this with great earnestness.
'After all, it seems to me that people of such background
simply couldn't understand . . .'

'Of all the goddamned nonsense!' shouted Leventhal.
'Look, I've got things to attend to. I have a phone call to
make. It's important. Tell me what in the name of hell you
want and make it snappy.'

'I assure you, I wasn't trying to be malicious. I was only
discussing this . . .'

'I assure you, you were trying, I assure you!' Leventhal

flung out. 'Now what are you after? Probably a few bucks for whisky.'

Allbee laughed aloud. 'They say drinking is only another kind of disease,' he said. 'Like heart disease or syphilis. You wouldn't be so hard on anyone with heart disease, would you? You'd be more sympathetic. They even say crime is only a sort of disease and if you had more hospitals you'd need fewer prisons. Look how many murderers are let off and get treatment instead of execution. If they're sick it's not their fault. Why can't you take that attitude?'

'Why?' Leventhal involuntarily repeated. He was bewildered.

'Because you've got to blame me, that's why,' said Allbee. 'You won't assume that it isn't entirely my fault. It's necessary for you to believe that I deserve what I get. It doesn't enter your mind, does it – that a man might not be able to help being hammered down? What do you say? Maybe he can't help himself? No, if a man is down, a man like me, it's his fault. If he suffers, he's being punished. There's no evil in life itself. And do you know what? It's a Jewish point of view. You'll find it all over the Bible. God doesn't make mistakes. He's the department of weights and measures. If you're okay, he's okay, too. That's what Job's friends come and say to him. But I'll tell you something. We do get it in the neck for nothing and suffer for nothing, and there's no denying that evil is as real as sunshine. Take it from me, I know what I'm talking about. To you the whole thing is that I must deserve what I get. That leaves your hands clean and it's unnecessary for you to bother yourself. Not that I'm asking you to feel sorry for me, but you sure can't understand what makes a man drink.'

'All right, so I can't. What then? What did you stop me for, to tell me that?'

'No, you never could and I'll tell you why. Because you people take care of yourselves before everything. You keep your spirit under lock and key. That's the way you're brought up. You make it your business assistant, and it's safe and tame and never leads you toward anything risky. Nothing dangerous and nothing glorious. Nothing ever tempts you to dissolve yourself. What for? What's in it? No percentage.'

Leventhal's expression was uncomprehending and horrified. His forehead was wrinkled. His heart beat agonizingly, and he faltered out, 'I don't see how you can talk that way. That's just talk. Millions of us have been killed. What about that?'

He seemed to be waiting for a reply, but before it could be given he turned and walked away rapidly, leaving Allbee alone under the lamp.

12

LEVENTHAL strode home blindly and rapidly, his stout body shaken by the unaccustomed gait. Perspiration ran from his bushy, lusterless hair over his dark skin. He was thinking that he should have done something, slammed Allbee on the head, not let him off. He felt he had answered stupidly, although he did not know what he should have told him; he was unable to remember all that had been said. But as the first throbs of anger began to pass into soreness, it began to appear to him that he had known all along, all through the conversation, what to do and had failed to do it, that he had been unequal to what was plain, clear, and necessary. 'I ought to have done it,' he thought, 'even if it meant murdering him.'

Just then, the blink of a yellow light in the middle of the street started him into a trot. An eddy of exhaust gas caught him in the face. He was behind a bus. A tearing of gears carried it forward, and he came up on the curb, breathless. He rested a moment and then went on, gradually slowing to his ordinary pace. His head ached. There was a spot between his eyes that was particularly painful; the skin itself was tender. He pressed it. It seemed to have been the dead center of all his staring and concentration. He felt that his nerves were worse than ever and that his rage had done him harm, affected his very blood. He had an impression of bad blood as something black, thick, briny, caused by sickness or lust or excessive anger. His heart quickened again. He cast a glance behind. Several people were going in the other direction. 'Let him better not come near me,' he muttered. His brain was clearer, and the single thought of murder that had risen in it was gone. However, he regretted not having hit Allbee and would almost have welcomed another chance. What was the use of wasting words on such people? Hit them! That was all they understood. A woman in the movies whom Mary had asked to remove her hat, two or three years ago, had turned around and uttered some insult about the 'gall of Jews.' Woman or no, Leventhal had had a powerful desire to drive his fist into her head, tear the hat off. He had afterwards argued with Mary that there were times when that should be done. 'Where would it get you?' was Mary's answer. Practically, she was right, no doubt; she knew the value of staying cool. But he regretted it. Oh, how he sometimes regretted not slapping off that hat. With his father it had at least been '*gib mir die groschke*,' a potentially real compensation. 'But what about me?' Leventhal asked with an arrested upward glance of his large meditative eyes. There was a murky redness in the clouds, absorbed from the neon lights and the clock tower on Fifth Avenue. His father had believed in getting his due, at any rate. And there was a certain wisdom in that. You couldn't say you were master of yourself when there were so many people by whom you could be humiliated. As for Mary, she must have been thinking, in answering, of the night he had pushed her, years ago in Baltimore. Perhaps she wanted to remind him of it. Of course, there was no excuse for that. But he still felt that the woman's hat should have been snatched off and hurled away.

And he uttered a low, unwilling laugh when he recalled how he had stood, just stood, without the presence of mind to realize that he was being insulted. It did have to do with presence of mind, exactly as in the case of Dunhill, the linotyper who sold him the unwanted ticket. With Allbee there was the added confusion that he brought off his insults with an air of discussion. When he started out, even though he made a crooked joke here and there, he seemed to be speaking impersonally. But all at once he said something in earnest that was terrible. Of course, he was sick. He himself had brought up the subject of disease, so he must be aware of it. But did his sickness, whatever it was, account for what he said, or would good health only have given him the strength to keep it to himself? Some people, gentle to begin with, were kind when they were sick. Leventhal said to himself, impatiently, 'There are two billion people or so in the world and *he's* miserable. What's he so special?'

Mrs Nunez was standing on the brownstone stoop. She and her husband had just returned from a Sunday outing. She carried gloves and a red patent-leather bag. Her hat was a white straw with cherries on the brim. Her Indian face was small, but she had an ungainly, full-hipped figure. She wore a close-fitting striped suit, her shoulders were raised, her bosom was high, and her lips were parted as if at the end of a long breath. Mary, whom nothing escaped, had once said about Mrs Nunez' suits, 'I don't see why she wears them. She could look very pretty in silk prints.' Till then Leventhal had scarcely noticed her. Now, when she said good evening and he nodded to her, he remembered this and had a moment of intense longing for his wife.

'Were you caught in the rain?' said Mrs Nunez.

'No, I slept through the whole storm.'

'We were in Prospect Park to see the flowers. My brother works in the hothouse. My, it was terrible. A tree fell down. The lightning hit it.'

'That must have been frightening.'

'Terrible. We were inside. But I was scared. Oh, awful,' she said with a release of breath. 'Your missis coming back already?'

'Not yet.'

She drew the gloves out and worked them with her long brown fingers whose size and strength he noted in absent-minded surprise.

'Coming soon?'

'I don't think so.'

'Oh, too bad, too bad,' she said in her light, flat, rapid

way. Leventhal had often paused at the Nunez' door to listen, entertained, to their quick-running Spanish, not a word of which he understood. 'Too bad,' she repeated, and Leventhal, with a glance of surmise at her small face under the white brim, wondered what hint her sympathy might contain. There was a burst of music above them; a window was thrown open.

'I'll be a bachelor for a month or so yet,' he said.

'Oh, maybe you enjoy yourself anyhow; makes you a change for a while.'

'No,' he said bluntly.

He went into the foyer where Nunez' dog scampered at him, jumping up. He bent and clasped the animal, and rubbed its head. It licked his face and pushed its muzzle into his coat under his sleeve.

'She's crazy about you,' said Nunez from the doorway. 'I think she smells you coming.' He was polishing his glasses with a flowered handkerchief of his wife's. Beside the bed, in his room, there were beer cans and newspapers.

'That's a friendly dog. I have a soft spot for dogs myself.'

'Up, Smoke,' said Nunez. 'Do hounds ever faint, Mr Leventhal? Sometimes I think this one is going to faint when you rub her belly.'

'I don't know. Do animals faint? Does anyone faint from pleasure?'

'Somebody,' Nunez joked. 'A lady with a weak heart, maybe. Look a' that, on her back. Look a' that chest on her.' He put on his glasses and held the edge of the door. The red of the foyer and the yellow of his flat were drawn on its black panels. His sport shirt was open, and a religious medal swung over the twist of hair between the muscles of his dark, reddish breast.

'Come in and have a beer,' he said.

'I can't, thanks, I have something to do.' Leventhal remembered that he had not yet reached Elena. It occurred to him, moreover, that Nunez had been a witness to his scuffle with Allbee in the hall. He looked at him uncomfortably and moved toward the stairs.

For the third time he got no answer at Villani's and he began to be anxious. The Villanis had young children, and young children had to be put to bed. It was already after eight. 'Maybe I'd better go out and see Elena and Phil,' he said to himself. 'I don't have anything to do tonight.' But his concealed thought was that Villani's absence was a bad sign. He set out again, nodding to Mrs Nunez on the stoop as though he saw her for the first time.

He found Villani and the old woman sitting with Philip and Elena in the parlor. They had just returned from the hospital, and he gathered that Mickey was worse. He appeared to be losing weight. Villani betrayed his misgivings by the pitch of his optimism. He cried, 'Don't worry about them, out there. They make them eat. There's no such thing in a hospital, not eating. They see to it. They can handle the kids; they got experience.' Elena was coldly silent. Evidently she had accused the hospital of not feeding the child. Her look was waxen. Everything – her black hair, dark nostrils, and white lips; her lack of stir at his arrival; even the fact that she was dressed for the street and not in her gingham with the nightgown under it – made Leventhal uneasy.

'Give them time,' said Villani. 'He ain't been there long. What do you say?'

Leventhal gave out a sound of confirmation and glanced from Elena to the old woman in her dark colors. Her lean wrists, marked with raised, dull blue veins, rested in her lap. He observed that her ankles, above her unfashionable black shoes, were swollen – probably from walking the long hospital corridors. Her mouth was thin, the underlip not quite matching the expressionless upper because her chin was sunk. The tilt of her body in the Morris chair, her crossed feet, suggested rest, and yet rest was what she seemed to be resisting, drawing off her shoulders from the cushion behind her. Her eyes, whenever her lids went up, disclosed a fierceness as piercing as a rooster's. Leventhal, in spite of himself, was arrested by her face. Other people might change themselves still; it was hard, it might not work, but they could try. This woman, as she was, was finished forever.

He took the first opportunity to whisper to Villani that perhaps Max ought to be sent for now, and Villani shut his eyes in agreement. It was serious, then. He would phone the doctor in the morning and get a report. Denisart had promised to tell him when to send for Max.

He got away to the kitchen for a while, ostensibly for a glass of water. Actually he was afraid that if he sat opposite Elena much longer he might lose control of himself. His face might twitch, perhaps, or his voice crack. Worst of all, he might ask her why she thought he was to blame, and that would be utterly wrong and possibly dangerous. She did hold him responsible, plainly. He had urged her to send the boy to the hospital. But the doctor had done that, too. And what could he look for later, if she blamed him now? This was only the beginning, judging from the signs Villani gave; there was more to expect. They themselves, the parents, were responsible insofar as anyone was. Especially Max. Why did he postpone coming home? Because he thought he could get by? He could get by, though, only if Mickey, hanging on in the hospital, got by. Not that Max's being at home now could make a real difference to the child, but at all events he might not seem so given up to that enormous hospital, and on Max's side an acknowledgment would be made. After all, you married and had children and there was a chain of consequences. It was impossible to tell, in starting out, what was going to happen. And it was unfair, perhaps, to have to account at forty for what was done at twenty. But unless one was more than human or less than human, as Mr Schlossberg put it, the payments had to be met. Leventhal disagreed about 'less than human.' Since it was done by so many, what was it but human? 'More than human' was for a much smaller number. But most people had fear in them – fear of life, fear of death, of life more than of death, perhaps. But it was a fact that they were afraid, and when the fear was uppermost they didn't want any more burdens. At twenty they had vigor and so were careless, and later they felt too weak to be accountable. They said, 'Just let me alone, that's all I ask.' But either they found the strength to meet the costs or they refused and gave way to dizziness – dizziness altogether, the dizziness of pleasures before catastrophes. Maybe you could call it 'less than human' to refuse; he liked to think 'human' meant accountable in spite of many weaknesses – at the last moment, tough enough to hold. But to go by what happened in the majority of cases, it was the last dizziness that was most typical and had the best claim to the name.

He went back to the parlor for a while. When he announced that he was leaving, Elena looked at him but did not say good night.

Philip, heavy eyed and dejected, sat outside the circle of adults, his arms wound around the back of the chair. His shirt was pulled out at the sides and his shoes untied.

'Tired from trotting after them all day,' Leventhal observed to himself. He was filled with tenderness toward him. 'Go to sleep, Phil,' he said.

'I will.'

'Did you have a good time yesterday?'

'Yes, swell.'

'When the kid gets out we'll take one of those boat excursions around the island. I understand they're really beautiful.'

Philip laid his cheek on the top rung of the chair in a way that fatigue alone could not have explained. Leventhal passed his hand over his short hair, saying, 'All right, boy.' But beyond that he could bring nothing out. He foundered, the thread of reassurance lost, the very breath with which to make reassurances driven out of him by his pity for the children. He hurried down the dirty tile stairs. A bus loomed up, half a block away, and he ran across the street. Though there were empty seats around him he stood up, supporting himself on the shining pole, hardly hearing the escape of air from the brakes and the pneumatic doors, and seeing only chaotically shapeless colors with his brimming eyes. Philip must have noticed him whispering to Villani. But probably he had begun to understand earlier. He knew, Leventhal was convinced. And perhaps even little Mickey in the hospital comprehended it all, after a fashion, affected as a candle flame is by varying amounts of air, as all that wants to be what it was made responds to whatever feeds or endangers it.

Looping and swerving the bus reached the waterfront. The smell of the harbor and the flash of the arcades came to Leventhal. He made his way through the dim space of the shed to the bow of the boat and looked out on the water, the sharp stars, and the crimson and yellow spots hung from the cranes and hulls swinging between the slip and the incandescent low crust of the shore.

13

THE week that followed was a miserable one for him. Dr
Denisart was not optimistic on Monday, and, since he had
proved before that he was anything but an alarmist, Leventhal saw that in his professional way he was giving notice that
there was very little hope. On Tuesday he said he thought it
advisable that Max should come home. Leventhal cried into
the phone, 'What do you mean? Is this it?' The doctor
answered, 'The father ought to be on hand.' 'It's the showdown, in other words,' Leventhal said. He sent the wire, and
that evening and the next he went out to the hospital, making
every effort to avoid meeting Elena. Mickey was now unconscious, and they fed him intravenously. Hot and grimy after
his long trip, Leventhal bent over the bed. The boy's face was
darkened with fever; the needle was taped to his arm with
strips broad enough for a grown man. The level of the liquid
in the flask held by a clamp on the long stand did not seem to
change. Leventhal moved to the window and lifted the edge
of the shade an inch or two with his forefinger, peering down
at the stone jars of vines and geraniums, too massive for the
small sunken court. Then he went out, with a hesitation at
the foot of the bed. He traveled two hours in order to spend
ten minutes in Mickey's room.

He kept telling himself, 'The showdown is coming' –
guiltily, for at heart he had no hope. The word itself was an
evasion, and he, not the doctor, had introduced it. But it was
a comprehensive word; it embraced more than Mickey's crisis,
or Elena's, or his own trouble with Allbee. These were in-
cluded; what had been going on with Allbee, for example,

could not be allowed to continue indefinitely. But what he meant by this preoccupying 'showdown' was a crisis which would bring an end of his resistance to something he had no right to resist. Illness, madness, and death were forcing him to confront his fault. He had used every means, and principally indifference and neglect, to avoid acknowledging it and he still did not know what it was. But that was owing to the way he had arranged not to know. He had done a great deal to make things easier for himself, toning down, softening, looking aside. But the more he tried to subdue whatever it was that he resisted, the more it raged, and the moment was coming when his strength to resist would be at an end. He was nearly exhausted now.

It was nearly midnight when he came home on Wednesday. Even before he unlocked the door, he heard the refrigerator panting as though it were trying to keep up a charge of energy in the air of the empty flat. He turned on the lights in the front room and in the bathroom where he undressed and put on pajamas. Opening the medicine chest, he stared like someone who has forgotten what he is looking for; in reality, his mind was empty. His hand touched his razor and, unthinkingly, he changed the blade and set it back in the red velvet groove of the case. Barefooted he walked into the front room. There was paper on the desk, and it occurred to him to send a note to Mary. He sat down, twisting his legs around the legs of the chair, wrote a few words, and stopped to consider what he ought or ought not to say. There was plenty to choose from. That he missed her? That it was still hot? He put down the pen and leaned on the desk, pressing his chest against the edge of the leaf. Dumb and motionless in the silent room, he heard the slamming of car doors and the racing of motors outside. Suddenly there was a prolonged, tearing peal of the bell. A finger screwed the pusher mercilessly in the socket. Hurrying to the door he shouted, 'Yes?' He heard his name pronounced several times and called back, 'Who is it?' Stooping over the banister, he caught sight of Allbee on the landing below and he withdrew into the vestibule and shut the door. Presently the handle was turned, turned again quietly, and then shaken.

'Yes, yes, what do you want now? What do you want?' he said.

Allbee knocked. Leventhal jerked the door open and saw him with his knuckles raised, ready to knock again.

'Well?'

'I want to see you,' said Allbee.

'Well, you're seeing me.' He made as if to close the door, and Allbee brought his head forward quickly in a movement of melancholy protest, looking at Leventhal without rancor, however.

'That isn't fair,' he said. 'I work up my courage to come and see you. It takes me nearly a day to do it.'

'To cook up something new.'

Allbee's expression was serious. The insane element usually manifested in his smiles was absent.

'The other night – last week – I was getting around to something,' he said. 'There was something I wanted to say to you.'

'I don't want any more discussions. I won't stand for any. Anyhow, it's after midnight.'

'Yes, I know it's late,' Allbee conceded. 'But there was something important to say. We were sidetracked.'

'You were,' Leventhal said heavily. 'I wasn't even in it.'

'I guess I know what you're referring to. But whatever I did say, I didn't intend to be personal. You shouldn't consider . . .'

'What? It was all theory, theoretical?' he said sarcastically.

'Well, partly. It was partly joking,' Allbee explained painfully. 'That's an ingrained habit with me. I know it's bad.'

'I'm sorry, but I don't understand you. Maybe I don't understand Emerson either. It goes together.'

'Please . . .' he said despondently.

142

There was a hush in the hall under the dull spokes of the skylight and the filmy glass.

'You take it all in the wrong spirit,' he went on.

'How should I take it?'

'You ought to realize that I'm not entirely . . .' he stumbled, 'that I'm not entirely under control.' The slant of the shadows on his pale, fleshy face made it look infirm. The marks beneath his eyes brought to Leventhal's mind the bruises under the skin of an apple. 'Things get away from me. I'm not trying to excuse myself. But you wouldn't believe how much . . .'

'Say, nowadays you can believe almost anything,' Leventhal said, and he laughed a little but without relish.

With a grave look, Allbee appealed to him not to persist in this. His brows went up, he pushed his fingers through his dirtyish blond hair, and Leventhal remarked to himself that there was an element of performance in all that he was doing. But suddenly he had a strange, close consciousness of Allbee, of his face and body, a feeling of intimate nearness such as he had experienced in the zoo when he had imagined himself at Allbee's back, seeing with microscopic fineness the lines in his skin, and the smallest of his hairs, and breathing in his odor. The same sensations were repeated; he could nearly feel the weight of his body and the contact of his clothes. Even more, the actuality of his face, loose in the cheeks, firm in the forehead and jaws, struck him, the distinctness of it; and the look of recognition. Allbee bent on him duplicated the look in his own. He was sure of that. Nevertheless he kept alive in his mind the thought that Allbee hated him, and his judgment, although it was numbed by his curious emotion of closeness – for it was an emotion – did not desert him. His burly, keen-set figure did not budge from the doorway any more than the spokes in the skylight moved.

'Will you let me in?' Allbee said at last.

'What for?'

'I want to talk to you.'

'I told you, it's late.'

'It's late for you, but it's all the same to me what time it is. You said you'd help me.'

'I don't want to start discussing your future now. Go away.'

'It's the present, not the future.'

Leventhal felt inexplicably weak against him. 'Am I forgetting all the things he said to me, how mad I was, all that ugly stuff?' he asked himself. And it was true that his sense of injury had not remained sharp; his self-reproach did not make it any sharper. The hall was airless, just as Mickey's room had been. He was starved for a free breath of air. His eyes were hot and tired, and the feeling of closeness seemed to have superseded and made faint all other feelings.

'What, the present?' he said.

'Well, you can go in, turn off the lights, and go to sleep,' said Allbee. 'It's nothing you have to think about. But I have nowhere to go. Not for the last few nights. I was put out.'

Leventhal studied him silently. Then he moved aside and said, 'All right. Come on.' He let Allbee precede him into the front room and pointed to a chair. He himself went to the window and put his head out, getting a glimpse of the reddened and darkened heavy forms of the street as he drew a long breath. He sat down on the creaking bed. It had not been made for a week, and papers and cardboard crescents the laundry put inside his collars were scattered over it. In crossing his legs, Allbee gave a twitch to his stained, loose-hanging trousers. His manner in some things was persistently gentlemanly. He knit his fingers around his knee.

'Now let's have it again. What happened, you were thrown out? Where were you, in a hotel, a room?'

'A furnished room. My landlord confiscated my stuff. Not that there was much of it.' Allbee's smile crept for a moment into the corners of his mouth and then was gone. 'But such as there was.'

'For back rent?'

'Yes.'

'Was it much?'

'I have no idea what I owed him. Or them. There's a land-lady, too. In fact she's the whole works. The Punts. They're a couple of Germans. She's a fat old woman with snag teeth. The nephew's a longshoreman. He's not so bad. It's that smelly old woman's fault. She kept after him. Old people, especially old women, are the hardest customers. They've made it, so to hell with everybody.'

'Made what? What are you talking about?'

'Lived so long. Pulled through. A long life,' said Allbee. 'All the hardships. The rich are rough on the poor for the same reason. The veteran is rough on the tenderfoot. All the way down the line. You know that yourself . . .'

'How much do you owe them? Ten dollars, twenty . . . ?' said Leventhal stopping him impatiently.

'More like forty or fifty. To be honest with you, I can't even make an estimate. I gave them a little on account, now and then. I don't know. Less than they say, you can be sure ot that.'

'Didn't they say?'

'I don't remember.'

'Don't tell me!'

Allbee did not speak.

'Don't you want to go back there, pay them a little? If it's forty dollars, I haven't got that kind of money on hand, but if you give them something . . . ?'

'No, thanks, the whole house smells. Pardon me, but that old Mrs Punt – I can't stand uncleanliness like that.'

'I'll bet you're a model roomer, too.'

'I'm not the worst.'

'Excuse me, but I forgot you were an aristocrat,' Leventhal muttered with a short laugh, Allbee looked at him simply. without a touch of reproof.

'Well, where have you been staying?'

'Fortunately the weather's been nice. I slept out. In the open. I could have gone to a shelter or a mission. I thought if the weather turned bad that I would. I'd go religious for a while. But it's been beautiful.'

'I don't know how you could let things get that bad. If you're telling me the truth.'

'If I told you the whole truth, it wouldn't sound plausible, so I'm only telling you part of it. I'm cutting it short. I suppose I shouldn't have let things get out of hand like this. Last week I kept warning myself to hurry up and do something, but I didn't pull myself together for some reason, and then Punt threw me out and there I was.' He turned his hand inward in a gesture of self-presentation. 'The way I look, pearl diving is about the only work I could get.'

'How much money did your wife leave you?' Leventhal asked suddenly.

Allbee colored. 'What business is it of yours?' he said.

'Why, man, you should have done something with it instead of just living it up.'

'You can't bring the world to its knees with a little insurance money . . .' He hesitated and added, 'I don't owe you any explanation, do I?'

'You don't owe me anything. I don't owe you anything, either.'

Allbee did not accept this, but he confined his disagreement to a shrug. Then he examined Leventhal at length. 'I had my reasons for doing what I did,' he said. 'I was in a peculiar state of mind and I wanted to get off the merry-go-round. Your wife is away, now. What if she were killed in an accident? Then you'd have the right to ask me such a question.'

'You're an idiot!' said Leventhal.

'I'm only saying that we're not in the same boat. Wait till we're in the same boat.'

'God forbid!'

'Of course. Who wants to see harm come to anyone? But accidents happen. You ought to realize that.'

'Look,' said Leventhal, 'it's as I say. I don't owe you anything. But I'll give you a few bucks. Go to your rooming house or to a hotel.'

'I can't go back. It's impossible. I can't ring Punt's bell at this time of the night. Besides, they have somebody else in the room. That's why they threw me out. And what sort of hotel would take me in? Like this? Without a bag? Unless you're suggesting a flophouse?'

'Well,' said Leventhal. 'Why beat around the bush? I see you've got your heart set on sleeping here tonight. I could see that all along.'

'Can you suggest a place for me to go?'

'You're just inviting yourself in. It's after one, do you know that?'

Allbee did not answer.

'After the way you've acted I should throw you out. And if you really believe half the things you said to me, you shouldn't want to stay under the same roof. You're a lousy counterfeit.'

'Why, you have the whole place to yourself. You can put me up,' Allbee said quietly smiling. 'I wouldn't be inconveniencing you. But if you want me to do this in the right spirit . . .' And to Leventhal's astonishment – he was too confounded when it happened to utter a sound – Allbee sank out of his chair and went to his knees.

Then he shouted, 'Get up!'

Allbee pulled himself to his feet.

'For Christ's sake, stop this damned clowning! What do you think this is?'

With a look of amusement, his eyes appearing fixed and large, Allbee seemed to taste first one lip and then the other.

'I warn you,' said Leventhal, 'I won't stand for your monkeyshines. Your jokes!' His disgust was passionate. 'You know they're not jokes; they're not supposed to be funny. You're trying to work something on me. You think you'll throw me off and I won't know what's happening.'

'You don't understand. I only wanted to do what was appropriate.'

'That's all right,' said Leventhal grimly, refusing to hear. 'I want you to get this – as far as I'm concerned, I'm letting you sleep here tonight to return a favor, and that's all. Do you hear me?'

'Oh, you *do* owe me something.'

'Am I the only one that does? Haven't you ever done anybody else a favor? It looks as if I'm the only one. And what do I owe you? You've pestered enough out of me already. I could shove you out in the hall and shut the door in your face with a clear conscience.'

'In your position – if I were in it, and I don't say that I could be – my conscience wouldn't be clear.'

'All right, conscience! I don't want to discuss my conscience with you,' said Leventhal. 'It's late.'

He took some bedding from the cupboard and, going into the dining-room, flung it onto the day bed.

'It's soft,' Allbee remarked feeling the mattress.

'Now what else do you need – you want to wash? There's the bathroom.'

'I'd like a shower,' said Allbee. 'It's been a long time since I had one.'

Leventhal gave him a towel and found an old bathrobe for him in the closet. He sat down on the bed in his crumpled pajamas and listened disquieted to the water pelting the shower curtain and streaming in the tub. Soon Allbee came out, carrying his clothes. Wet and combed, his yellow hair gave him quite a different look. Leventhal observed his feet with a queer feeling of aversion. The insteps were red, coarse, and swollen, his toes long and misshapen, with heavy nails.

'Amazing, what a shower can do for you,' said Allbee.

'I'm going to sleep,' Leventhal said. He switched off the bed lamp.

'Good night,' said Allbee. 'I'm really grateful for this hospitality.'

'Okay. There's milk in the refrigerator, if you want something.'

'Thanks, I may have a glass.' He went toward the dining-room. Leventhal covered himself and pulled the pillow into position. The door of the refrigerator clicked open and he thought, 'He is taking some.' He was already falling asleep when he heard it shut.

14

He slept but he did not rest. His heart beat swiftly and the emotions of the day still filled him. He had an unclear dream in which he held himself off like an unwilling spectator; yet it was he that did everything. He was in a railroad station, carrying a heavy suitcase, forcing his way with it through a crowd the sound of whose shuffling rose toward the flags hanging by the hundreds in the arches. He had missed his train, but the loud-speaker announced that a second section of it was leaving in three minutes. The gate was barely in sight; he could never reach it in time. There was a recoil of the crowd – the guards must have been pushing it back – and he found himself in a corridor which was freshly paved and plastered. It seemed to lead down to the tracks. 'Maybe they've just opened this and I'm the first to find it,' he thought. He began to run and suddenly came to a barrier, a movable frame resembling a sawhorse. Holding the suitcase before him, he pushed it aside. Two men stopped him. 'You can't go through, I've got people working here,' one of them said. He wore a business suit and a fedora, and he looked like a contractor. The other man was in overalls. 'I must, I've got to get to the tracks,' Leventhal said. 'There's a gate upstairs. This isn't open to the public. Didn't you see the sign on the door? What door did you come through?' 'I didn't come through any door,' said Leventhal angrily. 'This is an emergency; the train's leaving.' The second man appeared to be a thoughtful, sympathetic person, but he was an employee and couldn't interfere. 'You can't go back the way you came, either,' the contractor told him. 'There's a sign up there.

You'll have to leave through here.' Leventhal turned and a push on the shoulder sent him into an alley. His face was covered with tears. A few people noticed this, but he did not care about them.

He found himself not awake, precisely, but so nearly awake as to be conscious that he lay in the dark. He had a sense of marvelous relief at the end of the dream. He was, it seemed to him, in a state of great lucidity, and he experienced a rare, pure feeling of happiness. He was convinced that he knew the truth, and he said to himself with satisfaction, 'Yes, I do know it, positively. Will I know it in the morning? I do now.' For what he thought would have been very strange to his waking mind, difficult to accept if not downright foolish. But why was that? 'Why?' he reflected. 'Dear God, am I so lazy, so weak, is my soul fat like my body?' His heart was jolting painfully; nevertheless he felt confident and happy. What was it? What did he and others do? Admittedly, like others, he had been in the wrong. That was not so important, either. Everybody committed errors and offences. But it was supremely plain to him that everything, everything without exception, took place as if within a single soul or person. And still – here he was almost tempted to smile at himself – still he suspected, more than suspected, knew, that tomorrow this would be untenable. 'I won't be able to hold onto it,' he thought. Something would prevent it.

He had a particularly vivid recollection of the explicit recognition in Allbee's eyes which he could not doubt was the double of something in his own. Where did it come from? 'Speak of black and white,' he mused. Black and white were Mr Schlossberg's words, to which he frequently returned. Either the truth was simple or we had to accept the fact that we could not know it, and if we could not know it there was nothing to go by. 'There's just so much that we can do. What's the use of wearing yourself out for nothing?' Leventhal said to himself. No, the truth must be something we understand at once, without an introduction or explanation, but so common and familiar that we don't always realize it's around us.

Gripping the pillow, he turned over and shut his eyes. He was too stirred to sleep, however. He could hear Allbee's breathing, and he got up and closed the connecting door.

He had forgotten to set the alarm and he woke up late. The day was gray and hot. Irritated at oversleeping, he dressed and shaved hastily. After he washed off the lather he still looked unshaven. He shook some powder onto a towel, rubbed it on his chin, and slipped a shirt over his head. He had no time to stop for breakfast. In the kitchen he picked up an orange to eat on the way to the subway.

He went into the dining-room where Allbee lay face down, closely wrapped in the sheet. His broad calves were bare, his arms thrown forward, one hand touching the chair on which his clothes were heaped. Leventhal pulled at the mattress, but Allbee did not stir, and he was about to shake him but hesitated, nervously and angrily, and decided it would be unwise. For if he got him up now he was liable to lose half the morning in getting him out of the house. Leventhal did not know what to do about him. However – he looked at his watch – there was no time to deliberate now. Full of misgivings, he started for the office.

He almost welcomed his green metal desk with its hundreds of papers. The great, cloud-filled gray space his windows opened on seemed stationary. The activity around him, the swinging of the gates as the girls strode through them, the tremor and shimmer of the long-stemmed fans, had a settling effect on him. He worked hard. By eleven o'clock he had finished a complete set of galleys and he went in to Mr Beard to discuss a lead article for the next number. Millikan, the son-in-law, was there, sitting beside the old man. He took no part in the conversation. Beard made a few remarks of tentative opposition, merely, Leventhal felt, for the sake of his authority, because he wanted to avoid agreeing at once, not because he had countersuggestions. His eyeshade, dividing his forehead with its white blots from the rest of his face, hid his expression somewhat, but there were indications that he was pretty well satisfied. His mouth and jaw showed it. 'Well, can I handle your goddamned job?' Leventhal wanted to ask. He did not say this, he looked casual. Nevertheless a deep quiver of vindication went through him. 'Everything is going smoothly,' he remarked. Neither of them answered. Leventhal prolonged the silence for nearly a minute, until he forced a nod from Beard, and then he stalked out. He didn't claim to be indispensable; on the other hand, they might admit occasionally, without killing themselves, that he was valuable to them. With all his troubles and distractions, he was still finishing his work well within the deadlines. And Beard realized how efficient he was, that was why he had said that unpleasant thing to Mr Fay. 'What really bothers him,' Leventhal thought, 'is having to admit that he needs anyone for his business. He wants to be the one, the only, and the all-important. That's not the way a modern concern is run. He'll always be small potatoes.'

On the way back to his desk, he encountered Mr Fay. The fact that Fay had made an effort that day to defend him had led Leventhal to hope for more, a hint as to what had happened, an attempt to warn or advise him. One sign was all that was necessary. It wouldn't hurt to have a friend in the office. Moreover he wanted to thank Fay for putting in a word for him. 'Maybe he will talk, one of these days,' Leventhal told himself. Fay stopped him and mentioned an advertiser who was finishing a new plant that ought to be written up. He had spoken of it before. This time Leventhal was attentive, asked for more of the details, made notes on his pad, and said, 'That's easy to fix up.' He looked at Fay so expectantly that the latter seemed to think he was going to say more and paused, his dark eyes actively questioning under his graying, short brows and behind the shining circles of his glasses. 'Yes,' said Leventhal, 'I'll get the story for you,' and, with a mixture of impressions and, principally, the feeling that Fay was going to disappoint him, he turned away.

The ringing of the phone, reminding him of his sick nephew and of Allbee whom he had left sleeping, brought the blood to his face. He jerked his neck awkwardly as he fixed the receiver between his shoulder and his ear, praying that it might be a business call. With one hand he feverishly worked at the tangled wires.

At first he heard no one and he tried to signal the operator. Presently she broke in casually with, 'Somebody by the name of Williston, for you.' To restore his self-command, he stopped his breath for an instant. Then he said, 'Put him on.' He swung slowly back in the leather-backed chair, pulling a drawer open with the tip of his shoe and throwing his leg over it.

'Hello,' Williston said.

'Hello, Stan, how've you been?'

'Pretty fair.'

'You calling about Allbee?' Leventhal knew perfectly well that this directness was what Williston least wanted; Williston preferred to be roundabout. But why should he permit it?

He did not answer immediately.

'Well, aren't you?'

'I suppose I am. Yes, I am,' Williston said, sounding reluctant. 'I was wondering if you had seen him.'

'Oh, I've seen him. He's been coming around. As a matter of fact, he showed up last night; said he was kicked out of his rooming house. I put him up. He stayed over.'

'Kicked out?' Williston doubtfully said.

'What's the matter, you think I'm exaggerating? You haven't seen him. One look at him and it wouldn't sound so impossible.'

'What does he aim to do?'

'I wish I could tell, but he probably couldn't say himself. If you want to know, I think he's probably sick. There must be something wrong with him.'

Williston seemed to consider this; there was no reply for a while. Then he said, 'Hasn't he given you any clue as to what he wants?'

'Too many clues. I can't get any single thing out of him, that's the trouble.' He slipped his leg from the drawer and bent over the desk, cradling the phone in both hands. 'You should hear him; you'd find out in a hurry there was something wrong.'

Williston's voice came back in a drawling laugh. 'He's trying to calm me down,' thought Leventhal, feeling discouraged. 'He thinks I'm overdoing the complaining and wants to kid me out of it.'

'Oh, it isn't that bad, is it?' said Williston.

'It's plenty bad. You don't know how bad it is. I tell you, you haven't seen him or heard what he's got to say, what his line is. I did go wrong with Rudiger, I know, and that whole business was unfortunate. I won't try to duck out of it, although I could if I wanted to. But listen, you have no idea what he's like. Probably the thing to do is to get him a job. Whether he'll take it or not is another story. Maybe he doesn't want to work. I can't tell you. He wants everything, and I don't think he wants to do anything. He keeps play acting with me.' He stopped and grumbled to himself, 'I'll put him straight whether he wants to be put straight or not.'

'Oh, now, that's just boyishness,' said Williston. Leventhal was unable to decide to which of them the boyishness was attributed. He hunted for words, bluntly bracing his face against the difficulty of carrying on this conversation. It was purposeless, an added burden.

'Well, maybe you can make a useful suggestion, Stan.'

'I said I'd do whatever I could.' Williston appeared to feel himself accused.

'After all, I'm supposed to be his enemy. You're his friend.'

He did not hear all of his answer. He only caught a reference to a 'practical step' and understood that Williston was impatient with the way the conversation was going.

'Sure I'm in favor of something practical,' he replied. But as soon as the words were out he was aware that he and Williston had swung farther than ever, hopelessly far, from the real issues. Over the telephone the 'practical step' was vague enough and when he tried to apply it to Allbee it dissolved into irrelevance. For himself, the practical step was to get rid of the man, and this was not what Williston had in mind. 'You think of something,' he urged. 'You know him. Maybe you can figure out what would satisfy him.'

'He must have a definite object. If I could talk to him I might find out.'

'How would you get to talk to him? He doesn't want you to know anything about him. He was mad when he found out I talked to you about him. But I'll suggest it to him and see what happens.'

'I'll expect to hear from you, then,' said Williston. 'You won't forget to call, will you?'

'I'll call you,' Leventhal promised. He hung up and, setting the phone on some of his papers as a weight, he made an abstracted survey of his desk, slipped his jacket from the back of the chair, and started out to lunch.

He went down in the elevator amid a crowd of girls from the commercial school upstairs, largely unconscious of the pleasure that he took in their smooth arms and smooth faces. The elevator sank slowly in the musty shaft with a buzz of signals and a sparking of tiny arrowheads. On the street Leventhal bought a paper and glanced through it in the cafeteria. After lunch, he walked toward the river, passing through the sidewalk markets, between the sacks of coffee beans. The roasting odor was mixed with the smell of gas. The occasional piping of a tug or the low blurt of a steamer came through the trample and jamming of trucks, and booms bristled like the spikes of a maguey, dividing the white of the sky as the piers did that of the water.

He was the first to return to the office; the place was empty. A breeze passed over the papers on the desk or left rolled in the typewriters, and shadowed the green linen blinds on the crosspieces of the windows. He stepped out onto the fire escape to finish his cigar, and had just ground it out on the rail and tossed it into the air when one of the phones began to ring. In the violence of his turn, he struck his shoulder on the doorframe and for an instant he could not see – the interior of the office seemed black. The ringing filled the air wildly, coming from all four corners of the room simultaneously. He felt a clutch of horror at his heart, and the thrilling, piercing run of the bell was infinitely faster than the flow of his blood. He reached his desk. The call was for him.

'Yes? Who wants me?' he cried to the operator.

It was Villani.

Leventhal closed his eyes. It was what he had been expecting. Mickey was dead. He listened awhile to Villani and then roared out, 'Where is my damned brother!'

'He came in last night,' said Villani. 'He went straight out to the hospital. It was too late already. Poor little boy.'

Leventhal put the phone down. He could not restrain the play of muscles in his throat. He held himself off from the edge of the desk, as if about to stand up, and with the sick drop of fuller realization his broad face lost all color and his features grew thick.

After a time he picked up a pad and, printing Mr Beard's name in large crayon strokes, wrote under it, 'Death in the family' and, rising, went to lay it on his desk.

He walked with angry energy to the toilet and began to bathe his head. He had a crushing headache. Over the sink, when his face was wet, he began to cry. He snatched a paper towel from the box and covered his eyes. Then he heard someone approaching and turned blunderingly into a stall. He shut the door and, with his back against it, gradually, with silent effort, brought himself under control.

15

ON the ferry there was only a current of brackish air instead of the usual fresh breeze. The boat took the water with a sullen thudding beneath the broad lip of its bow. The air was chalky and the afternoon sun looked pale. One of the deck hands sat with his naked back touching the pilothouse, his head lying on his knees, his big forearms locked about his legs. At the slip, he dragged himself down the ladder to take down the chain, and Leventhal sprang past him and hurried through the shed. His bus was just pulling away from the curb, and he ran alongside and slammed at the door with his open hand. The bus stopped, the door folded open, and he squeezed in among the passengers on the lower step. The driver raised himself in his seat and called out something, stridently. His throat was taut and angry, his gray collar blackened with sweat. No one answered and, after a delay, he ground down the gearshift and they started again. Leventhal was panting. He did not heed the streaming of his face or the stinging of his hand. He was thinking, as he had thought on the boat, that he must expect to be blamed. Elena was bound to blame him and her mother sure to egg her on. He had argued for the hospital, he had brought the specialist; he had meddled. The old lady did not matter, but his dread of Elena was intense. Probably the disease was already in the fatal stage when Denisart took the case. In the hospital Mickey had at least had a chance, and if she had listened to the first doctor's advice he might have been saved. So it was her fault, if anyone's. But it was precisely because of the unreasonableness of the blame that he feared her. Nevertheless he was obliged to face her. He could not stay away now.

He hunted among the rows of bells, found his brother's, rang, and climbed up. The door of the flat was open a few inches. He pushed it and was startled to feel a resisting weight on the inside. Letting the knob go, he retreated a step. It ran swiftly through his mind that it was not a child behind that door, not Philip. And why should Max try to keep him out? Could it be Elena? A hot wave of fright passed over him at the thought that the energy of madness had held back his push. 'Who's there?' he said hoarsely. 'Who is it?' He went up to the door again. This time, merely at his touch, the door swung open. Elena's mother was in the hallway. He understood at once what had happened. Standing at the hinge to see who was coming she had been caught against the wall in the narrow vestibule.

'What are you doing?' His tone was harsh.

She was silent, and he was baffled by her look; behind its vindictiveness there was something crazily resembling amusement.

'Where is everybody?'

'Go out. I alone,' she said in her rough voice. He had never before heard her speak English. It surprised him. As for the amusement, he must have been mistaken about that. It was the concentration of her look that had suggested it. The boy was, after all, her grandson.

'Where did they go?'

Either she did not know or was unable to explain. She uttered a few sounds. Steam was coming from the kitchen; he saw it behind her. Was she cooking dinner?

'Where are they, at the chapel? Is the funeral today?'

She merely shrugged; she refused to answer, and she gave him another of those frightful glances of spite and exultation, as though he were the devil.

'They're going to come home to eat, aren't they – *mangare*? When?'

It was a waste of time. She only wanted to get rid of him. He turned from her and went downstairs.

No one responded to his knock at Villani's. His headache was becoming severer. He frowned and hit at the door despairingly. Then it occurred to him to try the superintendent. He found him in the court, reading the paper in the shade of the furnace room stairs.

'Do you know where I can find my people?' he said. 'I'm Max Leventhal's brother.'

The superintendent got up. Old and slow, he rested his weight on bent, swollen knuckles.

'Why, the boy's being buried out of Boldi's parlors.'

'The old mother-in-law is upstairs, but she wouldn't tell me. Where is this Boldi place?'

'Two blocks down. Turn left when you leave the building. Same side as this. There's a church on the corner.' He bent to gather up the paper which had unfolded over his brown felt slippers.

The sun had come round to a clearer portion of the sky and its glare was overpowering. Leventhal took off his jacket. The heat of the pavement penetrated his soles and he felt it in the very bones of his feet. In a long, black peninsular yard a row of scratchy bushes grew, dead green. The walls were flaming coarsely, and each thing – the moping bushes, the face of a woman appearing at a screen, a heap of melons before a grocery – came to him as though raised to a new power and given another quality by the air; and the colors, granular and bloody, black, green, blue, quivered like gases over the steady baselines of shadow. The open door of the grocery was like the entrance to a cave or mine; the cans shone like embedded rocks. He had a momentary impression of being in a foreign city when he saw the church the superintendent had mentioned – the ponderousness, the gorgeousness, the decay of it, the fenced parish house, the garden, and the small fountain thick with white lead and flimsily curtained with water.

He passed through Boldi's office and entered the lounge. There he saw Philip sitting in a wicker chair. His legs were crossed on a footstool and his head rested on his raised shoulder.

'How are you, boy?' Leventhal said quietly.

'Hello, uncle,' said Philip. He looked listless.

'I hear your father's back.'

'Yes, he came in.'

Leventhal caught the flush of candles through the oval windows of the studded leather door. He went into the chapel. It was cool. A master fan murmured somewhere in the building. Beyond the heaped-up, fiery glasses of the altar hung a Christ of human size. Taking off his hat, Leventhal walked up to the coffin. He was struck by the softness of the boy's face, the absence of signs of recoil or fright. He noted the curve of his nose, the texture of his brushed-up hair, the ends of which touched the folds of the satin, the poise of his small chin over his breast and decided, 'He was going to turn out like Max and me. A Leventhal.' Reflectively he fingered the smooth copper rail with its knot of dark plush and glanced upward. The chapel displeased him. Elena had undoubtedly insisted on a Catholic funeral. That was her right. But from the Leventhals' side, and the boy was one of them, too, it was peculiar, after so many generations, to have this. Prompted by an indistinct feeling, he thought to himself, 'Never mind, thanks, we'll manage by ourselves ...'

He turned from the rail and encountered his brother.

The sight of him hit Leventhal with a terrible force. He had been prepared to meet him in anger; his very first word was to have been a rebuke. But now, instead of speaking, he took in his brother's appearance, the darkness and soreness of his swollen face, the scar at the corner of his mouth from a cut received in a street fight years ago in Hartford. Outdoor work had weathered him; the loss of several teeth made his jaw longer. His suit – it was a suit such as laborers used to buy in his father's store. His new black shoes were dusty.

'I didn't make it in time,' he said.

'I heard, Max.'

'I left as soon as the telegram came. I got in about ten minutes late.'

'When's the funeral?'

'Four o'clock.' Max motioned him to come aside. In the aisle near the wall, clasping Leventhal's hand and stooping over it, he burst into tears. He whispered, but occasionally one of his sobs or half-articulated words broke out of key and reverberated through the place. Leventhal stiffened his arm and supported him. He heard him say, 'He was covered up,' and bit by bit, through many repetitions, he learned that Max had come into the room unaware that Mickey was dead and found the sheet drawn over his head.

'Awful,' he said. 'Awful.'

He gazed at Max's burly back and his sunburnt neck, and, as his glance moved across the polished rows of benches, he saw Elena sitting between Villani and a priest. The look she gave him was one of bitter anger. Though the light was poor, there was no mistaking it. Her face was white and straining. 'What have I done?' he thought; his panic was as great as if he had never foreseen this. He was afraid to let her catch his eye and did not return her look. Helping Max up the aisle, he sat down beside him, still holding his arm. What would he do if then and there – imagining the worst – she began to scream at him, accusing him? Once more she turned her face to him over her shoulder; it seemed to be blazing in its whiteness. She must be mad.

She was mad. He did not allow himself to use the word again. He held it back desperately like a man who is afraid to whisper lest he end by shouting.

He rode out to the cemetery with Villani and the priest, behind the limousine with Max, Elena, Philip, and Mrs Villani. During the burial he sheltered himself under a tree, hanging back from the others at the graveside in the full blast of the sun. When the shoveling of the earth began he walked back to the car. The chauffeur was waiting on the running board at the edge of the stonedust driveway. The glow of the sun in the locust trees gave a yellowish shine to his uniform. He had white hair, his eyes were bloodshot and his long lips impatiently drawn as he endured the heat moment by moment and breath by breath. Soon Villani and the priest came up. The priest was a Pole, stout and pale. He gave a push to his black Homburg, lit up, drawing deeply, and let the smoke out between his small teeth. Pulling out a handkerchief, he wiped his face and neck and the back of his hands.

'You're a relative, huh?' he said, addressing Leventhal for the first time.

Villani answered for him. 'He's the man's brother, Father.'

'Ah, yeah, tough deal.' His fingers, virtually nailless and curving at the tips, pinched the cigarette. He looked keenly into the sky, creasing the thick white skin of his forehead, and made a remark about the heat. The family were now approaching the cars and the chauffeurs started up the motors.

'Too hot back there for three,' said Leventhal, and climbed into the front seat. He wanted to avoid the priest. Touching the heated metal of the handle, he said mentally, 'So long, kid,' and peered out of the moving window at the yellow and brown of the large-grained soil and at the two booted men working their shovels. He occasionally saw Max in the back seat of the Cadillac and tried to recall Elena, persistently picturing how she had looked on the way to the grave, walking between Max and Villani, the fullness of her figure in the black dress, the grip of her hands on each arm, the jerking of her head. Poor Max, what was he going to do with her? And what about Philip? 'I'd take him in a minute,' he thought.

He did not say good-by to the family. It was after sunset when he reached the ferry. The boat went slowly over the sluggish harbor. The splash of a larger vessel reached it and Leventhal caught a glimpse of the murky orange of a hull, like the apparition of a furnace on the water. The searchlight

163

on the bridge passed over it and it was lost in a moment, put out. But its giant wading was still audible seaward in the hot, black air.

After getting off the subway he delayed going home. He stopped in the park. The crowd was extraordinarily thick tonight. The same band of revivalists was on the curb. A woman was singing. Her voice and the accompaniment of the organ were very dim, only a few notes emerging from the immense, interminable mutter. He searched for a long time before he found a seat near the pond where a few half-naked children were splashing. The trees were swathed in stifling dust, and the stars were faint and sparse through the pall. The benches formed a dense, double human wheel; the paths were thronged. There was an overwhelming human closeness and thickness, and Leventhal was penetrated by a sense not merely of the crowd in this park but of innumerable millions, crossing, touching, pressing. What was that story he had once read about Hell cracking open on account of the rage of the god of the sea, and all the souls, crammed together, looking out? But these were alive, this young couple with bare arms, this woman late in pregnancy, sauntering, this bootblack hauling his box by the long strap.

Leventhal fell to thinking that to his father what had happened in Staten Island today would be incomprehensible. In Hartford the old man used to point at the baskets of flowers in the doorways and remark how many foreign children, Italian or Irish, died. He was amazed at the size of the families, at the numbers born and dying. How strange if he could know that his own grandson was one of these, buried in a Catholic cemetery. With flowers, like the others. And baptized. It occurred to Leventhal for the first time that Elena must have had him baptized. And that a son of his was a workingman, indistinguishable from those who came to the store to buy socks, caps, and shirts. He would not have understood it.

Heartsick and tired, Leventhal started home at ten o'clock.

He did not think of Allbee till he began to go up, and then quickened his step. Twisting the key, he threw the door back with a bang and turned on the lights. On the couch in the dining-room, sheets, bathrobe, and towel were twisted together. There was half a glass of milk on the floor.

He went back to the front room and stretched out on the bed, intending to rest awhile before taking off his clothes and shutting off the lights. He put his hand to his face with a groan. Almost at once he fell asleep.

During the night he heard a noise and sat up. The lights were still burning. Someone was in the flat. He went softly into the dark kitchen. The dining-room door was open, and by the window he saw Allbee undressing. He stood in his underpants, pulling his shirt over his head. The fear that Leventhal felt, though deep, lasted only a second, a single thrust. His indignation, too, was short lived. He returned to the front room and took off his clothes. Switching off the lights, he went toward his bed through the dark, mumbling, 'Go, stay – it's all the same to me.' He was in a state of indifference akin to numbness, and he lay down more conscious of the heat than of any emotion in himself.

16

MR MILLIKAN, who attended to make-up at the printer's, was representing the firm at an all-industry conference, and Leventhal, at midday, had to go to the shop in Brooklyn Heights to replace him.

He waited on the subway platform in the dead brown air, feeling spent. He did not know how he was going to get through the day. The train rolled up and he sat down spiritlessly under the slow-wheeling fan that stirred the heat. Again and again he thought about the child's death. So soon closed over, covered up. So soon. He repeated it involuntarily while his head rocked with the bucketing of the cars in the long pull under the river that ended below the St George Hotel. He left the train and rode up to the street level in the elevator.

Millikan had made up four pages, leaving him four more. The work went slowly; he became drowsy and made mistakes and tedious recounts. Toward four o'clock, he began to drop off. 'It's the machine,' he thought. The presses were upstairs and they ran without interruption all day. He took time out for a walk. It was curious that he should feel so dull and heavy, and yet at the same time so apprehensive.

He went into a restaurant for a cup of coffee. The chairs were standing on the tables and a boy with a red, bluff head and freckled, rolling shoulders was mopping the tiles. The waitress made a detour of the advancing line of dirty water to ask Leventhal to move out of the way. He drank his coffee at the counter, wiped his mouth on the oblong of a paper napkin he did not bother to unfold, loitered through the lobby of the St George, examining a few magazines, and returned to the shop. Contemplating the pages with their blank spaces, he sighed and picked up the scissors. The presses had stopped before he was done. At half-past six he pasted his last strip and rubbed his hands clean with a piece of wastepaper.

On his way to dinner, he stopped at his flat to look in the mailbox. There was a note from Mary saying that she was writing a long letter which she expected to mail in a day or two. Disappointed, he slipped the note into his shirt pocket. He did not go upstairs. Near the corner he met Nunez, in his dungarees and straw hat, carrying a webbed market bag full of groceries.

'Eh, eh, hey! How are you, Mr Leventhal? I see you got yourself some company while your wife is away.'

'How do you know?' said Leventhal.

'Us supers, we keep track of everything around a building. We're supposed to be nosey. That's not what it is, you find out even if you don't care. You can't help it. The tenants get surprised. *Brujo*, I see through the wall. They don't know, eh?' He described a spiral with his fingers, enjoying himself greatly. 'No. You go out in the morning and then I hear your radio play. This afternoon the dumb-waiter goes up to the fourth floor. Later on, what's in it? – A empty soup can and rye bottle.'

'So that's what he's doing?' thought Leventhal. 'Guzzling all day. That's what I let him in for.' He said to Nunez, 'I've got a friend staying with me.'

'Oh, I don't care who you got.' Nunez gave a suggestive laugh and wrinkled his nose with pleasure, the veins on his forehead puffing out.

'Who do you think I've got?'

'That's okay. The way the dumb-waiter went up, there was no lady pulling on the rope, I know that. Don't worry.' He swung the bag with his big-jointed, muscular arm tattooed with a bleeding heart. Leventhal continued toward the restaurant. 'No money for rent,' he said going down the stairs and bending under the awning. 'But for hooch he has it. For hooch he can raise it. Where?' It occurred to him that Allbee had stolen some article from the house and pawned it. But

167

what valuables were there? Mary's sealskin coat was in storage. Spoons? The silver was not worth stealing. Clothing? But a pawnbroker would be running a great risk, seeing how Allbee was dressed, to deal with him. No, hockshops had to think of their licenses. Leventhal did not really fear for his clothes. He had a tweed suit sealed in a mothproof bag in his closet; the rest was not worth pawning. And the suit was a small enough price to pay for getting rid of Allbee. Allbee was certainly clever enough to realize that. Drunks, of course, when they were thirsty enough, desperate enough, turned reckless. 'But it isn't the few bucks he's after,' Leventhal reasoned. For he had already offered him money. Allbee must have some of his own, since he could afford to buy whisky. Then what about his being evicted, was that an invention? But what of his appearance, that filthy suit of his, his shirt, his long hair? Leventhal tentatively concluded that he kept a little money for whisky by economizing on rent and other things. 'But I better lock up the valuables, meanwhile,' he told himself.

He ate a small dinner of baked veal overseasoned with thyme, had a glass of iced tea with sandy, undissolved sugar, and lit a cigar. Max and the family had replaced Allbee in his mind. Should he phone? Not just now, not tonight – he busily supplied good excuses, flinching a little at the shadow of his own weakness which lay behind them. He knew it was there. But this was not really the time to call. Later, when things had settled down, Max would soon find out – assuming that Elena's last look in the chapel signified what he thought it did – what he had on his hands. Though perhaps there was nothing so unusual in that look under the circumstances. Perhaps – Leventhal studied the seam in the long ash of his cigar – he had let his imagination run away with him. Grief, overloading of the heart . . . 'Horror, you know,' he silently explained. People crying when their faces were twisted might appear to be laughing, and so on. 'Well, I hope to God I'm wrong,' he said. 'I hope I am. And if he can run the old woman out of the house, maybe they can come through.' The boy's death ought to bring the family closer together, at least. The old woman's influence on Elena was bad; and now especially she could work round her. For Philip's sake, Max ought to show the old devil the door. With her cooking and housekeeping she might try, at a time like this, to make herself a power in the house. He must impress the danger of this on Max, who might be inclined to let her stay. 'Throw her out, don't give her a chance!' Leventhal exclaimed. If Max came to rely on her, why . . . And he might, if it freed him, go where he liked and leave Philip in her hands. No, she must be pitched out. He sat awhile at his gloomy corner table, his black eyes giving very little evidence of the gloomy anxiety that filled him.

At home he took off his jacket in the vestibule. Through the window, in the clear depth over the wandering brown smoke and the low-lying red of twilight clouds, he saw the evening star. He went through the narrow kitchen into the dining-room, which was empty. Coming back to the front room, he was not immediately aware of Allbee's presence. It was only after he had dropped into a chair beside the window that he discovered him sitting between the desk and the corner, and he cried out fiercely, 'What's the big idea!'

He shot up and turned on the desk lamp. His hands were shaking.

'I was enjoying the evening.'

'My foot, the evening,' Leventhal grumbled. 'Drunken bastard!'

He was stubbornly silent, after this, determined that Allbee should speak first. The electric clock whirred swiftly. Allbee's head lay on the back of the chair, his large legs were thrown wide apart, their weight supported on his heels. His hands, loose-wristed, were folded on his chest. After some time he moved a little and sighed, 'This killing heat, it takes my energy away.'

'It couldn't be something besides heat that takes it away, could it?'

'What – ?'

'Whisky,' Leventhal said. 'You're supposed to be looking for work. What have you been doing? Sitting here, drinking? When you came I understood you were going to get something to do and find yourself a room.'

Allbee brought his head forward.

'I don't want to rush into anything,' he said beginning to smile. 'In any deal – you know that, you must know it by instinct – the worst thing of all is to hurry. Before you make up your mind . . . if you settle for buttons, peanuts . . . You have to think things over,' he ended with an unsteady, delighted, foolish look of self-congratulation. Was he drunk? Leventhal wondered.

'*You*, a deal,' he said contemptuously. 'What kind of a deal have you got?'

'Oh, I might have. I might have something.'

'Furthermore, how do you get in and out of here? I locked the door last night. I'm sure I locked it.'

'I hope you don't mind. There were some keys in the kitchen and one of them fitted.'

Leventhal scowled. Had Mary forgotten her key? Or was this an extra? 'Originally the agent gave us two,' he thought, 'and the mailbox keys and the key to the locker in the basement. Or were there three house keys?'

'I wasn't sure I was coming back,' said Allbee. 'But as long as there was a possibility of it, I thought it would be more convenient to have a key. I tried to call you at your office yesterday, but you weren't in.'

'Don't start bothering me at the office,' Leventhal said excitedly. 'What did you want?'

'I wanted to ask your permission about the key, for one thing. And then there was something else that occurred to me, that on an outside chance there was an opening for someone like me at Beard and Company, and I might apply. You're in a position to help me there.'

'At Beard's? – It didn't just occur to you! I don't believe it.'

'It did so,' Allbee quickly began, but stopped. His large full lips were parted and his loud breathing suggested repressed laughter; he looked at him with comic curiosity. But, seeing him stare back, he started over again, more seriously. 'No, it did, it struck me all of a sudden as I was eating breakfast. "Why shouldn't Leventhal help me get a job at his place?" And it's fair enough, isn't it? I introduced you to Rudiger. We won't count what happened. We'll forget about it. Let's think of it only as a return courtesy. You make an appointment with Mr Beard for me – does he do the hiring over there in person? – and we'll be square.'

'They don't need anybody.'

'Let me find that out for myself.'

'Anyway, they couldn't give you the type of job you want.'

'But you don't care what kind of job I want. It wouldn't make any difference to you, what,' he said grinning. 'Whether I became a dish washer or scavenger, or hired myself out as human bait.'

'No, it wouldn't, that's true,' Leventhal replied.

'Then why should you worry about the type of work they offer me at your place?'

'Didn't I hear you talking about a deal?' said Leventhal. He went to the mantel, fumbled for a cigarette in a jar, and, sitting down, slid his hand across the window sill toward the packet of matches lying in the ash tray. Allbee watched him.

'You know, when I see how your mind works, I actually feel sorry for you,' he said finally.

Leventhal pulled deeply at the cigarette; it stuck to his lips and he plucked it away.

'Look, the answer is a straight no. Never mind the discussion. I have plenty of trouble as it is. Skip the discussions.' His self-possession was temporary, like a reflection in water that may be wiped out at the first swell.

'I understand. You're afraid I'll turn around and do to you what you did to me at Dill's. You think I want to go there and retaliate by getting you fired. But your introduction isn't necessary. I can make trouble for you without it.'

'Go ahead.'

'You know I can.'

'Well, do!' he began to be shaken by the swells. 'You think the job is so valuable to me? I can live without it. So do your worst. Hell with it all!'

'I took Williston's word about you. He said you were all right, so I made the appointment for you with Rudiger. See? I wasn't suspicious. It's not in my make-up, I'm happy to say. I didn't even know who you were, except from seeing you a few times at his parties.'

'I feel too low to horse around with you, Allbee. I'm willing to help you out. I told you so already. But as far as having you in the same office where I could see you every day – no! As it is, there are plenty of people over there I don't care to see every day. You'd fit in with them better than I do. I don't have any choice about them. But I do about you. So it's out of the question. No! – and finished. I couldn't stand it.'

Allbee seemed to be considering something in Leventhal's words that pleased him, for his smile deepened.

'Yes,' he admitted. 'You don't have to have me around. And you're right. I think you really are right. You have a choice. I envy you, Leventhal. Because when it came to the important things in my life, I never had the chance to choose. I didn't want my wife to die. And if I could have chosen, she wouldn't have left me. I didn't choose to be stabbed in the back at *Dill's* either.'

'Who! I stabbed you in the back?' Leventhal furiously said, making a fist.

'I didn't choose to be fired by Rudiger, do you like that better? Anyway, you're in an independent position and I'm not.' He was already falling into that tone of speculative earnestness that Leventhal detested. 'Now I believe that luck . . . there really is such a thing as luck and those who do and don't have it. In the long run, I don't know who's better off. It must make things very unreal to have luck all the time. But it's a blessing, in some things, and especially if it gives you the chance to make a choice. That doesn't come very often, does it? For most people? No, it doesn't. It's hard to accept that, but we have to accept it. We don't choose much. We don't choose to be born, for example, and unless we commit suicide we don't choose the time to die, either. But having a few choices in between makes you seem less of an accident to yourself. It makes you feel your life is necessary. The world's a crowded place, damned if it isn't. It's an overcrowded place. There's room enough for the dead. Even they get buried in layers, I hear. There's room enough for them because they don't want anything. But the living . . . Do you want anything? Is there anything you want? There are a hundred million others who want that very same damn thing. I don't care whether it's a sandwich or a seat in the subway or what. I don't know exactly how you feel about it, but I'll say, speaking for myself, it's hard to believe that my life is necessary. I guess you wouldn't be familiar with the Catholic catechism where it asks, "For whom was the world made?" Something along that line. And the answer is, "For man." For every man? Yes, for every last mother's son. Every man. Precious to God, if you please, and made for His greater glory and given the whole blessed earth. Like Adam. He called the beasts by their names and they obeyed him. I wish I could do that. Now that's clever. For everybody who repeats "For man" it means "For me." "The world was created for me, and I am absolutely required, not only now, but forever. And it's all for me, forever." Does that make sense?'

He put the question with an unfinished flourish and Leventhal looked at his sweating face and only now realized how drunk he was.

'Who wants all these people to be here, especially forever? Where're you going to put them all? Who has any use for them all? Look at all the lousy *me*'s the world was made for and I share it with. Love thy neighbor as thyself? Who the

173

devil is my neighbor? I want to find out. Yes, sir, who and what? Even if I wanted to hate him as myself, who is he? Like myself? God help me if I'm like what I see around. And as for eternal life, I'm not letting you in on any secret when I say most people count on dying . . .'

Leventhal had an impulse to laugh. 'Don't be so noisy,' he said. 'I can't help it if the world is too crowded for you, but pipe down.'

Allbee also laughed, strenuously, with a staring expression; his entire face was distended. He cried out thickly, 'Hot stars and cold hearts, that's your universe!'

'Stop yelling. That's plenty, now. You'd better go to sleep. Go and sleep it off.'

'Oh, good old Leventhal! Kindhearted Leventhal, you deep Hebrew . . .'

'Enough, stop it!' Leventhal interrupted.

Allbee obeyed, though he went on grinning. From time to time he released a pent-up breath and he sank deeper into the armchair.

'Are you really going to do something for me?' he said.

'You've got to stop the tricks, first of all.'

'Oh, I don't want to see old man Beard,' Allbee assured him. 'I won't bother you up there, if that's what you mean.'

'You've got to try to do something about yourself.'

'But will you really try? You know, use your connections for me?'

'For the love of Mike, I can't do much. And as long as you behave the way you do . . .'

'Yes, you're right. I've got to get next to myself. I have to change. I intend to. I mean it.'

'You see that yourself, don't you?'

'Of course I do. Don't you think I've got any sense at all? I must take myself in hand before everything wriggles away from me . . . get back to what I was when Flora was alive. I feel worthless. I know what I am. Worthless.' Delirious tears came to his eyes. 'There were good things in me.' He struggled and fumbled, half revolting in the fervor of his self-abasement, but half – ah, half you could not help feeling sorry. 'Williston will tell you. Flora would if she was here to speak and forgive me. I think she would. She loved me. You can see how I've come down if I talk to you like this. If she were alive, it wouldn't hurt me so much to be a failure.'

'Ah, quit – !'

'I'd still be ashamed, but at least I wouldn't have so much to blame myself for.'

'You? You hypocrite, you'd never blame yourself in a thousand years. I know your type.'

'I am to blame. I know it. My darling!' He put the heel of his hand to his wet forehead, spread his mouth open crudely, and wept.

Leventhal regarded him with a kind of dismayed pity. He rose and stood wondering what to do.

'The thing to do is to make him coffee, I suppose,' he decided. He hurried to fill the pot and, striking a match, held it to the burner. The flames spurted up in the star-shaped rows. He tapped the jar with the spoon and measured out the coffee.

When he came back to the front room, Allbee was asleep. He shouted, 'Wake up, I'm fixing coffee for you.' He clapped his hands and shook him. Finally he lifted one of his lids and looked at his eye. 'Passed out,' he said. And he thought with grim distaste, 'Can I let him stay here like this? He may slide out of the chair and lie on the floor all night.' The idea of spending the night like that, with Allbee on the floor and perhaps waking up, frightened him somewhat. Besides, he was beginning to be aware of the disgusting smell of alcohol that came from him. He hauled Allbee from the chair and began to drag him from the room. At the kitchen door he lifted him onto his back, holding him by the wrists, and he carried him to the dining-room and dropped him onto the day bed.

17

LABOR DAY was approaching; the coming week was shortened. Press time had been moved back and all copy had to be ready by Friday. Beard called a meeting of the editors to announce this. He was in a talkative mood and he swiveled back and forth, catching the red threads of the carpet in the casters of his chair. At every other sentence he lifted his hand and let it fall slackly. He made it an official occasion because of the holiday. He wouldn't keep them long. They had their work and brevity was the soul of wit. But this had been a good year for the firm, and he wanted the personnel to know how much he appreciated their loyalty and hard work. When you said work you said decency. They went together. So he wasn't thanking his people so much as complimenting them. It was better to wear out than to rust out, as was often quoted. He was a hard worker himself. He lived five miles as the crow flies from the office and he always allowed himself enough time so that if the subway broke down he could still walk the distance before nine o'clock. If a job was worth holding it was worth being loyal to. Life without loyalty was like – Shakespeare said it – a flat tamed piece. Leventhal in his white shirt, his face concealing his somber, weary annoyance, knew this was aimed at him. He kept his eyes on the image of the light striped window shade filling like a sail in the glass of the desk which was already cleared for the holiday.

'*Grosser philosoph.*' Leventhal, walking through the office, repeated his father's phrase with all his father's satire. Of all days to waste time. He got back to work even before the lamp over his papers had come to its full blue radiance. He had promised himself to take a breather today in order to think things over. But he was not really sorry to be too busy.

Mr Millikan, his face pale and his nostrils widened, strode through the office carrying galley sheets in each hand. Mr Fay stopped by to remind Leventhal about his manufacturer who wanted a spread.

'First thing next week, I'll take care of it,' Leventhal said. 'On Tuesday.'

'Say, I'm sorry to hear you had such bad luck in your family – bereavement.' Mr Fay's lips thinned, his tone was formal, and the skin began to gather on his forehead. 'Who was it?'

'My brother's kid.'

'Oh, a child.'

'A little boy.'

'That's awfully tough. Beard mentioned it to me.' The severity of his lips gave him a look of coldness bordering on suffering. Leventhal understood what caused it.

'Any other children?'

'They have another son.'

'That makes it a little easier.'

'Yes,' Leventhal said.

He let his work drift briefly while he gazed after Mr Fay. He at least was decent. Beard might have taken a moment off to say something. And Millikan rushed by and didn't even have time to nod. It showed the low quality of the people, their inferiority and meanness. Not that it made any difference to him. This Millikan, when he finally did get around to ask a personal question, never listened to the answer, only seemed to. He was like a shellfish down in the wet sand, and you were the noise of the water to him. Leventhal glanced over his desk – the papers, the glassful of colored pencils, the thick inkstand, the wire letter tray. There were several messages on his spindle and he tore them off. One, dated yesterday, was from Williston; he wanted him to call. Leventhal held the slip of paper in his palm, against his chest, and looked down at it. He thought, 'I'll call him when the pressure's off me. It couldn't be so urgent or he would have tried to reach me at the shop or at home, last night.'

At noon the receptionist rang to say that there was a man in the waiting-room looking for him.

'What's his name?'

'He didn't give any.'

'Well, ask him, will you?' The phone went silent. There was no response when he tried to signal her a few minutes later. He walked into the aisle to look at the switchboard. Her place was vacant. He took his straw hat from the hook and put it on. It had been his first guess that the visitor was Max. Max, however, would have given his name. It was probably Allbee. So much for his promise not to bother him at work. The waiting-room was deserted. Leventhal, trying to force open the opaque glass slide to see whether she had returned to her switchboard by another entrance, heard her behind him. She was coming through the office door.

'Well, did you locate him?'

'Yes, he's in the corridor, but he doesn't want to give his name or come in.' She was laughing, perplexed, and her small eyes seemed to ask Leventhal what was up. He stepped into the corridor.

Allbee was watching the cables and the rising weight at the back of the elevator shaft. He was carrying his jacket wrapped around his arm; his face was yellow and unshaven, his soiled shirt open; he stood loose-hipped, one hand bent against his chest. His shoes were untied. He appeared to have dragged on his clothes as soon as he got out of bed and set out, without losing a second, to see him. No wonder the girl had laughed. But Leventhal was not really disturbed either by her laughing or by Allbee himself. The lower half of the red globe above the doors lit up and the elevator sprang to a soft stop. He and Allbee crowded in among the girls from the commercial school upstairs.

'Nice,' Allbee whispered. They were forced to stand close. Leventhal could scarcely move his arms. 'Nice little tender things. Soon you and I, we'll be too old to take notice.' Leventhal was silent. 'Last night he was crying for his wife,' he was thinking as they sank slowly along the wall.

Allbee followed him through the lobby and into the street.

'I thought you said you weren't going to come around?' said Leventhal.

'You'll notice that I waited outside.'

'Well, I don't want you around. I told you that.'

Allbee's eyes shone at him with reproachful irony. They were quite clear, considering how drunk he had been. His voice was thick, however. 'I promised you I wasn't going to make trouble for you here. Since things are like this between us, you ought to have a little faith in me.'

'Yes?' said Leventhal. 'How are things between us?'

'Besides, I had a look at the goings-on inside. That's not for me.'

'Well, what's on your mind? Make it quick. I have to have lunch and get right back.'

Allbee was slow to begin. Could it be, Leventhal wondered, that he was unprepared and improvising something? Or was it part of his game to appear awkward, like this?

'I know you're suspicious of me,' he finally said.

'Come on, let's have it.'

He wiped his hand over his eyes. There were lines of strain about the root of his nose.

'I've got to get myself in motion.'

'What, are you going away?'

'No, I didn't say I was. Well, yes, as soon as I can. That's understand. I mostly wanted to say . . .' He reflected. 'I was in dead earnest last night; I want to do something about myself. But before I can start there are certain things I'll have to have . . . clean up, make myself look a little more respectable. I can't approach anybody this way.'

Leventhal agreed.

179

'I should get a haircut. And this shirt,' he plucked at it. 'My suit should be cleaned. Pressed, at least. I need some money.'

'You find money for whisky. You don't have any trouble about that.'

Allbee's look was earnest and even somewhat impressive, despite the sullen sickliness of his face.

'I suppose you weren't drunk last night. What did you do it on, sink water?'

'That was absolutely the last of Flora's money, the last few dollars. The last connection with her,' he uttered the words slowly, 'in something tangible.'

Leventhal raised his eyes to him skeptically. His gaze contained all the comment he thought necessary. He shrugged and turned his face away.

'I didn't expect you to approve of that or even sympathize. You people, by and large – and this is only an observation, nothing else, take it for what it's worth – you can only tolerate feelings like your own. But this was good-by to my wife. That wasn't sentimental. Just the opposite. To get a haircut or a new shirt with those last few dollars of hers would have been sentimental. Worse. That would have been hypocrisy.' His large lips made a burst of disgust. 'Hypocritical! The money had to go the way the rest did. It would have been cheap and dishonest to use the last dime differently from the first.'

'In other words, it was all for your wife.'

'It was. I wasn't going to use a single cent of it to advance myself with. I felt bound to do it that way no matter how much it hurt me. And it did hurt me.' He put his hand to his breast. 'But this way I've been decent, at least. I didn't become a success at her expense. I didn't become what I wasn't before she died. And consequently I can face myself today.' He stood swaying over him, ungainly, his mouth beginning to swell out derisively. 'You wouldn't have done that, Leventhal.'

'Maybe I wouldn't have to,' Leventhal said disgustedly.

'It's easy for you to say. You haven't been touched. Wait till you're touched.'

'Pardon?'

'Wait till something happens to your wife.'

Leventhal blazed up. 'You stop that harping on something happening . . . and that hinting. You've done it before. Damn you, you stop!'

'I don't want anything to happen,' Allbee said. 'All I've been trying to show is that you've been luckier than I. But you shouldn't forget that luck cuts both ways and be prepared, and when you're in my position – *if* you ever are. That's the whole thing, that *if*.' He had recovered his favorite key and he brightened. '*If* swings us around by the ears like rabbits. But *if* . . . ! And you have to square it with yourself, every mistake you ever made, all your sins against her, then maybe you'll admit it isn't so simple. That's all I want to say.'

'Oh, now we're on my sins.'

'I'm not talking about cheating on your wife. I don't know how it stands, but that's a very unimportant part of it – your cheating on her, or her cheating on you. What I'm talking about holds good regardless. You mustn't forget you're an animal. There's where a lot of unnecessary trouble begins. Not that I'm in favor of infidelity. You know how I feel about marriage. But you see a lot of marriages where one partner takes too much from the other. When a woman takes too much from a man, he tries to recover what he can from another woman. Likewise the wife. Everybody tries to work out a balance. Nature is too violent for human ideals, sometimes, and ideals ought to leave it plenty of room. However, we're not monkeys, either, and it's the ideals we ought to live for, not nature. That brings us back to sins and mistakes. I heard of a case . . .'

Leventhal cried, 'Do you think I'm going to stand here and listen to your cases?'

'I thought you might be interested,' Allbee said pacifyingly.

'Well, I'm not.'

'All right.'

Leventhal started toward the restaurant and Allbee walked beside him. The slanting parallels of shadow from the elevated tracks passed over them. The windows and window metals trembled and flashed.

'Where do you eat around here?'

'Down a way.'

They came to a corner. 'No use going on with you,' said Allbee. 'I had my coffee before getting on the subway.'

'Good-by,' Leventhal said indifferently, hardly pausing; he glanced at the traffic light. Allbee hung on, a little to the rear.

'I wanted to ask you – will you lend me a few dollars? Five or so . . . ?'

'To start life over?' said Leventhal, still looking away.

'You offered me some, awhile back.'

'Tell me why I should give you anything.' Leventhal turned squarely to him.

Allbee met this with an uncertain, puzzled smile while Leventhal, on the other hand, felt more steadily balanced and confident.

'You tell me,' he said again.

'You offered it. You'll get it back.' Allbee dropped his glance, and there was a curious flicker not only in his lowered lids, over the fullness of his eyeballs, but over his temples.

'Yes, naturally I will,' Leventhal said. 'You're a man of honor.'

'I want to borrow ten bucks or so.'

'You raised it. You said five, before, and five is what I'll let you have. But I'll give you notice now that if you show up drunk . . .'

'Don't worry about that.'

'Worry? It's not my lookout.'

'I'm not a drunkard. Not a real one.'

Leventhal had half a mind to ask what he was, really, what he genuinely thought he was. But he said instead, with casual irony, 'And here I believed you when you said you were so reckless.' He opened his wallet and took out five singles.

'I appreciate it,' said Allbee, folding the money and buttoning it up in his shirt pocket. 'You'll get every penny back.'

'Okay,' Leventhal replied dryly.

Allbee turned away, and Leventhal thought, 'If he takes one shot – and he probably thinks he'll have one and quit – he'll take two and then a dozen. That's the way they are.'

There was a letter from Mary waiting for him that evening. He pulled it out of the mailbox thankfully. Allbee's hints had bothered him more than he knew. He had brushed them aside. What reason did he have to be anxious about her? Nevertheless there were coincidences; things were mentioned and then they occurred. He worked his finger under the flap and tore open the envelope. The letter was thick. He sat down on the stairs and read it in absorption and deep pleasure. It was dated Tuesday night; she had just come back from dinner at her uncle's. She asked for news of Mickey – Leventhal had put off writing about him – and she complained mildly about her mother. It was comical and strange that her mother treated her like a child. She didn't make coffee enough for two in the morning, assuming that her daughter still drank milk, unable to grasp the fact that she was not merely a grown woman but a woman no longer so young. This morning a few gray hairs had showed up. Old! Leventhal smiled, but his smile was touched with solicitude. He turned the page. She had so much time on her hands and so little to do that she had bought yardgoods and was sewing herself some slips, trimming them with lace from old blouses of her mother's, 'still in good condition and very pretty as you'll see when I get home.' The rest of the letter was about her brother's children. He put it to his mouth as though to cover a cough and touched the paper with his lips.

If she were still in Baltimore, he would have gone down for the holiday. But unless he flew, he could not get back from Charleston by Tuesday. And besides there was her mother in Charleston, recently widowed and no doubt difficult. He would wait and have Mary to himself in a few weeks, when things were quieter. She would make them quieter. He had great faith in her ability to restore normalcy.

The thought of reunion made entering the house all the harder. He listened at the door before going in. He wanted to avoid being taken by surprise again. There were no sounds. 'Let him just come back drunk,' Leventhal said to himself. 'That's all I ask.'

Within a few days the flat had become dirty. The sink was full of dishes and garbage, newspapers were scattered over the front-room floor, the ash trays were spilling over, and the air stank. Depressed, Leventhal opened the windows. Where was Wilma? Didn't she generally come on Wednesdays? Perhaps Mary had forgotten to ask her to continue in her absence. He decided to ask Mrs Nunez tomorrow to clean the place. Picking up an ash tray, he took it to the toilet to empty. The tiles were slippery. He grasped the shower curtains for support; they were wet. In the dark his foot encountered something sodden and, setting the ash tray in the sink, he bent to the floor and picked up his cotton bathrobe. He took a quick, angry step into the front room and spread the dripping robe to the light. There were shoeprints on it and, around the pocket, pale blue stains that looked like inkstains. He emptied it and found several ads torn from the paper, Jack Shifcart's business card, the one jokingly intended for Schlossberg, and, bent and smeared, the two postcards he had received from Mary a few weeks ago. He hurled the robe furiously into the tub. His face was drawn, his mouth gaping with rage. 'The . . . sucking bitch!' he brought out, almost inarticulate and struggling ferociously against a stifling pressure in his throat. He flung aside the chair before his desk, threw the writing leaf down, tore papers out of the pigeonholes and drawers, and began to go through them – as if, in his numbness and blindness, he could tell what was missing. Awkwardly, his hands stiff, he spread them out: letters, bills, certificates, bundles of canceled checks, old bankbooks, recipes that Mary had pasted on cards and put away. Heaping them together again he picked up the blotter, banged up the leaf with his knee, and pushed them, blotter and all, into a drawer. He locked it, put the key in his watch pocket, and sat down on the bed. He still retained the cards and the clippings he had taken from the pocket of the robe. 'I'll kill him!' he cried, bringing his fist down heavily on the mattress between his knees; and then he was silent and his large eyes stared as though he were trying to force open an inward blindness with the sharp edge of something actual. He rubbed his fingers thickly on his forehead. Presently he began to read Mary's cards, the words of intimacy meant only for him. There were a few private references and abbreviations that no one else could understand; the drift of the rest was hard to miss. 'To carry them around like that, to keep them to look at!' he thought. He felt a drench of shame like a hot liquid over his neck and shoulders. 'If that isn't nasty, twisted, bitching dirty!' It sickened him. If Allbee had seen them accidentally . . . that too would have been hateful to him. But it was not accidental; Allbee had gone into his things, his desk – Shifcart's card proved that, for Leventhal was certain he had put it away – and snooped over his correspondence and kept these cards to amuse himself with. And perhaps he had seen Mary's earliest letters, the letters of reconciliation after the engagement was broken. They were in the desk, somewhere. Was that the reason he had made those remarks today about marriage and the rest? He might have made them without knowing, on the chance that he was susceptible. Nearly everyone was. Leventhal thought with a stab of that incident before his marriage and Mary's behavior, which he still did not understand. How could she have done that? But he had long ago decided to accept the fact and stop puzzling about the cause. To Allbee, who might have read the letters, it must have seemed a wonderful opportunity: Mary away, and so why not drop a hint? What he did not know was that Leventhal's old rival was dead. He had died of heart-failure two years ago. Mary's brother had brought the news on his last visit North. It wasn't to be found in a letter.

To himself he said, 'A lot a dirty drunk like that would know about a woman like Mary.'

18

THE dark came on. He did not light the bed lamp but sat, still with the cards in his hand, waiting for Allbee, listening for footsteps and hearing instead a variety of sounds from below, the booming of radio music through the floor, mixed voices, the rasping of the ropes in the dumb-waiter; the cries of boys scudding down the street rose above the rest, as distinct as sparks from fire. With the setting of the sun, the colored, brilliant combers of cloud rolled more and more quickly into gray and blue, while red lights appeared on the peaks of buildings, pilot warnings, like shore signals along a coast. The imperfections of the pane through which Leventhal gazed suggested the thickening of water at a great depth when one looks up toward the surface. The air had a salt smell. A breeze had begun to blow; it swayed the curtains and rattled among the papers on the floor.

After a time, Leventhal held his wrist up to the faint, gold bits of light under the window and studied his watch. It was well past eight; he had been sitting for more than an hour. He looked meditatively into the street. His first anger had passed over. From waiting to confront Allbee, he had lapsed gradually into a state of inert rest and now he felt hungry and got up to go to dinner. No use waiting for Allbee, who was probably drinking up the last of the five dollars in some bar and was in that case disposing of himself the quickest way. It was just as well, he reflected, that Allbee had not showed up, for what he obviously wanted was to be taken seriously. Once he had succeeded in this he could work him, Leventhal, as he liked. And that, quite plainly, was his object.

The restaurant was full; there was a crowd around the small bar. He moved to the rear in search of a table. 'I got customers next at the bar,' the bony, dark waiter said, 'but I'll see what I can do for you.' He had a cup of coffee in either hand and he hurried away. Leventhal was undecided whether to wait with the others or stand at the kitchen door. It was not very likely that the waiter would give him a table out of turn if he got into the crowd. He continued toward the leaning wall of the kitchen passage. Through the arch he saw one of the cooks beside the brick oven wiping the flour from his arms and waving his apron to cool his face. Leventhal brushed against someone who seemed to have stretched an arm into his path accidentally. Without looking, he said, 'Beg your pardon.' A man said laughingly, 'Why don't you watch?' And though it was peculiar that this should be said with a laugh, he did not turn but merely nodded, and he was going on when he felt his jacket being pulled. It was Williston. Phoebe was with him.

'Well, hello,' she said. 'Don't you talk to people any more?' It came over Leventhal that she was accusing him of deliberately avoiding them.

'My mind was somewhere else,' he said, his cheeks darkening coarsely.

'Sit down. Are you alone?'

'Yes, I am. They promised me a table, so don't let me . . .'

'Oh, come ahead. Here.' Williston pushed back a chair.

Leventhal hesitated, and Phoebe said, 'What's the matter, Asa?' in a manner that indicated it was impossible to show reluctance for another moment without offending her.

'Oh, Mary's out of town,' he said, 'and I don't bother too much about meals. I just run out and grab something. And you're almost through.'

'Now sit down, will you?' said Williston.

'What does your wife's being away have to do with it? My Lord!'

Leventhal looked at her dead-white complexion, her thick

level eyebrows, and the short, even teeth her smile revealed. The noise of the place cut off their conversation for a moment. He accepted the chair, massively crowding the table as the waiter passed behind him. With an anxious face he struggled up again to catch his attention. He sat down again, telling himself not to be so nervous. Why should they rattle him? He read the menu with his hand to his forehead, feeling the heat and moisture under his fingers, and putting his swarming emotions in order. 'What's the matter; can't I stand up to them?' he asked himself. The challenge strengthened him. When he closed the menu he was surer of himself. The waiter came up.

'What's special?' he said.

'Soup, you want bean soup? *Lasagna*, we got tonight.'

'I see mussels.' He pointed to the shells.

'Very good,' said Phoebe.

'*A la possilopo*.' The waiter wrote.

'And a bottle of beer; a plate of soup to start.'

'Right up.'

'I've been trying to reach you,' Williston said.

'Oh?' Leventhal turned to him. 'Anything in particular?'

'The same matter.'

'I got your message. I was going to call back, but I've been tied up.'

'By what?' said Phoebe.

Leventhal considered his answer. He was unwilling to speak of his family; he did not want to appear to be soliciting sympathy, and besides he was incapable of mentioning Mickey's death conversationally. The thought was repugnant to him.

'Oh, things,' he said.

'Labor Day pile-up, eh?' said Williston.

'That and some private things. Mostly work.'

'What are you doing with yourself over the week end?' Phoebe asked him. 'Planning to go somewhere? We're invited to Fire Island.'

'No, I'm not going anywhere.'

'Are you facing three days in town alone? You poor man.'

'I'm not what you might call alone, exactly.' Leventhal glanced at her, speaking quietly. 'I have a friend of yours staying with me.'

'Of ours?' she cried. He saw that he had her off balance. 'You mean Kirby Allbee?'

'Yes, Allbee.'

'I wanted to ask you about that,' said Williston. 'Is he still with you?'

'Still.'

'Tell me, how is he?' Phoebe said. 'I didn't know you came about him, the other night. I wouldn't have stayed in the kitchen.'

'I didn't realize you were so interested.'

'Well, now I'd like to know how he is,' she said. Leventhal wondered how much of his description Williston had repeated.

'Didn't Stan tell you?'

'Yes, but I want to hear more from you.' Her habitual cool, good temper was missing. A faint color appeared below her eyes, and he commented to himself, 'Out in the open, for a change.' He delayed, thinking that Williston might intervene. The waiter put the black and green mussels before him, and he said, taking up the fork as if to weigh it, 'Oh, he's getting around.' He began to eat.

'Is he very broken up about Flora?'

'His wife? Yes, he's broken up.'

'It must have been terrible for him. I never thought they'd separate. They started out so brilliantly.'

'Brilliant?' Leventhal thought. He paused, letting them see that the word had struck him. 'What does she mean? That's only the way women talk about marriage. What could be brilliant? He, Allbee, brilliant?' He made an indifferent movement of concession.

'I attended the wedding, if you want to know why it interests me,' she said.

'Phoebe and Flora were roommates at school.'

'Were they?' said Leventhal, somewhat curious. He poured the beer. 'I met her a few times at your house.'

'Yes, you must have,' Williston said.

Phoebe for a brief moment regained her usual manner. 'At the church I remember they were going to have a singer and they didn't on account of his mother. They didn't want to hurt her feelings. Everybody humored her about her singing. She studied in Boston for years and years. She was about sixty, and she might have had a voice once, but she certainly didn't have one then. She sang anyway. She was bound to, at her son's wedding. They couldn't stop her. Poor Kirby. But the old lady was very nice. She told me she had beautiful legs when she was a girl and was so proud of them, wasn't it a shame she had to wear long skirts? She said she was born too soon.'

'Excuse me for asking,' put in Leventhal, 'but was this marriage supposed to be a good thing from his wife's point of view?'

'What do you mean?'

'Did her family like him?'

'They were suspicious. But I thought he was very promising. Intelligent and charming. So did lots of other people. I always believed he'd outdistance all our friends.'

Williston corroborated her. 'Yes, he's brainy and well read, too. He used to read an awful lot.'

'And suddenly the bottom falls out. I wonder whom you could blame for that.' Phoebe sighed and turned her long, handsome, pensive face with its marked, level brows to her husband first and then to Leventhal.

'Why, she wasn't to blame, was she?' said Leventhal. 'His wife?'

'No . . .' Phoebe appeared to be disconcerted. 'Why should she be? She loved him.'

'Well, if she wasn't to blame, who's left?' asked Leventhal. 'She left him, didn't she?'

'Yes, she did. We never learned why. She didn't take it up with me. We saw it from the outside, mostly. It was hard to understand because he was so charming.'

'Charming!' Leventhal scornfully repeated to himself. '– Brilliant start!' What could this woman actually have seen with those two eyes of hers? What did she allow herself to see? Could anything that started so well, so promisingly, have ended so badly? There must have been a flaw in the beginning, visible to anyone who wanted to see. But Phoebe did not want to see. And as for Allbee, no wonder he stayed away from the Willistons, they had such a high opinion of him.

He said reservedly, 'They say that drinking people usually make a good impression. They're supposed to be likeable.'

'Still drinking, eh?' Williston asked in an undertone.

'Still?' Leventhal shrugged, as if to say, 'What's the use of asking?'

'No, he was just what I say. Ask Stan. Even before he started drinking. But you haven't told me how he's making out and what he's doing.'

'He's doing nothing. And he hasn't told me what he's going to do, either.'

'Well, ask him to come over and see us, will you?' Her face was tremulous with hidden resentment.

'With pleasure.' Leventhal sounded rather sharp. Williston was turning over a spoon in his short fingers. He had spoken very little realizing, perhaps, that Phoebe was in the wrong, and was afraid to make matters worse by interfering. Leventhal hid his annoyance. They wanted to see Allbee – they could have him altogether, as far as he was concerned – but they didn't say they wanted him to stay with them, only to visit. And why, Leventhal wanted to know, didn't it occur to Phoebe to ask why Allbee was with him rather than with his friends? Logically, they were the ones for him to go to. But it struck him, in examining her white face, that there were certain logical questions she didn't want to ask. She did not want the facts; she warded them off. In a general way she understood them well enough, he was sure. She only wanted to insist that Allbee be taken care of. And chances were that she no more wanted to see him in his present condition than he wanted to see her. She probably knew what he was like. Oh, of course she knew. But she wanted him changed back to what he had been. 'My dear lady,' Leventhal protested in thought, 'I don't ask you to look at things my way, but just to look. That would be enough. Have a look!' However, and he always returned to this, the Willistons had been kind to him; he was indebted to them. – Although what Williston had done for him was nothing compared to what he was being told implicitly to do for Allbee.

Williston roused himself, or so it appeared to Leventhal. 'I don't think Kirby wants to see us now, dear,' he said. 'He would have come before.'

'Too bad he hasn't,' said Leventhal. He showed more feeling than he had intended, and Phoebe quickly took him up.

'I don't think I understand that, Asa,' she said.

'You ought to see him. From the way you're talking about him, I don't think you'd recognize him. I know I don't recognize the same man.'

'Well, that may not be my fault.' She stopped with a short release of breath. The red began to come out again under her eyes.

'I suppose he has changed,' said Williston slowly.

'Believe me, he's not what Phoebe says. I'm telling you.' Leventhal tenaciously limited himself to this in order to control his mounting sense of wrong.

'You ought to be more charitable,' Phoebe said.

At this he almost lost his head, staring at her while the color spread to her cheeks. He pushed away his plate, muttering, 'I can't change myself over to suit you.'

'What?' said Williston.

'I said, if I'm not, I'm not!'

'I don't think Phoebe meant what she said, exactly. Phoebe? I think Asa got the wrong impression.'

'I see that you misunderstood me,' she grudgingly said.

'Well, it doesn't make any difference.'

'I didn't mean anything except that Kirby *was* promising, and so on. I wasn't saying anything but that.'

What did she know about him? Leventhal thought bitterly. But he was silent.

'I phoned because I wanted to know if I could help out with a little money,' said Williston. 'I haven't been able to think of a job for him, but he must need things. I guess he can use a few dollars.'

'That's right,' Leventhal said.

'I want to give you ten or so. You don't have to tell him where it comes from. He might not want to accept money from me.'

'I'll give it to him,' said Leventhal. 'It's very nice of you.'

The Willistons left. Leventhal watched them in the blue mirror of the bar above the massed forms of the bottles. Stan waited while Phoebe stopped to give a touch to her hat and they went up the stairs together, passing under the awning.

19

FROM the foyer he saw Mrs Nunez sitting cross-legged on the divan, putting up her freshly washed hair. She held her chin against her breast, and there were pins in her mouth and others strewn on the brown and white squares of her skirt. He rapped, and she drew her hair back from her eyes but did not change her position or cover her unsymmetrically gartered legs.

'I don't want to disturb you,' he said, looking at them. 'I was thinking – the flat's pretty dirty. Could you give me a lead about a cleaning woman? Ours hasn't been around.'

'Clean? I don't know anybody. If it's straighten, I'll do it for you. I don't do the heavy work.'

'Nothing heavy, I just want the place to look a little neater.'

'Sure, I'll straighten it for you.'

'I'll be much obliged. It's getting to be too much for me.'

The look of his front room by lamplight disgusted him. It would have done Phoebe good to see it. He half regretted that he had not invited the Willistons home with him. He set to work gathering up the papers from the floor and spread clean sheets on his bed and laid out a pair of pajamas. In the bathroom he soaked and rinsed the robe and rubbed out the ink-stains with a brush and soap powder. Taking it to the roof he wrung it out and spread it on a line. There was a smell of approaching fall in the breeze. Leventhal walked over the pebbles and tar to the parapet. To the east the lights of the two shores joined in a long seam in midriver. Summer would end soon after the holiday and with the start of fall everything would change; Leventhal felt inexplicably convinced of this. The sky was overcast. He looked out awhile and then returned to the staircase, careful of lines and wires in the dark. He touched the robe in passing. It was drying rapidly in the breeze.

On the landing he heard someone coming and glanced below. It was Allbee. Regularly his hand clasped and released the banister as he made his way up. Catching sight of Leventhal at the last turn, he paused and raised his head and seemed to examine him. The low light crossed his face up to the brows and eyes and gave it an expression, most likely accidental, of naked malice. A stir of uneasiness went over Leventhal. He remembered immediately, however, that there were a few things Allbee had to answer to him for. And, to begin with, was he drunk? But he was already quite sure, he could sense that he was sober.

'Well?' he said.

Reaching the landing, Allbee gave him a restrained nod. His hair had been trimmed. Along the sides of his head and down his cheeks there was a conspicuous margin of shaven whiteness. His face shone. He had on a new shirt and a black tie and he carried a paper bag. When he saw Leventhal inspecting him he said, 'I picked these up on Second Avenue, in a bargain store.'

'I didn't ask you.'

'I owe you an accounting,' he said matter-of-factly. Leventhal listened for a provocative note in his answer; there was none. He looked at him suspiciously.

'I haven't had a drink today,' said Allbee.

'Come in here. There's something I want to find out.'

'What is it?'

'Not here; in the house.'

Allbee held back. 'What's the trouble?' he asked.

Leventhal seized his coat and pulled him forward. Allbee resisted, and he lay hold of him with both hands, and, with a sullen look of determination, his anger rekindled, dragged him into the house and flung the door shut with his foot. He twisted him around. Allbee tried to free himself anew, and Leventhal shouted, 'What the hell do you think I'll stand for!'

'What are you talking about?'

'You'll answer me. You won't duck out of it.'

He tore his coat out of Leventhal's grasp and swung away. 'What's the idea?' he said with a trembling, short laugh, wonderingly. 'Have you decided to beat me up?'

'How much do you think I'll take from you!' Leventhal was panting. 'Do you think you can get away with everything?'

'Don't lose your head, now.' His laugh was gone and he looked at him gravely. 'After all, I expect to be treated fairly. I'm in your house, and you have certain advantages over me . . . Anyway, you ought to tell me what this is all about.'

'This is what it's about.' Leventhal snatched out the cards. 'Going through my desk like a damned crook and blackmailer. That's what it's about.'

'Oh, is *that* it?' He swung his hand loosely toward them.

Leventhal's voice broke as he cried, '*That?* Isn't that anything? You followed me around and snooped, before. I let you in here and you get your dirty hands all over my things, my private business, my letters.'

'Well, now, that's not true. I haven't touched your letters. I'm not interested in your business.'

'Where did I find these!' Leventhal threw the cards down. 'In my bathrobe that you were wearing.'

'That's where I found them. I don't like to defend myself against such accusations. They're not fair. This is the kind of thing that gets people in trouble.'

'Isn't this yours?' Leventhal picked up a clipping from the classified ads.

'Oh, I know what was in that pocket. But some of it was there when I put the robe on. Maybe you object to the fact that I used the robe. I'm sorry, I . . .'

Leventhal refused to be deflected. 'You mean to say that you didn't go through my desk?'

Allbee made a movement of sincere, straightforward denial.

'How about this. Where did you get this?' Leventhal pointed to Shifcart's card.

'I found it on the floor. Now, there I'll admit . . . if I did anything really wrong it was to take that card. It was on the floor near your bed. I had no right to keep it. Perhaps you needed it. I should have asked. But I didn't think of that. I was interested in it. In fact, I was going to bring it up in connection with something I've been thinking about but kept forgetting.'

'You're lying.'

Allbee was silent. He stood looking at him.

'I didn't put the postcards in the bathrobe,' said Leventhal, 'and this card of Shifcart's was in the desk.'

Allbee answered simply, 'If you didn't put them there, then a third party must have. I know I didn't.'

'But you read them!' He said this violently, but he wanted to sink away.

'Yes, I did,' Allbee dropped his eyes as if to spare him.

'Damn you to hell!' Leventhal shouted in anguish and outrage. 'That's not all you read. What else!'

'Nothing.'

'You did!'

'No, that was all. I couldn't avoid looking them over. It wasn't intentional. But I took them out of the pocket and so I had to see what they were. It's mostly your wife's fault. She should have put them in an envelope – things like that. I never would have pulled a letter out of an envelope. But I read this before I realized what it was. It's not so serious, is it? What's so special about your cards? Any wife might write like that to a husband, or a husband to a wife. And an old married man like me . . . it's not the same as if a young person, say a young girl, got hold of them. And even then, I wonder if anybody is innocent. And last of all, I don't think it would matter

198

to your wife. This is not the kind of thing for postcards. If she cared, she'd have written it in a letter.'

'I still think you're lying.'

'Well, if you do, I can't change your mind. But I'm not. Why not keep your desk locked, as long as you don't trust me?'

'It is now.'

'You should have locked it sooner. Nobody likes to be jumped on like this. Keep it locked. You have a right to lose your temper when there's definite proof that somebody is monkeying with your private things. It's not very nice. But neither are such accusations. Suppose I did look in your desk, and I absolutely deny it, why should I want to carry the cards around?'

'Why should you? Search me!'

'Like a mental case? Not me, you've got the wrong party.'

Leventhal did not know what more to say. Perhaps he was wrong. Except when Allbee spoke of young girls he made sense and even that, fully explained, might not be irrelevant. Besides, the haircut, the shirt and tie, and the fact that he was sober made a difference. It was the haircut mainly; it gave him a new aspect. His face appeared more solid. Leventhal all at once felt nothing very strongly; he only had a certain curiosity about Allbee. He sat down beside the desk. Allbee sank into the easy chair and stretched his legs out.

After a few minutes of silence he said, 'Did you see this morning's paper?'

'Why, what's in the paper?'

'There was an item in it I thought you might have picked up. It's about Rudiger. Really about Rudiger's son, but he was mentioned too. The son's in the army and he was promoted, yesterday. To the rank of major.'

'What about it?'

'I just happened to notice. I was in the barber shop looking at the paper and saw the boy's picture. He worked in the office for a while. He's a very ordinary boy. Nice . . . I can't criticize him. Just a college boy; very ordinary, no special spark. It's no business of mine; that is, it can't do me any good or harm. But I'm always interested in the way things work themselves out. Now somebody without influence spends twenty years in the service, first in this hole of a garrison and then in that one, lives with native girls because he can't afford to marry. Maybe he gets a little rank in the end, becomes a second lieutenant. You can't tell me it isn't a matter of influence.'

'It probably is,' said Leventhal idly.

'Yes. Not that I have anything against him because he happens to be his father's son. Why shouldn't he take advantage of the old man's position? And what else can the old man do for him?' He suddenly changed the subject with a quick laugh. 'Notice my haircut?'

'I see.'

'I didn't drink, either. That's not what you expected, is it?'

'Go ahead, surprise me.'

'No, you thought I'd get looped again.'

'Maybe.'

'I told you I wasn't that far gone.'

'I'm glad to see it.'

'Are you?' There was a break of excitement in his hilarity.

'Sure,' said Leventhal. He felt a responsive laugh forming in his chest and he held it down. 'What do you want, a basket of roses?'

'Why not?'

'A medal?' Leventhal began to smile.

'Yes, a medal.' He coughed thickly. 'I ought to have one.'

'You ought to get one.'

'Well, I wasn't even tempted, to be honest about it. I didn't have to fight a yen; not a bit of trouble.'

Allbee bent forward and laid his hand on the arm of Leventhal's chair, and for a short space the two men looked at each other and Leventhal felt himself singularly drawn with a kind of affection. It oppressed him, it was repellent. He did not know what to make of it. Still he welcomed it, too. He was remotely disturbed to see himself so changeable. However, it did not seem just then to be a serious fault.

'I had clippers on the sides.' Allbee brought the tips of his fingers to his head. 'I got into the habit. It's cleaner that way, I've learned. Because of nits. You wouldn't know anything about that, would you?'

Leventhal shrugged.

'Oh, if you got them in your hair, hair like that . . . Your hair amazes me. Whenever I see you, I have to study it. With some people you sometimes doubt if it's real and you want to see if your man is wearing a wig. But your hair; I've often tried to imagine how it would be to have hair like that. Is it hard to comb?'

'What do you mean, is it hard?'

'I mean, does it tangle. It must break the teeth out of combs. Say, let me touch it once, will you?'

'Don't be a fool. It's hair. What's hair?' he said.

'No, it's not ordinary hair.'

'Ah, get out,' Leventhal said, drawing back.

Allbee stood up. 'Just to satisfy my curiosity,' he said, smiling. He fingered Leventhal's hair, and Leventhal found himself caught under his touch and felt incapable of doing anything. But then he pushed his hand away, crying, 'Lay off!'

'It's astonishing. It's like an animal's hair. You must have a terrific constitution.'

Leventhal jerked his chair away, wrinkling his forehead in confusion and incipient anger. Then he bawled, 'Sit down, you lunatic!' and Allbee went back to his place. He sat forward, ungainly, his hands under his thighs, his jaw slipped to one side, exactly as on the night when he had first confronted Leventhal in the park. The white of his trimmed temples and his shaven face made the blue of his eyes conspicuous.

No further word was spoken for a while. Leventhal was

trying to settle his feelings and to determine how to recover the ground he had lost through this last piece of insanity.

'It's hard to have the right mixture of everything,' Allbee suddenly began.

'What are you driving at now?' said Leventhal.

'Oh, this about your calling me a lunatic when I give in to an impulse. Nobody can be sure he has the right mixture. Just to give you an example. Lately, a couple of weeks ago, there was a man in the subway, on the tracks. I don't understand how he got there. But he was on the tracks and a train came along and pinned him against the wall. He was bleeding to death. A policeman came down and right away forbid anyone to touch this man until the ambulance arrived. That was because he had instructions about accidents. Now that's too much of one thing – playing it safe. The impulse is to save the man, but the policy is to stick to rules. The ambulance came and the man was dragged out and died right away. I'm not a doctor and I can't say whether he had a chance at any time. But suppose he could have been saved? That's what I mean by the mixture.'

'Was he yelling for help? What line was that?' Leventhal said with a frown of pain.

'East-side line. Well, of course, when a man is spread-eagled like that. He was filling the tunnel with his noise. And the crowd! The trains were held up and the station was jammed. They kept coming down. People should have pushed the cop out of the way and taken the fellow down. But everybody stood and listened to him. Those are the real trimmers.'

'Trimmers?'

'They're not for God and they're not for the Old Scratch. They think they're for themselves but they're not that either.'

'What does he tell me this for?' thought Leventhal. 'Does he want to work on my feelings? Maybe he doesn't know why himself.'

Allbee began to smile. 'You should have seen how surprised

you looked when I showed up dead sober. You're going to be even more surprised, you know.'

'By what?'

'You were joking with me this morning about a new start. You wouldn't take me seriously.'

'Do you believe it yourself?'

'Don't you worry,' he said confidently. 'I know what really goes on inside me. I'll let you in on something. There isn't a man living who doesn't. All this business, "Know thyself"! Everybody knows but nobody wants to admit. That's the thing. Some swimmers can hold their breath a long time – those Greek sponge divers – and that's interesting. But the way we keep our eyes shut is a stunt too, because they're made to be open.'

'So. You're off again. You can do it without whisky. I thought it was the whisky.'

'All right,' cried Allbee. 'Now let me explain something to you. It's a Christian idea but I don't see why you shouldn't be able to understand it. "Repent!" That's John the Baptist coming out of the desert. Change yourself, that's what he's saying, and be another man. You must be and the reason for that is that you can be, and when your time comes here you will be. There's another thing behind that "repent"; it's that we know what to repent. How?' His unsmiling face compelled Leventhal's attention. '*I* know. Everybody knows. But you've got to take away the fear of admitting by a still greater fear. I understand that doctors are beginning to give their patients electric shocks. They tear all hell out of them, and then they won't trifle. You see, you have to get yourself so that you can't stand to keep on in the old way. When you reach that stage –' he knotted his hands and the sinews rose up on his wrists. 'It takes a long time before you're ready to quit dodging. Meanwhile, the pain is horrible.' He blinked blindly several times as if to clear his eyes of an obstruction. 'We're mulish; that's why we have to take such a beating. When we can't stand another lick without dying of it, then

203

we change. And some people never do. They stand there until the last lick falls and die like animals. Others have the strength to change long before. But repent means *now*, this minute and forever, without wasting any more time.'

'And this minute has arrived for you already?'

'Yes.'

'I don't know whom you're stringing, me or yourself.'

'Every word is sincere – sin-cere!' said Allbee inclining his head and gazing at him. He hesitated, his large lips remained parted, the upper, with its long groove, moving a little.

'Go on!' Leventhal abruptly laughed.

'Well, I thought I would *try* to explain it to you.' He turned slightly in his chair, resting one shoulder on the cushion, and slowly rubbed the side of his extended leg. 'I'm not religious or anything like that, but I know that I don't have to be next year what I was last year. I've been at one end and I can get to the other. There's no limit to what I can be. And even if I should miss being so dazzling, I know the idea of it is genuine.'

'We'll see what you are next year.'

'You'll be the same, I know. You people . . .' He shook his head and his cheek brushed his collar.

'If you start that again, you'll be on the steps in a minute.' Leventhal began menacingly to rise.

'All right, all right, let's drop it. Only when a man says something serious about himself he likes to be believed,' said Allbee. 'It makes sense to me that a man can be born again. – I'll take a rain check on the kingdom of heaven, but if I'm tired of being this way I can become a new man. That's all I'm saying.' Straightening himself in his chair he was silent and lightly held his big hands together. By the curve of his mouth Leventhal saw that he was very pleased with himself. Indeed the position of his hands spoke of applause rather than rest. The hump of shadow behind him was occasionally extended by the slight stirring of his head. The lamp in its green, watered-silk shade made a second, softer center of brightness in the polish of the desk. A rush of low sounds came up from the street, and a gust of air swelled and separated the curtains; they drifted together again.

At this moment Leventhal felt Allbee's presence, all that concerned him, like a great tiring weight, and looked at him with dead fatigue, his fingers motionless on his thighs. Something would have to happen, something that he could not foresee. Whatever it was, he would be too muddled and fatigued to deal with it. He was played out. His old weakness, his nerves, had never been so bad; he could not concentrate long enough to settle any of his difficulties, and had to wait for the occasion to bring this or that to his attention, and was slow and fitful in his thinking. He ought to have thought of what was going on in Staten Island, if only for Philip's sake, and he should have phoned Max at least once. Max had hung on to him in the chapel; he had no one else to hang on to. And by now he must have decided that he had no one at all. But the reason Leventhal shrank from calling was that he was unable to clarify his thoughts or bring them into focus, and he lacked the energy to continue the effort. And anyway the sparks, the clear spark of Mickey's life, the spark of Elena's sanity, the sparks of thought and courage, even courage as confident as Mary's – how such sparks were chased and overtaken, drowned, put out. Then what good was thinking? His dark, poring face with its full cheeks and high-rising dull hair was hung toward his chest. He drew a deep, irregular breath and raised his hands from his lap in a gesture of exorcism against the spell of confusion and despair. 'God will help me out,' passed through his mind, and he did not stop to ask himself exactly what he meant by this.

'About the card I picked up,' said Allbee. 'The business card: is that man a moving-picture agent of some kind? I want to explain why I picked it up. I suppose you know him.'

'A little.'

'What does he do? What's his line?'

'I think he looks for talent.'

'Is he influential? I mean, is he . . .' But Allbee canceled this question as if it were a mark of his persistent innocence or unworldliness.

'Is he what?'

'Oh . . . on the inside.' His lip began to curl; his eyes were distended and humorlessly direct. 'I've come to the conclusion that if you want to get along nowadays you have to go along with the powers. It's no use trying to buck them.'

'Who told you Shifcart was a power?'

Allbee declined to answer. He lifted his shoulders and looked away disdainfully.

'Who?' Leventhal repeated.

'Let's say he can help me, then, and leave out other considerations.'

'Do you want to become an actor?'

'Wouldn't I make a good one?'

'You?'

'Is that so funny?'

A faint smile crossed Leventhal's shadowed face. 'I understand your mother thought she was a singer,' he said. 'And you think you are an actor.'

'Oh, you've heard about my mother. Who told you about her, Phoebe?'

'Yes. She sang at your wedding, didn't she?'

'Sensationally,' said Allbee in an indeterminate tone; and, after a pause, 'No, of course I don't want to act. But I thought with all my experience on magazines that I might be able to get into movie work. I once heard about somebody – an acquaintance of an acquaintance – who was doing some preliminary scenario job, looking up stories, and making digests of them, and if I could get into that . . . Well, maybe your friend can tell me how to do it.'

'He's no special friend of mine. How long ago did you hear about this?'

'I don't remember, now. A few years ago.'

'Then how do you know you can still get such a job? Why

don't you find out from this acquaintance of yours? What have you got to go on? Ask him about it.'

Allbee answered quickly, 'I couldn't. I wouldn't know where to find him or how to start looking. Besides, he doesn't owe me anything, Leventhal. Why should I go to him?'

'Why? Well, why to me? It makes just as much sense.'

His reply tremendously aroused Allbee.

'Why? For good reasons; the best in the world!' He shocked Leventhal by clenching his fists before his breast as if passionately threatening to tear loose from all restraint. 'I'm giving you a chance to be fair, Leventhal, and to do what's right. And I want what's right from you. Don't drag anybody else in. This is just between the two of us.'

'Don't be crazy.'

'Just you and I. Just the two of us.'

'I never . . . I never. . . .' Leventhal stammered.

'I can't afford to fool around. The fooling has been kicked out of me. I've been put straight the hard way, the way you pay for with years of your life.' He lowered his head and stared at him before continuing. There was a noticeable pulsation in the sides of his face beside his eyes, and in his eyes there was a glint that astounded Leventhal; it resembled nothing in his experience. 'Look,' said Allbee firmly in a lower voice. 'You know that when I say I want an introduction to this man Shifcart it means I am ready to play ball. I'm offering a settlement. I'm offering to haul down my flag. If he helps me. Do you understand?'

'No, I don't understand,' Leventhal said. 'I don't even begin to get it. And as long as you keep on talking about settling, I won't lift a finger for you.'

'Listen,' said Allbee. 'I know you want to settle. And so do I. And I know what I'm talking about when I say I'll play ball. The world's changed hands. I'm like the Indian who sees a train running over the prairie where the buffalo used to roam. Well, now that the buffalo have disappeared, I want to get off the pony and be a conductor on that train. I'm not

207

asking to be a stockholder in the company. I know that's impossible. Lots of things are impossible that didn't use to be. When I was younger I had my whole life laid out in my mind. I planned what it was going to be like on the assumption that I came out of the lords of the earth. I had all kinds of expectations. But God disposes. There's no use kidding.'

Leventhal, his eyes raised to the ceiling, seemed to ask, 'You follow? I don't.'

There was a knock at the door.

20

IT was Max. He stood before Leventhal with a rolled news-paper under his arm, his shirt open at the throat, the black hair of his chest coming out, and his soft collar pulled over the collar of his coat, the same way Philip's had been on the day of the outing. The suit was the double-breasted one he had worn at the funeral. When the door opened, he seemed to hesitate on the landing, and Leventhal cried out in a cracked voice, 'Max! Come in, for heaven's sake.'

'You folks in?' Max asked huskily, still hesitant.

It struck Leventhal that his brother was behaving as if he were about to enter a stranger's house. He had never been here before.

'Well, I am, that's sure. I didn't get a chance to tell you the other day. Mary's out of town. But come on in.' And he led him over the threshold and turned to the front room, filled with anxiety at his new difficulty. He did not know what to expect from Allbee, what he would say when he learned who Max was. He was already leaning forward inquisitively. Leventhal stood arrested for an instant, incapable of speaking or moving forward. Glancing into the room and seeing Allbee, Max said, apologetically, 'Say, you're busy. I'll come back later.'

'I'm not,' Leventhal whispered. 'Come on.'

'I should have called up first.'

But Leventhal held him by the arm and forced him in.

'This is my brother Max. This is Kirby Allbee.'

'Your brother? I didn't know you had one.'

'Only one.'

Reticent and somber, Max looked down, perhaps partly to acknowledge his share in their estrangement.

'I don't know what made me think you were an only child, like me.' Allbee was conversational and bright, and Leventhal wondered what he was preparing and hid his dread in impassivity. He brought up a chair and Max sat down. The points of his dusty shoes were turned inward. The side of his lowered face and his large neck formed one surface, from the curve of his nose to the padded thickness of his shoulder.

'I often used to wish there were two of us,' said Allbee.

'How are things at home, Max?' asked Leventhal.

'Oh,' Max said. 'You know . . .' Leventhal expected him to finish the sentence, but it tailed off.

Allbee seemed to be commenting to himself smilingly on something in the appearance of the two brothers. Leventhal covertly indicated the door with his head. Allbee's brows curved up questioningly. His whole air said, 'Why should I?' Leventhal bent close to him and muttered, 'I want to talk to my brother.'

'What's the matter?' Allbee spoke out loudly.

Sternly Leventhal made the same sign with his head.

But Max had heard. 'Did you ask me what was the matter?' he said.

Allbee looked at Leventhal and shrugged, to confess his slip. He did not reply.

'I guess it must show on me,' said Max.

'We had a death in the family recently,' Leventhal said. 'My youngest son.'

An expression went over Allbee's face that Leventhal could not interpret, a cold wrinkling. 'Oh, sorry to hear it. When?'

'Four days ago.'

'You didn't mention it to me,' Allbee said to Leventhal.

'No,' Leventhal answered flatly, gazing at his brother.

Allbee came forward swiftly in his chair. 'Say, was that the boy . . . the other day?'

'No, not the one that was with me. He means Phil,' Leventhal explained to Max. 'I took him to the movies awhile back, and we ran into Mr Allbee.'

'Oh, Phil. Knock wood. That's my other son you saw.'

'Oh, I see, two children . . .'

'Are you going?' Leventhal said to him, aside.

'Will you fix it up for me with Shifcart?'

Leventhal fastened his hand on his arm. 'Will you go?'

'You said you'd help me.'

'We'll take it up later.' Leventhal was growing savage with impatience. 'Don't think you can hold me up.'

'I don't want to interfere with business,' said Max.

'What business! There's no business.'

Allbee rose and Leventhal went into the hall with him.

'I'll be back for your answer,' Allbee said. He looked into Leventhal's face as though he saw something new there. 'I'm really surprised. Here this happens to you – your nephew. I'm in the same house and you don't even say a word about it.'

'What do I want to talk to you about it for?' Before Allbee could speak again, he had shut the door.

'Who is he?' said Max, when Leventhal came back. 'A friend?'

'No, just a guy who keeps coming around.'

'He's peculiar looking . . .' Max checked himself and then said, 'I hope I didn't butt in on anything.'

'Oh, hell no. I was going to call you up, Max. But I thought I'd better wait awhile.'

'I was kind of expecting you to, since you took an interest and came to the funeral, and all.'

Max addressed him diffidently, a little formally, feeling his way with a queer politeness, almost the politeness of a stranger. Subdued, worn, and plainly, to Leventhal's eyes, tormented, he was making an effort, nevertheless, to find an appropriate tone, one not too familiar. The blood crowded to Leventhal's heart guiltily. He wanted to say something to Max about it. He did not know how and he was afraid of creating a still greater difficulty. How should they talk when they had never, since childhood, spent an hour together? And he surmised also that the flat, the contrast between his upholstered chairs and good rugs and the borax furniture in Staten Island, shabby before half the installments were paid, made Max deferential.

'So how are things going?' he said. He thought Max would speak about Elena. He was in fact certain that the main object of his visit was to discuss her with him.

'I guess as good as I can expect.'

'Phil all right?'

'Well, when one kid passes on it's pretty hard on the other one.'

'He'll come around.'

Max said nothing to this, and Leventhal began to think he was debating whether to mention Elena at all, undecided at the last moment, and struggling with himself.

'Yes, kids come around,' Leventhal repeated.

'I wanted to ask you,' said Max. 'I want to straighten it up with you about the specialist. He says you gave him ten dollars the first visit.' His hand dropped inside his coat.

'Oh, no.'

But Max opened his wallet and, half rising, laid a ten dollar bill beside the lamp on the desk.

'That's not necessary.'

'I want to pay you back. Thanks.'

'Now he takes over,' was Leventhal's unspoken comment. His original vexation with Max revived and he said, a shade coldly, 'You're welcome.'

'Not just for the money,' said Max. 'The rest, too.'

Leventhal's temper got the better of him.

'For doing a small part of what you should have been here to do.'

Max reflected, raising his rough-skinned, large-jawed face with its high-ridged, freckled nose. 'Yes,' he said. 'I should have been here.' He was submissive, seeming to find nothing in himself with which to resist.

212

Leventhal could not hold back his next question.

'What does Elena say?'

'About what?'

'About me?'

Max appeared surprised.

'What should she say? All she said was that she wondered why you didn't come to the house after the funeral. But she doesn't say much. She's in bed most of the time, crying.'

Leventhal had edged forward. The lamplight shone into his hair and over his shoulders.

'Does she give you a lot of trouble, Max?'

'Trouble? You've got to consider. It's a rough deal. She cries. That's pretty natural.'

'You might as well be open with me.'

Max's surprise grew.

'What's there not to be open about?'

'If you don't know, I don't either. But you've got a chance to talk it out, if you want to. I realize we're not so close. But do you have anyone else to talk to? Maybe you have friends. I didn't notice many at the funeral.'

Max said uncertainly, 'I don't catch your drift, exactly.'

'I asked if Elena gives you trouble.'

The blood rose darkly in Max's face under the full mask of his ill-shaven beard. There was a show of fear and bewilderment in his eyes and, reluctantly, he began a motion of denial with his black-nailed hands; he did not finish; he gave it up.

'She's calming down.'

'What does she say?'

'All kinds of things,' Max said with obvious difficulty, still shunning a direct answer.

But Leventhal did not need a direct answer. He could picture Elena in the brass bed where Mickey had lain, in that terrible room, crying and raging; and Max sitting just as he saw him sitting now, abjectly listening. For what could he do? And Philip had to listen, too. The thought struck into him.

But how could the boy be protected? He would have to hear and learn. Leventhal believed what he had said to Max about children coming through. They were mauled in birth and they straightened as they grew because their bones were soft. Mauled again later, they could recover again. She was his mother, so let him see and hear. Was that a cruel view of it? He was full of love for the boy. But it did not do to be soft. Be soft when things were harsh? Not that softness was to be condemned, but there were times when it was only another name for weakness. Softness? Out of the whole creation only man was like that, and he was half harsh.

'Have you had a doctor for her?' he asked.

'What makes you think she needs one?'

'Remember Mamma!'

Max started. 'What are you talking about?' he said with a sudden flash of indignation.

'I don't blame you for not wanting it brought up.'

'Why do you bring Ma into this? Does she remind you of Ma?'

Leventhal hesitated. 'Once in a while, she does . . . But you admit you have trouble with her.'

'What do you expect? She carries on. Sure she carries on. It's a kid, after all. That hits. But she'll be all right. She's getting better already.'

'Max, I don't think you understand. People go overboard easily. I guess they're not as strong that way as they used to be and when things get rough they give in. There's more and more of that all the time. Everybody feels it. I do myself, often. Elena was very queer about the kid and the hospital. – That's what she yells about, isn't it? The hospital?' He grew increasingly unsure of himself. 'And I thought . . .'

'I remember Ma pretty often, too, and Hartford, and all. You're not the only one.'

'No?' Leventhal said. He looked at him searchingly.

'And you're wrong about Elena.'

'You don't think I want to be right, do you?'

'The main trouble I'm having with her is that I want to move the family down south. I was looking for a place in Galveston. That was what took so long. I found one and I have a deposit on it. I was going to bring them all down there.'

'That's good. The best thing you could do. Take Philip out of New York. It's no place to bring him up.'

'But I can't talk Elena into it.'

'Why?'

'Maybe I started in too soon after the funeral. But she says she doesn't want to go.'

'Tell me, is the old woman around much – her mother?'

'Oh, she's in and out all the time.'

'For God's sake, throw her out!'

His vehemence astonished Max.

'She doesn't have anything to do with it.'

'Don't let her get a hold. Protect yourself against her.'

Max for the first time began to smile.

'She won't hurt me.'

'I'll bet she's telling Elena not to go. How do you know what she tells her? You don't understand what they're saying.'

Max's look changed; he became grave again and his mouth sank at the corners. 'I understand a little,' he said. 'I guess you think I should have married a Jewish girl.'

'You never heard me say so,' Leventhal answered vigorously. Never.'

'No.'

'You never will. I'm talking about her mother, not Elena. You told me yourself that the old woman hated you, years ago. She'll do you all the harm she can. Maybe you're used to the old devil and don't notice what she's like any more. But I've watched her. It's as clear as day to me that she thinks the baby's death was God's punishment because Elena married you.'

Max started and then his lips stiffened, and there was a

submerged flaming of indignation beneath his natural darkness and the added darkness of care. 'What kind of talk is that!' he said. 'I never heard anything so peculiar in all my life. First you've got ideas about Elena and now the old woman.'

'You've been away,' said Leventhal. 'You don't know how she's been acting. She's poison.'

'Well, you've sure turned into a suspicious character.' Max's face began to soften and he sighed.

'She's full of hate,' Leventhal insisted.

'Go on, she's a harmless old woman.'

If he were wrong about Elena, thought Leventhal, if he had overshot the mark and misinterpreted that last look of hers in the chapel, the mistake was a terrible and damaging one; the confusion in himself out of which it had risen was even more terrible. Eventually he had to have a reckoning with himself, when he was calmer and stronger. It was impossible now. But he was right about the old woman, he was sure. 'You must get rid of your mother-in-law, Max!' he said with savage earnestness.

'Ah, what are you talking about?' he said rather wearily. 'She's just an old widow, old and cranky. Elena is her only daughter. I can't tell her to stay away. This week she helped, she kept house and cooked for us. I know she doesn't like me. So what? A worn-out old woman. I feel sad, sometimes, when I look at her. No, we'll go to Galveston. Phil will start school there in the fall. He wants to go, and so does Elena. I can talk her into it. She wants to leave New York, only she's still mixed up. But she'll come. I've got to get back to my job, and we don't want to be separated again. I don't see why you're so disturbed about the old woman. If she's the worst I'm ever up against . . .' The large fold of his jacket reached kiltwise almost to his knees on which his hands were set. His unshapely fingers thickened where they should taper and the creases at the joints resembled the threads of flattened screws. 'You don't know Elena when there's a tight spot,' he resumed.

'She's excitable all in pieces before something happens, but usually when it happens she's stronger than I am. During the depression when I was laid up, she went out and peddled stuff from door to door.'

'I never heard that you were laid up.'

'Well, I was. And then when we were on relief, she has a brother who's a hood and he wanted to take me into a kind of racket he had out in Astoria. I could've seen a little money, but she said no and went all the way out against it, so it was "No" and we stayed on relief. Another woman would have said, "Go ahead."'

'I see.'

'Afterwards things started to pick up and we thought we could add on to the family. Mickey wasn't ever a healthy kid like Phil. And then we must have made mistakes, too. But what can you do? It's not like with God, you know, in the Bible, where he blows his breath into Adam, or whoever. I think I told you that I asked a nurse what room he was in, when I got to the hospital. I went in there and he was lying covered up already. I pulled the sheet off and had a look at him.'

'Those fools!' Leventhal exclaimed. 'Not to have somebody posted there.'

Max excused them with a downward wave of the hand. 'All the nurses didn't know. It's a big place.' He added, consecutively, 'I'm going south with the idea of a new start. I paid a deposit and so on. But to tell the truth, I don't expect much. I feel half burned out already.'

Leventhal felt his heart shaken. 'Half burned?' he said. 'I'm older than you and I don't say that.'

Max did not reply. His large trunk was ungainly in the double-breasted jacket.

'There have been times when I felt like that, too,' Leventhal went on. 'That's a feeling that comes and goes.' His brother turned his crude, dark face up to him and his voice died.

They sat together in silence and at last Max stirred and got up. Leventhal went with him to the subway. A heavy mist lay over the street. At the turnstile he dropped two nickels into the slot and Max said over his shoulder, 'You don't have to wait with me.'

But Leventhal pushed through. They stood at the edge of the platform till the grind of the approaching train reached them.

'If you need me for anything . . .' Leventhal said.

'Thanks.'

'I mean it.'

'Thank you.' He extended his hand. Leventhal clumsily spread his arms wide and clasped him. They felt the concussion of the train, and the streaked face of the lead car with its beam shot toward them in a smolder of dust; the windows ran by. Max returned his embrace. 'Call me,' Leventhal said hoarsely in Max's ear. The crowd swirled around them at the doors. When the train started, he saw Max gripping a strap and bending over the heads of passengers, peering out.

Pulling out a handkerchief, Leventhal wiped his sweat. He began to labor up the long, steel-striped concrete flights, opening his mouth to assist his breathing. Halfway up he stopped, squeezing against the wall to let others past, looking as if the lack of air maddened him. He felt faint with the expansion of his heart.

Then he continued. The mist had gathered to a light rain. At the top of the stairs he saw an umbrella flung open, like a bat in the chill current of air. The bars of the revolving door raced and clinked. Buttoning his coat, he raised the collar, and his eyes moved from the glare of the cars flowing up in the street to the towering lights that stood far ahead, not quite steady in the immense blackness.

21

In the Saturday mail there was an invitation from Mrs
Harkavy to a party that same evening in honor of her granddaughter's seventh birthday. The postman whom Leventhal
encountered in the fog on the outer stairs handed it to him.
There was nothing from Mary and he was secretly glad of it,
for the truth was that he felt he was stealing away and leaving
Allbee in possession of the house. Ostensibly he was going out
for coffee. He had risen to find the flat cold, and the windows
dripping and gray as tin. Allbee was still asleep in the dining-
room, his naked arms locked around the narrow mattress,
sprawling, uncouth. His clothes lay on the floor and the air
was stifling. Leventhal had gone into the kitchen and put on
the coffee but, when he pictured himself sitting down in the
cheerless front room to drink it, he made a face, shut off the
gas, and went down to eat at the Greek's. But he had no
intention of coming back after breakfast.

Around Mrs Harkavy's invitation he half unconsciously
and in a complicatedly indirect fashion made out a schedule.
He was at first uncertain about attending the party. Should
he go so soon after Mickey's death? But, having decided that
it would be a good thing for him to be among people, he rode
uptown to buy the girl a present. And finding himself near the
library at noon, he spent a few hours glancing over some of
the trade papers to see what others were doing. So it was
nearly evening and he was coming out of a newsreel theater
in Times Square before he realized that behind everything he
had contrived to fill this weary day was his unwillingness and
inability to deal with Allbee. He had set off purposefully down

Broadway, and now something seemed to hinder the steady action of his legs and he faltered and began to go slower.

'All right, I'll send him to Shifcart,' Leventhal decided. 'What do I care? I'll do it, and if that isn't enough for him, we'll see. Only what will Shifcart think?' But he was already in disfavor with Shifcart, who had looked at him peevishly in the cafeteria when he failed to laugh at his joke. 'It would be better to come in cold than with a recommendation from me. But as long as he believes so much in connections let him go and find out for himself.'

He stopped at home before dinner to put on a clean shirt. Allbee was out. The dirt and disorder of the place sickened Leventhal. There was rubbish on the kitchen floor and the remains of a meal on the table. 'He'd behave better in a flophouse. He's just trying to show me,' thought Leventhal. He swept out the kitchen. Bending down with the dust pan, he experienced a curious tightness in the skin of his face. He threw the broom into the corner, washed his hands, and left.

Mrs Harkavy met him in the entry and she disconcerted him by saying, 'I was awfully upset to hear about your nephew.' For he had just then, in the elevator, been thinking about Mickey. 'Doctor Denisart told me about it. I'm sure he did his best.'

Leventhal muttered that he thought so too. Because he was disturbed, he was more conscious than usual of the bracing process he went through on meeting one of the Harkavys. He was fond of them, they were kind, but he had never been able to work out a satisfactory balance with them. Mrs Harkavy's expression was like her son's, lively and erratic. Yet there was a durable, underlying melancholy in her animation, and occasionally it came uppermost and took him by surprise.

'Someday science will conquer death,' she said. 'Last Sunday there was a symposium in the *Times* about it.'

Leventhal pulled himself together sufficiently to reply, 'I hope . . .'

'Oh, it looks definite. Then the size of the population will have to be controlled. But science will figure that out, too. There are brains enough for everything. This man discovered something to make the tissues live forever. I don't think we can expect much in our lifetime. It's for future generations. Meanwhile, we have to make the best of it. I think Mr Banting's father died of diabetes about a year before insulin was discovered. And this Mr Bogomolets couldn't use his own serum on account of a bad heart, and he died. Asa, how old was the child?'

'Three and a half, four . . .'

The freakishness seemed to leave her. Only her eyes moved, meeting his own with a familiar, instantaneous significance.

'That's the brother who lives in Queens?'

'Staten Island.'

'Asa, sometimes I feel wicked still to be here at my age while children die.'

He was at a loss for an answer.

'But I'm not taking it away from anybody,' she said, falling back into her eccentricity; it quivered at the corners of her green-ringed eyes.

'Mamma,' Julia called.

'The men are in the dining-room, Asa. There's wine and liquor on the sideboard.' Her face was flushed and she turned away, wide-hipped in her blue dress with its ornamented shoulders.

The guests, none of whom he knew, were playing pinochle. He was disappointed. He had hoped to see Schlossberg or Shifcart.

'Take a hand,' said Harkavy.

'No, I don't think I will. Is anybody else coming, Dan?'

'We're expecting a few more people,' said Harkavy. He was engrossed in his cards.

Leventhal poured himself a glass of wine and took a diamond-shaped biscuit sprinkled with sugar. Suddenly he remembered the present he had brought and he drank down the wine, tugged the package out of his pocket, and went into the kitchen. There was a cloud over the range. Julia was raising a colander of fried potatoes from the oil, averting her face from the sputter and crying nervously, 'Mother, Mother, keep Libbie back.'

'Stay away, honey. Julia, don't rush those potatoes. They'll be raw.'

Leventhal came forward with his package.

'I brought something for the girl.'

'Oh, how thoughtful of you,' said Mrs Harkavy. 'With all your own troubles.'

Leventhal was impassive.

'Here,' he said. 'Happy birthday.'

There was a gold seal pasted on the tissue paper and Libbie, after one quick glance at him, began picking it off.

'Not even "thank you, Uncle Leventhal."' Julia looked furious.

'Julia, it's only shyness, nervousness.'

'Say thanks, you little animal.'

The girl ran into the hall and Leventhal returned to the dining-room. He had a second glass of the sweet wine, and a third.

'Come, sit in,' Goldstone said to him.

He shook his head and slouched against the sideboard, leaning on his elbow and sipping. This was his fourth glass and he was beginning to feel a heavy, solvent, milky warmth. He was conscious of being extremely clear-eyed, of seeing everything, catching every movement as if under extraordinary illumination. As the cards slapped and flicked over the red leather pad, he diverted himself by observing the hands, shuffling, dealing, manipulating the money, the variety of knuckles and fingers. Harkavy's were white, pointed, and simple looking. The hands of the man next to him were strung with veins and overgrown with hair, his thumb was turned back and blackened, perhaps by lead – he might be a printer. The flesh of his palm was red and brutally cross-hatched.

'Used hard,' reflected Leventhal. Yet these hands were limber with coins, and counted and tossed them with the ease of deep familiarity.

Leaving the sideboard he strolled into the dark living-room and lit a cigar. He felt the blood at his heart and brain to be a very rich and powerful mixture, for the most part pleasurable. A little painful also. The slight distress, however, was part of the pleasure. He took a sip of wine, licked the base of the glass and wiped it on his wrist to prevent a ring, and set it on a little table. Mrs Harkavy's voice came down the hall. 'Future generations!' he grinned. 'My Lord!' He sat down, lame and heavy limbed.

After some time he saw Harkavy come in to the room apparently looking for him. He spoke up from his corner.

'Hey, here!'

'Oh, hiding out, having a quiet cigar. The house is filling up. Mamma and Julia are starting to serve.' Leventhal heard the scrape of chairs on the parquet floor of the dining-room.

'Say, do you expect Shifcart tonight?'

'I don't think he was asked. What do you want him for?'

'Do you think I made a bad impression on him that day?'

'I know you did on me. I've never seen such an exhibition of ghetto psychology. The attitude you took toward Disraeli amazed me.'

'No, I don't mean that. Did he say anything to you?'

'Nothing. Is this an attack of your old weakness – worrying whether people like you?'

'I wanted to sound him out about something ... To see what he'd say. If he'd help me out with someone.'

'Who's the favor for?'

'It doesn't matter who, does it?' Leventhal said.

'No, it doesn't. You don't have to tell me.' There was already a ring of exasperation in his voice.

'It doesn't make any difference who.'

'I asked to be helpful. But I won't play button-button with

223

you. Especially since you have an edge on. I saw you drinking.'

'Ah, you could have had a lot of opportunities to be helpful,' said Leventhal.

'Why, it must be that what's-his-name that's been bothering you,' said Harkavy with a sudden nicker of amused discovery. 'That's who, isn't it?'

Leventhal dumbly nodded.

'Then what's the mystery?'

'No mystery,' Leventhal muttered.

'Why do you need help with him? What does he want?
I don't understand how Shifcart comes into the picture.'

'Well, Dan, this Allbee is interested in scenario work and
since he once got me an introduction at Dill's he wants me to
do the same for him with Shifcart, seeing he's in the movie
line. It's mostly for the record that I'm doing it.'

'You know Shifcart has nothing to do with scenario. He
deals with actors, talent.'

'Allbee thought he might have a connection somewhere.
I didn't think so, but he asked me, and I thought . . . Well,
to tell you the truth, Dan, I didn't know what to think. I had
my doubts. But he did get me the interview with Rudiger.
So I thought, "Well, let him go and see Shifcart. Why should
I answer for Shifcart? I'll show my good intentions and return the favor," and so on. That's the story.'

'I don't believe it. It seems to me that he's got you on the
merry-go-round.'

One of Mrs Harkavy's plants stood behind Leventhal. He
felt a leaf graze his hair as he shut his eyes and leaned backwards.

'How did he ever sell you such a bill of goods?' said Harkavy. 'Where did he hear of Shifcart?'

'He happened to be at the house and saw a card of Shifcart's.'

'So he keeps coming around. You must be encouraging him.
I thought we came to the conclusion he was off his nut.'

'*You* did!' Blindly roused, Leventhal flung out his arm. 'You were the one. That was what you said. You compared him to your aunt.'

'Well, you're impetuous tonight. Both of us came to the same conclusion.'

'No, no!' Leventhal refused to hear him. 'I absolutely deny it. Absolutely!'

'Where did I get it from, if you didn't say it? I can't understand you. I haven't seen the man. Anyhow, what's the odds? Why should that be an issue? I can see you're losing your bearings. Of course, you've got quite a little wine in your system; maybe that partly accounts for your funny behavior. Yes, it is very funny. I always thought you didn't know how to take care of yourself. I can see this man has you eating out of his hand. He comes around, you get excited when you talk about him, you're going to send him to Shifcart . . .'

'I'd send him anywhere to get rid of him,' said Leventhal.

'There, you wouldn't say anything like that unless you were in pretty deep. I can tell that you're keeping back information; don't have to be much of a mindreader to see that. I can't help you any more than to remind you that you're playing for keeps. You're not a boy, any more.'

'Dan, you know Shifcart. This has to be done. Tell me . . .' He caught Harkavy's hand.

'Take it up with him yourself.'

'Yes, I will, but I want to ask you . . .'

'We'd better go in. They must be waiting for us. We'll discuss this tomorrow when your head is clearer and if you want to be open with me.'

The guests, all men, had taken off their jackets and were sitting in the high-backed chairs. In the kitchen door, talking with Mrs Harkavy, was Mr Schlossberg who had just arrived and was still wearing his brown topcoat. Leventhal said good evening to him and Schlossberg answered, 'How are you?' He did not seem, however, to remember him. 'Fourteenth Street a couple of weeks ago,' said Leventhal.

'His memory is bad,' Harkavy whispered. He drew Leventhal into the row of chairs along the buffet.

Across the table, Leventhal recognized the possessor of the red hands he had watched during the card game. His name was Kaplan and his face, like his hands, was red and creased. He had a sharp blue squint, as though – Leventhal thought – he had made an effort to pierce heaven and distorted his eyes. Just now he was holding up a glass of brandy and saying, 'Here's to all.'

'Drink up,' someone said. 'Next year in Jerusalem.'

Leventhal heard Julia say, 'We had a children's party last year. It was too nerve racking. This time we decided we would have older people.'

'Shall we begin eating?' asked Goldstone.

'We ought to have the cake brought in first,' Mrs Harkavy said. She explained to the company, 'They weren't very careful with it at the bakery. Some of the frosting came off with the wax paper. We did our best to repair it.'

Julia put the cake with its seven candles on the table. Libbie stood staring into the flames. Her eyes were much like her grandmother's and her uncle's.

'Blow, kiddie,' said Harkavy. 'Once, that's luckiest.'

But Libbie reached out and tried to capture a drop of the melting wax.

'Libbie, dear . . .' her father urged.

'People are waiting,' Julia cried impatiently. 'Would you rather be hanging upside down in the closet?'

The child lowered her face to the clear ring of candles. Leventhal saw the liquid image of them in her eyes and on her white forehead. She blew, and the whitish, odorous wax smoke drifted over the table. The guests clapped and cried out.

'Sweet little kid,' said Harkavy to Leventhal, who nodded and still gazed heavy eyed at the candles. Julia and her grandmother kissed the girl.

The supper began. Leventhal's clothing, especially his shirt, bound and chafed him, and he opened his collar, grumbling to Harkavy, 'It's cutting my neck.' But Harkavy had resumed an argument begun earlier in the evening with a Mr Benjamin who sat between Goldstone and Julia. Leventhal had noticed him in the hall before, clumping on a specially built shoe. He had the complexion of a Hindu, a head of grizzled short curls, and scornful brown-freckled lips; there was a drop of yellow in his wide-set black eyes. Benjamin sold life insurance, and Harkavy had assailed the insurance companies. 'It's all in the Cardozo investigation. Does any more have to be said? The same money that's taken from the customers is used against them.' 'I don't see, Harkavy,' said Mr Benjamin, 'why one business has to be run down more than another. You ought to be against them all. And against government. You're an amateur, Harkavy, an amateur. I've heard your argument from experts. You have to pay for regulation and for order. It's one kind of harness or another. Men need a harness. This is light harness compared to some.' 'Oh, my dear man, you're as reactionary as they come,' said Harkavy. 'Are you against all banks and business?' asked Benjamin. 'Damn it, certainly I am.' Harkavy's voice rose. 'Let's hear what kind of a system you're thinking about?' Mr Benjamin's acerbity almost wiped out his smile.

'Stop the wrangling, Dan, for God's sake,' said Goldstone.

'I'll make it easier for you,' said Benjamin. 'Don't you want to provide for the people you love? Let's not argue about the best system. This one is standing yet.'

'It may not be for long. You never know when everything will be swept away overnight.' 'But meantime . . .' Mrs Harkavy interrupted. 'Daniel, you're just being sensational. I don't like to hear such talk from you.' 'Mamma, what I say is perfectly true. There have been big organizations before and people who thought they would last forever.' 'You mean Insull?' said the man on his left. 'I mean Rome, Persia, the great Chinese empires!'

Mr Benjamin shrugged his shoulders. 'We have to live

today,' he said. 'If you had a son, Harkavy, you'd want him to have a college education. Who's going to wait for the Messiah? They tell a story about a little town in the old country. It was out of the way, in a valley, so the Jews were afraid the Messiah would come and miss them, and they built a high tower and hired one of the town beggars to sit in it all day long. A friend of his meets this beggar and he says, "How do you like your job, Baruch?" So he says, "It doesn't pay much, but I think it's steady work."' There was an uproar at the table. 'There's a moral, for you!' cried Benjamin in a suddenly strengthened voice. Leventhal felt himself beginning to smile. 'It is!' shouted Mr Kaplan, laying his hand on Benjamin's shoulder. Mrs Harkavy, flushing, raised her delighted brows and covered her mouth with her handkerchief.

'Anyway, I don't think it's right,' said Harkavy, 'to go frightening people the way you do.' 'Oh? What now?' Harkavy knitted his brows. 'I know how you insurance gentlemen work,' he said. 'You go in to see a prospect. There he is, behind his desk or his counter, still in pretty fair shape, you may say. He has his aches and his troubles, but in general everything is satisfactory. Suddenly you're there to say, "Have you considered your family's future?" Well and good, every man dies, but you're playing it unfair and hitting where you know it hurts. He thinks about these things alone at night. Most of us do. But now you're undermining him in the daytime. When you've frightened him good he says, "What'll I do?" And you're ready with the contract and the fountain pen.' 'Now, Dan,' said Goldstone restrainingly. Benjamin glanced at him with his yellow and black eyes as though to say that he needed no defender. 'So what,' he said. 'I do them a favor. Shouldn't they be prepared?'

'Oh, Death!' someone quoted at the far end of the table. 'Thou comest when I had thee least in mind.' 'Yes, that's the thing,' Benjamin said lifting himself with a scuff of his heel and pointing. 'That's it.' 'My heavens,' said Mrs Harkavy. 'What a morbid thing for a birthday party. With all this food

on the table. Can't we find something lighter to talk about?'
'The funeral baked meats did furnish forth the marriage
feast.' 'Where the blazes is this poetry coming from?' said
Goldstone. 'It's Brimberg. His father died and he was able to
go to college.' Goldstone smiled. 'Be serious, down there,' he
said. 'Cousins of mine,' he explained to Leventhal, happening
to catch his glance. 'My mother sewed her own shroud,' said
Kaplan, raising his distorted shining blue eyes to them. 'That's
right, it was the custom,' said Benjamin. 'All the old people
used to do it. And a good custom, too, don't you think so,
Mr Schlossberg?' 'There's a lot to say for it,' Schlossberg
replied. 'At least they knew where they stood and who they
were, in those days. Now they don't know who they are but
they don't want to give themselves up. The last funeral I went
to, they had paper grass in the grave to cover up the dirt.'
'So you're on Benjamin's side?' said Harkavy. 'No, not
exactly,' said the old man. 'Sure, Benjamin's business is to
scare people.' 'So you're on my side, then?' Mr Schlossberg
looked impatient. 'It's not a question of people's feelings,' he
said. 'You don't have to remind them of anything. They don't
forget. But they're too busy and too smart to die. It's easy to
understand. Here I'm sitting here, and my mind can go
around the world. Is there any limit to what I can think? But
in another minute I can be dead, on this spot. There's a limit
to me. But I have to be myself in full. Which is somebody who
dies, isn't it? That's what I was from the beginning. I'm not
three people, four people. I was born once and I will die once.
You want to be two people? More than human? Maybe it's
because you don't know how to be one. Everybody is busy.
Every man turns himself into a whole corporation to handle
the business. So one stockholder is riding in the elevator, and
another one is on the roof looking through a telescope, one is
eating candy, and one is in the movies looking at a pretty face.
Who is left? And how can a corporation die? One stockholder
dies. The corporation lives and goes on eating and riding in
the elevator and looking at the pretty face. But it stands to

reason, paper grass in the grave makes all the grass paper . . .'

'There's always something new with Schlossberg,' said Kaplan. He strangely altered his squint by raising his brows. 'What's on his lung is on his tongue.'

'Really,' Julia broke in. 'Mamma is right. What kind of talk is this for a birthday?'

'Never out of place,' said Benjamin.

'Out of place?' said Brimberg at the foot of the table. 'It depends on your taste. I heard about a French lady of easy virtue who dressed in a bridal veil for her clients.'

'Sammy!' came Mrs Harkavy's scolding scream. And there was more laughter and a hubbub out of which grew a new conversation to which Leventhal, however, did not listen. Harkavy was not watching and he poured himself another glass of wine.

22

BEFORE he was fully awake, Leventhal, on Harkavy's couch where he had spent the night, realized that his head was aching, and, when he opened his eyes, even the gray light of the overcast day was too strong for him and he turned his face to the cushions and hitched the quilt over his shoulder. He was in his undershirt and his feet were bare but he had not taken off his trousers. His belt was tight and he loosened it, and brought his hand out, pressing and kneading the skin of his forehead. Over the arm of the couch he gazed at the period furniture, the ferns, the looped and gathered silk of the unmodish lamps, and the dragons, flowers, and eyes of the rug. He knew the rug. Old Harkavy had gotten it from the estate of a broker who committed suicide on Black Friday.

Occasionally the windows were slammed by a high wind, and when this occurred the curtained French doors shook a little. Steam hissed in the pipes and there was a fall smell of heating radiators. Leventhal's nose was dry. The mohair was rough against his cheek. He did not change his position. Shutting his eyes, he tried to doze away the oppressiveness of his headache.

At a stir behind the French doors he said loudly, 'Come!' No one entered, however, and he pushed away the covers. The strap of his watch was loose and it had worked round to the wrong side of his wrist. The lateness of the hour made him frown – it was nearly half-past one. He sat up and leaned forward, his undershirt hanging shapeless over his fat chest. He was about to reach for his shoes and stockings, but his hands remained on his knees and he was suddenly powerless to move and fearfully hampered in his breathing. He had the strange feeling that there was not a single part of him on which the whole world did not press with full weight, on his body, on his soul, pushing upward in his breast and downward in his bowels. He concentrated, moving his lips like someone about to speak, and blew a tormented breath through his nose. What he meanwhile sensed was that this interruption of the customary motions he went through unthinkingly on rising, despite the pain it was causing, was a disguised opportunity to discover something of great importance. He tried to seize the opportunity. He put out all his strength to collect himself, beginning with the primary certainty that the world pressed on him and passed through him. Beyond this he could not go, hard though he drove himself. He was bewilderingly moved. He sat in the same posture, massively, his murky face trained on the ferns standing softly against the gray glass. His nostrils twitched. It came into his head that he was like a man in a mine who could smell smoke and feel heat but never see the flames. And then the cramp and the enigmatic opportunity ended together. His legs quivered as he worked his feet back and forth on the carpet. He walked over to the window and he heard the loud crack of the wind. It was pumping the trees in the small wedge of park six stories below, tearing at the wires on rooftops, fanning the smoke out under the clouds, scattering it like soot on paraffin.

He dressed, feeling a little easier. His shirt cuffs were soiled; he turned them underside up and transferred the links. He stuffed his tie into his pocket; he would put it on after washing. Stripping the couch, he folded up the sheets and the silk quilt and laid them on a chair. When he opened the French doors, he expected to meet Mrs Harkavy or one of the family in the hall and he wondered why the house was so silent. Harkavy's dark room was open, the bed empty. Leventhal switched on the light and saw trousers hung neatly from the top drawer of the dresser and the suspenders coiled on the floor. An open magazine covered the lamp.

Harkavy was sitting alone in the kitchen. At his elbow the toaster was ticking, and a pot of coffee was warming on the electric heater. He was wearing a corduroy jacket over his pajamas, a belted jacket with large leather buttons. His bare feet were crossed on a chair. His green slippers had fallen to the floor.

'Good morning,' Harkavy's look was amused. 'The reveler.'

'Good morning. Where's the family?'

'Gone to Shifcart senior's for the birthday dinner.'

'Why didn't you go?'

'To Long Island City when I have a chance to sleep late? They left at nine.'

'I hope you didn't stay here because of me.'

'You? No, I wanted to sleep. Holidays are poison if I have to get up early.' He stroked the golden-green jacket. 'I like a late, peaceful breakfast. Bachelor habits. As long as I'm not married, I've got to stand pat on my advantages.'

The kitchen light, reflecting from the tiles and the white refrigerator, was too sharp for Leventhal. He winced away from it slightly.

'How do you feel – not very well?'

'Headache.'

'You're not used to drinking.'

'No,' said Leventhal. The banter annoyed him.

'You were bright-eyed, last night.'

He looked rather sullenly at him. 'What if I was?'

'Nothing. I'm not blaming you, you understand, for getting a little tight. You probably have good reasons.'

'Where's your aspirin?'

'In the bathroom. I'll bring you some.' Harkavy started to rise.

'Stay put; I'll find it.'

'Have a cup of coffee. It'll do you more good.' He removed his feet from the chair. They were very long and white, with toes as slender as fingers.

Leventhal poured himself a cup of black coffee. It was

233

bitter and coated his tongue with a sediment, but he felt it would do him good.

Harkavy sighed. 'I'm a little under the weather myself. Not from drinking; the excitement, the arguing, and such. Mamma, though, she was up at seven and got everything in order. What vitality she's got! Her mother – there was another dry old fire for you. She lived to be ninety-four. Do you remember her? Down on Joralemon Street?'

'No.' Leventhal, trying to recapture the feeling that had interrupted his dressing, found he retained almost nothing of it.

'I'm a different type,' Harkavy said. 'The sword that wears out the sheath. But some of these old people. . . . Take Schlossberg, for example, still supporting his family, his good-for-nothing son and his daughters. The old man is a blowhard, sometimes, but you have to hand it to him. With him it's a case of "touch me and you touch a man," and these days you can't always be sure what you're touching. I set myself up against him, now and then, because I like a good argument. I don't trust people who won't argue.'

Gradually Harkavy's manner underwent a change. He was slouching in his chair, his heels were set wide apart on the linoleum and his arms were hanging over the back of the chair; his hands with their whitish hairs were full veined. Beneath the clear water lines, his lids suddenly appeared flushed and irritated, and when he began again to speak it was with a nervous dodge of the head, as if he were already putting aside an objection.

'Why don't you come clean now on this business we were talking about last night?' he said.

'What's there to come clean about?'

'It baffles me. I've been giving it some thought. After what you said about him, that you should be trying to arrange this . . .'

Leventhal did not stir his face from the cup. 'We went over that yesterday. I told you about *Dill's*.'

'He must have you by the tail.'

Leventhal reflected, 'This is just curiosity on his part. Why should I satisfy it? That Sunday when he could have helped me out he went away with Goldstone and his friends, and now, because he's itching to know, *I* should talk.' He resolved to give him no satisfaction. Nevertheless, the saucer shook in his hand and he held it against his chest, bending his head until folds of skin appeared under his chin and along his jaw. He meditated on his weakness. How weak he was becoming. Even Harkavy could make him tremble.

'How come you changed your mind about him? You said he was loony.'

'No, you did.'

'On your information. What you told me was all I had to go by. It looks as if he really did a job on you, sold you a bill of goods.'

Leventhal doggedly refrained from answering. He kept his head down with a look of worn endurance.

Harkavy persisted. 'Didn't he?'

Leventhal drew his lips against his teeth as he wiped his mouth. 'I must have wanted to buy,' he said.

'It's beyond me. When you came to talk to me about him, you were mad enough to hang him. He was accusing you of some crime and blaming you for what happened to his wife and what not. Now you want to send him to Shifcart with a reference. And unless I'm mistaken you were fishing for me to help you. I couldn't believe my ears when you asked me about Shifcart. What kind of impression will a man like that make on him? And why do you let him hang around? Didn't you tell me he picked up Shifcart's card at your house? Besides, you know Shifcart can't do anything for him.'

'I suppose not.'

'And where does he get the idea that Shifcart can help him?'

Though he knew he was making a mistake, Leventhal said, and to some extent it was involuntary, 'I think he believes it's

235

all a Jewish setup and Shifcart can pull strings for him . . . Jews have influence with other Jews.'

'No!' Harkavy cried. 'No!' His hands flew to his head. 'And you're trying to do something for him? You're willing, regardless? Boy, do you know what this does to my opinion of you? Are you in your right mind?'

His horror shook Leventhal.

'Look, Dan, I don't want to go into this any further. Don't push me. I asked you about Shifcart. You told me what you think . . . Let that be the end of it.'

'But how does he do it?' Harkavy's voice rang. 'What's he got on you? Is it blackmail? Have you done something?'

'No, nothing . . . I've been having a lot of trouble. My family – you heard about that. And Mary's away, that's been hard on me, too. My nerves aren't in very good shape. I feel I've been trying to throw something off. You aren't being very helpful. Just let me alone to handle this in my own way.' This was a great deal for him to say; it was exorbitant, like a plea. His hands were less steady than ever. He set down the coffee, splashing some of it into the saucer.

'What's between you? How does he work you? First you come to complain about him. Next thing I know he sounds like the Protocols, but it's all right with you.' He furiously pounded the metal table, his face and his elongated throat flaming. 'Influence with Jews!' he shouted.

Leventhal silently reproached himself. 'That was a real mistake. I shouldn't have said that. Why did I let it slip out? I'm not even sure Allbee means that.'

To Harkavy, he said, 'Don't fly off the handle. I realize it seems bad, but you don't know the facts. I can judge this better than you.' He kept his voice low in order to control it.

'The facts? What are you letting this man do to you? Are you going off your rocker?'

'Don't be foolish, Dan,' he cried. 'I know you mean well, but you're being carried away. And please remember my mother before you say a thing like that. You know about my mother. I told you about her as friend to friend. The meaning of it hasn't sunk in.'

This silenced Harkavy briefly. He seemed to scowl. In reality he was clearing his throat. After considering him for a while he said, 'Well, you *are* a privileged character. You're the only man living whose mother lost her mind and died.' Immediately he changed his tone, clapping his hands sharply. 'As friend to friend, what are the facts? This thing about Shifcart is such nonsense it isn't even worth talking about. But you, you must be in a trance. Tell me, what's going on. Just look at you!'

'What's the matter?'

'You look like the devil.'

'Do I? Well, I told you. There was the kid's death, first of all.'

'You were more honest when you were drunk, last night. You admitted that you wanted to get the man off your neck. Don't hide behind the child. That's not good. It's dishonest. Wake up! What's life? Metabolism? That's what it is for the bugs. Jesus Christ, no! What's life? Consciousness, that's what it is. That's what you're short on. For God's sake, give yourself a push and a shake. It's dangerous stuff, Asa, this stuff.'

Leventhal looked at Harkavy in blank perplexity.

'Well, I'm damned if I can see it,' he finally said. 'In the first place, when I came to you, you were the one who told me about Williston . . .'

'And?'

But Leventhal would not continue.

'And? What next?' said Harkavy, sitting forward.

There was a short pause and then Leventhal said, 'Say, I've got to have that aspirin.' He rose.

'All right, you don't want my help. I can't make you take it. God bless you. You had a chance to unburden yourself and get some advice. How many friends have you got?' He put a slice of bread in the toaster and rammed down the lever.

Among the bottles of lotion and cologne and the powder boxes in Mrs Harkavy's medicine chest, Leventhal found the aspirin and swallowed a tablet with a sip from the tap. He filled the sink with warm water and pushed back his sleeves; the light green color gave him a kind of pleasure. He dipped in his hands and then glanced at the tub with its thick nickled spout. The linen closet stood open, giving out a dry perfume of soap. Leventhal took a towel and let the metal stopper fall. 'I'm going to take a bath, if you don't mind,' he called to Harkavy.

'Go ahead.'

The faucet ran loudly and Leventhal shut the door and began to undress. The room grew hot. He sat on the edge of the tub in the roar of the steaming water and lathered his hairy dark body, energetic and all absorbed. The tumult of the faucet relieved him, for some reason. As he lay back in the charge and sway of the water, he observed to himself, as if in compliment, 'He didn't get anything out of me.' He stroked his chest, releasing tiny bubbles from the hairs. 'I'll be better off taking care of things by myself,' he thought. He turned off the cold tap and the hot water ran on, green with a white inner shape and a thread of vapor.

He wondered what success Max was having with Elena. He was concerned for him, of course, but he worried mainly about Philip whom, if it turned out that Max was wrong about Elena, he would go to any lengths to save. He postponed thinking about himself. Eventually he would have to – provided that Max was right about Elena and he wrong. The reason for a mistake like that could not be neglected; it had to be dug out. But dug out when he had the strength for the operation, not now. A ring of soap, melting from the bar in his hand, spread over the water.

While he dried himself, his heart beat rapidly. However, his headache was almost gone, and he felt freshened and almost cheerful. He went into the kitchen. Harkavy had set out plates and was scrambling some eggs.

It was not until the meal was nearly over that he suffered a recoil, a raw, painful current through his overtried nerves. He could not continue this way with Allbee. It was enough. It had to be ended. Any day he expected to hear that Mary was coming back. What if she should come back before it was ended? He freed himself from this fear much as one might brush away a clinging insect from one's face. And Allbee might think, because he had not slept at home last night – what might he think, that he was afraid of him? It would give him the confidence to make new demands. He could have the introduction to Shifcart. More than that, no. And he would have to get out of the house. 'Enough!' he silently decided. 'Enough, enough!' He dropped his fork noisily. Under Harkavy's questioning eyes he looked, as usual, unperturbed; moping somewhat, but steady and calm. He recovered the fork and touched his food with it. But he was unable to swallow another bite.

23

HE started home at half-past four. The wind had dropped, the sky was cold and darkening rapidly. In the little park the turned-up rusty shells of leaves scraped in the path and cracked underfoot. Very little green remained in those that streamed raggedly in the trees. A damp warmth, smelling of stone, rose from the subway, and through the gratings Leventhal caught a glimpse of the inert light on the roadbed and of the rails, hard and gray in their simultaneous strike. The close brownstone houses looked autumnal and so did the foot-burnished, steel manhole lids; they were glinting sharply. Summer seemed to have ended prematurely in chill and darkness. The people who had gone out of town for the holiday would be building fires on the beaches, those who were not already crowding the trains into the city.

Leventhal halted on the sidewalk opposite his flat. All the windows in the building were dark. The tiny red lamp in the foyer appeared to be embedded in the fanlight and sent its bloody color into the corners and as far as the polished, florid head of the banister at the rear. Mrs Nunez' vines, spreading thickly upwards, swayed in a mass on the taut strings. 'He's out,' said Leventhal to himself. He was exasperated, almost as if Allbee had gone away to thwart him. But actually it was to his advantage to be the first one home, for so far he had not decided how to deal with Allbee. And now, while going up the stairs, he occasionally touched the dust-hung concave of the wall and thought, 'What will I do?' He was, however, far too agitated to make any plans. He climbed rapidly, rather struck by the number of landings and, until he recognized a fire bucket with cigarettes buried in the sand, wondering why the place did not look more familiar. Reaching the fourth floor, he put his back against the wall while he felt in both pockets for his key. He brought out a handful of change and keys, and began to pick it over under the weak light. Then it seemed to him that someone was moving in the flat. It could be that Allbee had been sleeping and had just gotten up. That would explain the dark windows. He rapped and put his ear to the panel. He was sure that he heard steps.

He was far from calm when he turned the key in the lock. The door yielded a few inches, and then bumped and held with a rattle. He thrust his hand into the opening and felt the chain. Were there thieves in the house? He was on the point of running down to fetch Nunez or to phone the police when he heard Allbee say, 'Is that you?'

'What's the chain up for?' he demanded.

'I'll explain to you later.'

'No, you won't, you'll explain it right now.'

But the chain remained in place. Leventhal urged himself not to lose his head and an instant later he punched at the door so that it shook and waited, staring at its ancient black trickles and tears of enamel. Then he began to pound again, enraged, shouting, 'You! Open!' When he stopped he heard a low sound and, peering into the crack, he saw Allbee's face or rather a segment of his face, his nose, his full lip, and, with the lingering effect of a trance, his eye and the familiar stain beneath it.

'Come on!' he said to him.

'I can't,' Allbee whispered. 'Come back a little later, will you? Give me about fifteen minutes.'

'I'll give you nothing.'

'Ten minutes. Be decent.'

Leventhal threw himself at the door, whirling around and striking it with the side of his body and his lowered shoulder, his feet gritting on the tiles. He gripped the door posts and pushed. He now heard two voices inside. Again, more desperately, he lunged. The chain broke and he was thrown against the wall of the vestibule. He recovered and rushed into the front room. There Allbee, naked and ungainly, stood beside a woman who was dressing in great haste. He was helping her, handing her stockings and underwear from the heap on the chair beside the bed. She had on her skirt but from the waist up she was bare. Brushing aside his hand with the proffered stockings, she bent to squeeze her foot into a shoe, digging her finger in beside the heel. Her hair covered her face; nevertheless Leventhal thought he recognized her. Mrs Nunez! Was it Mrs Nunez? The horror of it bristled on him, and the outcry he had been about to make was choked down.

She stooped toward the light – only the bed lamp was lit and it cast a limited circle over the twisted sheets and the rug – and turned her blouse right side out. Her scared eyes glimmered at him and her breasts hung down heavily as she thrust her arm through the sleeve. Meanwhile, Allbee had hurried to the door and closed it. He came back and put on his shirt, the new shirt he had bought on Second Avenue. The stiff loop of the collar stood off from his neck. Next he drew on his pants, nearly losing his balance as he shifted from foot to foot. Breathing heavily, he looked down and, while he buttoned himself, he said quietly to Leventhal, 'At least, go into another room for a while, till she leaves.'

'You get out, too.'

He dropped his head, and Leventhal could not tell from his expression whether he was entreating or ordering him. He looked at him with anger and contempt, and began to walk toward the kitchen. The woman turned and he saw her plainly. She was straightening her hair, her elbows working quickly above her head. She was a stranger, not Mrs Nunez; simply a woman. He felt enormously lightened, but at the same time it gave him a pang to think of his suspicion. She was a big woman, large hipped; her shoulders were high and the straight lines of her blouse made them appear square. She was tall and her hair was black, and that was all there was to the resemblance. There was an irregularity in the shape of her eyes; one was smaller than the other. It was with the larger, more brilliant eye that she returned his stare. Her smile was unsteady and resentful. He hovered near her a moment, inhaling the strong odor of powder or perfume that emanated from her in the heat of the room. She pushed a white comb into her hair and moved away from him.

He banged the kitchen door and, in the dark, beside the throbbing refrigerator, he waited and heard the low sounds of a conversation. He did not try to follow it. There were footsteps; the tread was the woman's, she was going toward the door. It was for her sake primarily that he had withdrawn, in order to spare her. It wasn't her fault. Probably Allbee had not told her the flat was someone else's. The nerve of him, the nerve! Leventhal nearly cried aloud in revulsion. He distorted his face wildly, stretching his mouth. The nastiness of it! The refrigerator faltered and quivered but always recovered and ran, chaotically and interminably, ran and ran. Its white crown was on a level with his eyes; he could see blue sparks within. The only other thing visible in the room was the pilot light, also blue, a much deeper blue, in the black hollows and spidery bars of the gas range.

The woman's look remained with him. So did her scent; it seemed to cling to the rooms. The voices continued in the vestibule. Leventhal went into the dining-room. On the day-bed's crumpled sheets, the pillow gray, almost black, there were newspapers, underclothes, and socks. Between the curtains, on the sill, he discovered a cup of coffee in which drops of mold floated, and crumbs and scraps of food.

The outer door shut and he strode into the front room.

'Look here,' said Allbee, as soon as he came through the kitchen door. 'I thought you were out of town for the week end. You didn't come home last night. I thought . . .'

'You thought you'd bring a tramp in from the street.'

'No . . . now wait.' He gave a hasty, somewhat breathless

243

laugh. 'I know I have a fallen nature. I never pretended to be anything I wasn't. Why all the excitement? You might have given me a few minutes.' He spoke placatingly, with humorous chagrin. He looked sallow and his lips were dry. His smile persisted at the corners covertly, it was boastful.

Leventhal flushed thickly. 'In my bed!'

'Well, the day bed is so narrow. No place to take a lady . . . I wanted a little more space . . .' He was by no means sure of himself and his voice wavered as he made the joke. 'I fail to see what there is to fuss about.'

'Oh, you don't see! It gave you a bang to put your whore where I sleep.'

The vehemence of his loathing gave a different turn to Allbee's smile; it became jeering, and a yellowish hot tinge came over his bloodshot eyes. Leventhal heard him murmur something about 'fastidiousness.'

'You hypocrite! I thought you couldn't get over your wife.'

'Don't you mention my wife!' Allbee cried.

'Why not, you're always crying about her, aren't you?'

'I say don't! Leave things alone that you can't understand.'

'What can't I understand?'

'Not that, for sure!' Allbee said harshly. His face was inflamed; his cheekbones looked as if they had been branded. But he checked himself and slowly the color retreated. Only a few refractory spots remained. He seemed to force himself to make a gesture of retraction. 'I mean,' he said, 'she's dead. What does she have to do with it? I have needs, naturally, the same as anybody else.'

'What did she have to do with the other things? You mealy-mouth, you were using her to work on my feelings. All right, what do I care? Go to hell. But you weren't satisfied that you made this place so filthy I can't stand to come in; you had to bring this woman into my bed.'

'But what's there to be so upset about? Where else, if not in bed . . . ?' He looked amused again and blinked his bloodshot eyes. 'What do you do? Maybe you have some other way, more refined, different? Don't you people claim that you're the same as everybody else? That's your way of saying that you're above everybody else. I know.'

'Go get your stuff in the dining-room and clear out. I don't want any more of you.'

'You don't care about the woman. You're just using her to make an issue and break your promise to me. Well, and I thought I had seen everything in the way of cynicism. By God, you could give lessons! I never met anyone who could touch you. I guess there's an example in the world of everything a man can imagine, no matter how great or how gruesome. You certainly are not the same as everybody else.' He looked at him, keenly, brilliantly, triumphantly insolent. 'What do you care about my wife! But your instinct told you where to jab, in the way that insects know where they'll find the most sap.'

'You dirty phoney!' Leventhal cried huskily. 'You ugly bastard counterfeit. I said it because you're such a liar, with your phoney tears and your wife's name in your mouth, every second word. The poor woman, a fine life she must have had with you, a freak like you, out of a carnival. You don't care what you say. You'll say anything that comes into your head. You're not even human, if you ask me. No wonder she left you.'

'It's very interesting that you should take her part. She was like me. What do you think of that? We were alike,' he shouted.

'Well, get out! Beat it! I told you to leave when the woman did.'

'What about your promise?'

Leventhal pushed him toward the door. Allbee fell back a few steps and, seizing a heavy glass ash tray, he aimed it menacingly and cried, 'Keep off me!' Leventhal made a rush at him and knocked the ash tray down. Pinning his arms, he wheeled him around and ran him into the vestibule.

'Let go. I'll leave,' he panted.

The door, as Leventhal jerked it open, hit Allbee in the face. He did not resist when Leventhal thrust him out on the landing and, without looking back, he started down the stairs.

Winded, Leventhal stumbled into a chair, pulled at his collar. The sweat ran into his eyes and a pain, starting at his shoulders, passed downward through his chest. Suddenly he thought, 'Maybe he's still hanging around. I'd better look.' He forced himself up and went to the stairs. Holding the rail, he stared into the shaft. It was silent. He thought as he returned to the flat, 'He didn't even have the courage to fight back. As much as he hates me. And he's bigger; he could have killed me.' He wondered whether Allbee was stunned by the door when it struck him in the face. The sound of that did not leave him.

He stopped to examine the chain. The staple was only loosened and might have been hammered in. But one of the links had given. He tossed the severed half away. Over the furrows of the rug in the front room there was a long, curving trail of ashes. He wiped his sweat with his sleeve and took in the room, angry, but exultant also; he felt dimly that this disorder and upheaval was part of the price he was obliged to pay for his release.

The radiators were spitting and the room was unendurably hot. He flung up the window and bent out. Instantly he heard the tumultuous swoop of the Third Avenue train rising above the continuous, tidal noise of the street. People were walking among the stripes of light on the pavement, light that came from windows opening on carpeted floors and the shapes of furniture; they passed through the radiance of the glass cage that bulged before the theater and into shadows, tributaries that led into deeper shadows and led, still further on, into mighty holes filled with light and stifled roaring. 'Is he around somewhere?' Leventhal asked himself. He doubted that Allbee was near. Certainly he knew he had nothing more to hope for here after tonight. And what he had hoped for in the first place remained a mystery. The idea of an introduction to Shifcart lost all its substance; it was a makeshift demand, improvised. That he was able to see this gave Leventhal the feeling that he was becoming himself again after a long lapse.

The breeze was cooling him too rapidly. He drew his head in, shivering, and sat down, wiping the grit of the sill from his palms. His throat was bitter and raw, and there was a deadening weight in his side. But he sat and rested briefly and soon felt better. When he rose, he began unsystematically to set the flat in order, going slowly and desultorily from task to task.

He stripped the linen from the beds and threw it in the laundry hamper. Then, without taking the trouble to clean out the scraps in the drain, he spilled soap powder over the dishes in the kitchen sink and let the hot water run until the foam boiled up and covered them. He made up his bed with clean sheets, awkwardly shaking the pillows into pillow cases and dragging the bed away from the wall in order to tuck in the blankets. In the dining-room, he turned over the mattress of the day bed and forced up the seldom-opened windows. On one of the chairs he found a glossy haberdasher's bag with a Second Avenue address. It contained Allbee's old shirt and a few other articles that he did not examine. He threw the bag into the dumb-waiter, together with the socks and undershirts and the newspapers Allbee had accumulated. Next, in the bathroom, he took down the towels, turned on the shower to rinse the tub, and made an effort to clean the basin. After a few strokes he gave this up and returned the rag to its pipe beneath the sink.

He was moving chairs into place when he saw a comb on the carpet. It must have been the mate to the one the woman had fastened in her hair. Studying it, he could not help breathing its odor. It was a white comb, white bone, its teeth darkened yellow in an uneven fringe. On one side it was decorated with a diamond-shaped piece of glass; on the other, the bit of glass had fallen out of its setting. He did not linger over the comb very long; he let it fall into the waste-basket. He recalled the women in the wrangle he had watched on the corner several weeks back and even reflected that she might have been one of them. She might, easily. After all, where had Allbee picked her up? Probably in a tavern in the neighborhood.

A breeze blew through the flat while he swept the ashes from the rug. It brought the cold and vacancy of the outside into the room. Nevertheless, the smell of the comb occasionally returned, coming over him with some fragment of what had occurred that evening in its wake, like a qualm. It must have been frightening, sickening for her to hear the crash of the door and then to run out of bed – still another bed. And even granting that she could endure roughness better than another (many a woman would have cried from terror or sheer mortification), he was sorry to have subjected her to it. He found himself regretting the whole incident because of her and almost wished that he had listened to Allbee and gone away. He could have attended to him later. A few impressions of her remained vividly with Leventhal – the heaviness of her figure in the skirt, the way she had crouched to work her foot into the shoe, the look he had received from her queerly shaped eyes. It now struck him that there was more amusement in it than fear, and he could see, too, how with a grain of detachment it was possible for her to find the incident amusing. He began to remember how Allbee had stumbled in pulling up his pants and how comically he had held out the woman's stockings to her. It was low, it was painful, but it was funny. He grinned, his eyes dilated and shone; he gave way explosively to laughter, driving the broom at the floor. 'The stockings! Those damn stockings! Standing there without a stitch and passing those stockings!' He broke suddenly into a cough. When he was done laughing and coughing, his face remained unusually expressive. Yes, and he ought not to leave himself out of the picture, glaring at them both. Meanwhile, Allbee was burning, yet trying to keep his head. The woman must have grasped that he did not dare say what he felt. Perhaps he had been boasting to her, telling lies about himself, and that was why his predicament amused her.

But when he sat down for a moment on the bed, all the comedy of it was snatched away and torn to pieces. He was wrong about the woman's expression; he was trying to transform it into something he could bear. The truth was probably far different. He had started out to see what had happened with her eyes and had ended by substituting his own, thus contriving to put her on his side. Whereas, the fact was that she was nearer to Allbee. Both of them, Allbee and the woman, moved or swam toward him out of a depth of life in which he himself would be lost, choked, ended. There lay horror, evil, all that he had kept himself from. In the days when he was clerking in the hotel on the East Side, he had been as near to it as he could ever bear to be. He had seen it face on then. And since, he had learned more about it out of the corner of his eye. Why not say heart, rather than eye? His heart was what caught it, with awful pain and dread, in heavy blows. Then, since the fear and pain were so great, what drew him on?

He picked up the broom and returned to his tasks. As he bent on trembling legs to brush up the ashes, he was thinking, 'Maybe I didn't do the right thing. I didn't know what it was. I don't yet. And there had to be a showdown sooner or later. What was I going to do with him? He hated me. He hated me enough to cut my throat. He didn't do it because he was too much of a coward. That's why he was pulling all those stunts instead. He was pulling them on himself as much as on me, and the reason for that was that he hated himself for not having enough nerve, but by clowning he could pass off his own feelings. – All that stuff, the mustard and going on his knees and all that talk. That's what it was for. I had to do something with him. I suppose I handled it badly. Still, it's over; that's the main thing . . .'

The chairs did not look quite as they did when Mary

arranged them; the bed was unevenly made. A swath of ashes still remained on the rug. However, things began to right themselves and it soothed him to be busy. He opened a can of vegetable soup and set it on the stove. While it was heating, he washed the dishes and, for the first time in weeks, turned on the radio simply to hear a voice. The phone rang. It was Max, calling, he said, from a drugstore on Fourteenth Street. He did not want to come unannounced a second time. A good thing, too, Leventhal thought; he would not have answered the doorbell.

He was finishing his soup ten minutes later, when Max arrived. Elena had agreed at last to leave New York. That was his news. He was coming from Pennsylvania Station where he had picked up the reservations. Villani's brother, a secondhand dealer on Bleecker Street, was buying the furniture.

'It'll cost us twice what we're getting to buy new things down there,' he said.

'Ah, you don't want this stuff.'

'What's the matter with it? Shipping is too high, that's all.' Then he smiled at Leventhal. 'So . . . ?' he said.

'You mean I was mistaken about Elena.'

'I sure do. And about the old lady.'

'Oh. Well, you caught me in a bad mood the other night, Max. I'm not always like that. I hope I didn't hurt your feelings.'

The lines radiating out from Max's eyes deepened. 'Oh, I got a kind of a kick out of the way you built up the old woman,' he said.

'I'm glad you finally got Elena to come around. It's going to be all to the good. I'm glad for Phil's sake, especially. When you're settled we'll come down and visit.'

'Sure, you'll be welcome. Anytime. Is she going to be back soon?'

Leventhal noticed that Max did not mention Mary by name. Like Elena, he probably did not know what her name was.

'Mary? Just as soon as I can get her to come. I'm going to phone her tonight.'

'Your radio's on pretty loud. Got a drive on against spooks?'

They smiled together.

'I guess I really don't know where I'm at when she's away.'

Max poured himself a glass of water, declining to sit down for coffee. 'Too many things to take care of,' he said. He pulled his hat down. His sideburns were long and ill-trimmed, overgrowing his ears.

'I'll see you off,' said Leventhal. 'When are you leaving?'

'Friday, four o'clock on the Natchez Prince.'

'I'll be on hand.'

After talking to his wife, Leventhal prepared for bed in a kind of intoxication. He walked up and down the room, undressing, and stopped before her picture on the desk and caressed her face with his thumb over the glass. Under the arch of his chest, he felt a thick, distinct stroke that seemed to him much slower than the actual, remote, jubilant speeding of his heart. His legs were melting with excitement. Mary was probably packing her bags, for she had promised to leave on the earliest train tomorrow. From the way she spoke, he realized that she had been waiting for him to make this call. When he said, 'Can you come soon?' she replied, 'Tomorrow,' with an eagerness that astonished him. She would arrive very early on Tuesday, if the Labor Day crowd did not delay her too much. Meanwhile, he had to attend to the flat; she had to find it as she had left it. Half an hour ago he had thought it passable. Now it looked appallingly dirty. He slipped a coat over his pajamas and was about to go down to see Mrs Nunez. But he remembered in time that the Nunez' had a telephone and turned back. As usual, he chided himself; the easiest, sensible way came to him last. He found the number in Mary's alphabetized book and dialed it. In a moment he heard her aspirated Spanish ''Allo?' The thing was quickly arranged:

251

she would be up in the morning. After hanging up, he silently apologized to her for his suspicion. But there was no place in his present mood for penitence or even for thought.

He locked the front door. He ought to have spoken to Nunez about the broken chain while he was on the wire. And for that matter Allbee still had a key; the lock should be changed. He had not retained the number, and he picked up the book again and then decided to let the thing go until morning. Explanations were necessary. Why was the chain broken? Why did a perfectly good lock have to be taken out? He had to have time; he could not invent reasons on the telephone.

He got into bed, piled the pillows against the wall, and sat with a magazine in his lap. He did not read; he had no desire to, and besides nothing took shape before his eyes. Restlessly, he turned the pages and heard the interminable sleepy sigh of the steam in the radiators and the intermittent shock of the subway beneath the house. Finally he threw down the magazine and turned face down on the pillow. His impatience made him groan. He could hardly bear to lie still. Over and over again he saw the station platform, the cars in the tunnel, and made out Mary's face in the crowd of passengers – her hat, her light hair, and last of all her face. He embraced and kissed her, and asked, 'Did you have a good trip?' Would that do? He struggled over a choice of greetings. Then once more he imagined himself running on the platform. It was unendurable. He resolved to go to sleep and he turned off the lamp. But as soon as he had done this, he rose – the room was not entirely dark because the light was burning in the bathroom – and dragged the heavy desk chair to the door. He fixed the back of it tightly under the knob and returned to bed. 'For God's sake,' he muttered, 'let me get a night's rest.' There was a pallor on the windows; the moon had risen. Standing on the bed, he drew the curtains and dropped down. He pulled the blanket over his head and soon he was asleep.

At first he slept deeply, but after a time he began to stir.

He was too warm; he threw some of his covers off; his legs moved as if unwilling to be relaxed, and once or twice he was on the point of jumping up and turning on the lamp. But he held his head down between the pillows obstinately and presently he began to dream.

He was on a boardwalk in broad, open, blue summer weather. The sea was flaring on his right and the shore blackened with bathers. On his left, there was an amusement park with ticket booths, and he saw round yellow and red cars whipping around and bumping together. He entered a place that resembled a hotel – there was a circular veranda where people sat looking at the bay – but proved to be a department store. He was here to buy some rouge for Mary. The salesgirl demonstrated various shades on her own face, wiping off each in turn with a soiled hand towel and bending to the round mirror on the counter to draw a new spot. There was a great, empty glitter of glass and metal around them. What could this possibly be about? Leventhal wondered. For he was perfectly sure he had once seen a chart with all the colors. This work was unnecessary. Nevertheless, he watched her smearing the rouge on her sharp face and did not interrupt her. The odor of the towel had from the beginning seemed familiar. He made so strong an effort to identify it that he half roused himself, aware, all at once, that the odor came from his bed. His eyes were open and his unshaven chin rustled on the pillow. Could the woman's scent have penetrated the slip and the ticking? He raised his head, feeling stifled, and saw the dazzling wall of the bathroom, the yawning clothes hamper, the black fin of the scale. He thought he could hear the steam in the pipes, and yet the room was not warm. He shivered and lit the lamp. His heart nearly burst with fear, for the chair was down and the front door gaping. There were movements in the kitchen. He hunched forward in the gathered bedclothes, listening, and the wires of the spring sang out. His terror, like a cold fluid, like brine, seemed to have been released by the breaking open of something within him. 'My God!' he cried to himself. His mouth was parched and the taste of his lips was like that of dried blood. But what if the chair had slid down and the door opened by itself? And what if the kitchen were empty? His nerves again, his sick imagination. But why nerves – as an excuse for his cowardice? So that he would not have to go to the kitchen to investigate? Had he locked the door? He was ready to swear to it. And if it was open now, it was because Allbee, who had a key, had opened it. Leventhal's legs were braced to spring, but he held back, feeling that to be deceived now through his nerves would crush him. But suddenly he rushed from bed, dragging the sheets in which his foot had caught. He kicked free and ran into the kitchen. He collided with someone who crouched there, and a cry came out of him. The air was foul and hard to breathe. Gas was pouring from the oven. 'I have to kill him now,' he thought as they grappled. He caught the cloth of his coat in his teeth while he swiftly changed his grip, clutching at Allbee's face. He tore away convulsively, but Leventhal crushed him with his weight in the corner. Allbee's fist came down heavily on his neck, beside the shoulder. 'You want to murder me? Murder?' Leventhal gasped. The sibilance of the pouring gas was almost deafening.

'Me, myself!' Allbee whispered despairingly, as if with his last breath. 'Me ... !'

Then his head shot up, catching Leventhal on the mouth. The pain made him drop his hands, and Allbee pushed him away and flung out of the kitchen. He stumbled after him down a flight of stairs, trying to shout and bruising his naked feet on the metal edges of the treads. He heard Allbee jump and saw him running into the foyer. Seizing a milk bottle from a neighbor's sill, he threw it. It smashed on the tiles.

He raced back to turn off the gas. He feared an explosion. By the wildly swinging light, he saw a chair placed before the open oven from which Allbee apparently had risen when he ran in.

Leventhal threw open the front-room window and bent out,

254

tears running down his face in the cold air. The long lines of lamps hung down their yellow grains in the gray and blue of the street. He saw no one, not a living thing.

When he had had enough air, he limped to the bathroom. He had bitten his tongue and he rinsed his mouth with peroxide. In spite of the struggle, the revolting sweetness of the gas like the acrid sweetness of sewage, the numbness in his neck, and, now, the sight of blood, he did not seem greatly disturbed. He looked impassive, under the cloud of his hair. He rinsed and spat, washed out the sink, wiped the stains from the mouth of the peroxide bottle, and went to pick up the sheets he had dragged to the floor. By the time he had remade the bed, the flat was nearly free of gas. Though he scarcely thought that Allbee would be back again, he shut the door and barricaded it with the dresser. He would sleep undisturbed; he cared about nothing else. Drowsily, he went to check the stove again, to make sure no more gas was escaping. Then he dropped onto the bed. He was still sleeping at eleven o'clock when Mrs Nunez arrived to start the cleaning. Her repeated knocks woke him.

24

THAT fall, one of the editors of Harkavy's paper, *Antique Horizons*, went to a national magazine and, through Harkavy, Leventhal got the vacancy. Characteristically, Beard at first declined to meet the offer and then went two hundred dollars higher, but Leventhal left him.

Things went well for him in the next few years. The consciousness of an unremitting daily fight, though still present, was fainter and less troubling. His health was better, and there were changes in his appearance. Something recalcitrant seemed to have left him; he was not exactly affable, but his obstinately unrevealing expression had softened. His face was paler and there were some gray areas in his hair, in spite of which he looked years younger.

And, as time went on, he lost the feeling that he had, as he used to say, 'got away with it,' his guilty relief, and the accompanying sense of infringement. He was thankful for his job at *Antique Horizons*; he didn't underestimate it; there weren't many better jobs in the trade field. He was lucky, of course. It was understandable that a man suffered when he did not have a place. On the other hand, it was pitiful that he should envy the man who had one. In Leventhal's mind, this was not even a true injustice, for how could you call anything so haphazard an injustice? It was a shuffle, all, all accidental and haphazard. And somewhere, besides, there was a wrong emphasis. As though a man really could be made for, say, Burke-Beard and Company, as though that were true work instead of a delaying maze to be gone through daily in a misery so habitual that one became absentminded about it.

This was wrong. But the error rose out of something very mysterious, namely, a conviction or illusion that at the start of life, and perhaps even before, a promise had been made. In thinking of this promise, Leventhal compared it to a ticket, a theater ticket. And with his ticket, a man entitled to an average seat might feel too shabby for the dress circle or sit in it defiantly and arrogantly; another, entitled to the best in the house, might cry out in rage to the usher who led him to the third balcony. And how many more stood disconsolately in the rain and snow, in the long line of those who could only expect to be turned away? But no, this was incorrect. The reality was different. For why should tickets, mere tickets, be promised if promises were being made – tickets to desirable and undesirable places? There were more important things to be promised. Possibly there was a promise, since so many felt it. He himself was almost ready to affirm that there was. But it was misunderstood.

Occasionally he thought about Allbee and wondered whether Williston knew what had happened to him. But he had written to Williston, returning the ten dollars which, for one reason and another, he had failed to give Allbee. In his letter he made a special effort to explain his position, and, realizing that Williston believed he had a tendency to exaggerate, he gave a very careful and moderate account of what had taken place. Allbee, he said, 'tried a kind of suicide pact without getting my permission first.' He might have added, fairly, 'without intending to die himself.' For there were reasonable grounds to suspect this. But no reply came from Williston, and Leventhal was too proud to write a second letter; that would be too much like pleading. Perhaps Williston felt that he had kept the money from Allbee out of malice. Leventhal made it as clear as he could that he had had no opportunity to pass it on to him. 'Does he think I'm that cheap?' he asked himself resentfully. Repeatedly, he went over all that he had done during those confusing weeks. Hadn't he tried to be fair? Didn't he intend to help him? He considered that he and

Allbee were even, by any honest standards. Much difference ten dollars would have made! At first he was deeply annoyed; later he prepared some things to say to Williston if they should meet. But the opportunity never came.

From time to time he heard rumors about Allbee. Invariably, however, he heard them from people who did not know him personally, and he could never be sure that the man to whom they referred actually was Allbee. 'Some journalist, from New England, originally, who hit the bottle,' etcetera. In three years a dozen or so stories reached him, no two of which agreed. He did not attempt to follow up any of them. Although they always interested him, the truth was that he did not want to know precisely where he was and what he was doing. He believed that he had continued to go down. By now he was in an institution, perhaps, in some hospital, or even already lying in Potter's Field. Leventhal did not care to think too much or too literally about it.

But one night he saw Allbee again.

It happened that a dealer who had furnished some of the antiques for a play that was running on Broadway gave Leventhal two passes. He was reluctant to go; Mary, however, insisted. Mary was pregnant; she was expecting the baby in a month, and she would be tied down, she argued, for a long time to come. Leventhal said that the theater would be very warm – this was early June and prematurely hot – but offered no real opposition. The evening of the play he came home early. (They had moved to the uptown end of Central Park West, closer to the Porto Rican slum than to the blazoned canopies of the Sixties and Seventies.) During dinner he was heavy eyed. But before he had finished his dessert, Mary was clearing the table. He washed, shaved for the second time that day, and put on a Palm Beach suit, breaking it out of the brown paper wrapper in which the cleaner had sealed it eight months ago. The trousers were a little tight and short, for during the preceding winter he had put on weight.

The subway was hot enough; the theater was suffocating.

Leventhal sat and endured the play. He had no taste for plays in general, and this was sentimental and untrue – a complicated love affair in a Renaissance palace. He held Mary's hand. In the refulgence of the stage, he saw drops of moisture on her forehead, under the thick loop of her braid, and on her nose. Her skin looked very pure, and his heart rose as he watched her, intent on the play. Presently he brought his eyes back to the stage. His own dark face was damp, and his tight suit was already crumpled; his collar was soaked with sweat.

At the first curtain he quickly got to his feet and guided Mary through the crowd to the lobby. An usher opened the doors to the sidewalk, and they walked out. The tavern adjoining the theater was filling up. Leventhal and Mary lit cigarettes and gazed into the street and upward at the glow of yellow glass that passed into the haze. The afternoon had been almost tropical. A few large drops of rain had fallen; the air was moist, odorous, and black; one felt it like a soft weight. There were night clubs and restaurants in the block, and the traffic was heavy. Suddenly a taxi cut a dangerous curve from the far side of the street and made an abrupt, pitching stop in front of the theater. There was a terrific croaking of horns behind it. The door flung open and a woman was handed out. Something about the queerness of existence, always haunting Leventhal at a short distance, came very close to him when he saw her escort's face over her shoulder in the faint light. The glass slide in the roof of the cab was drawn aside, and the top of a straw hat circled and shone in the opening. The woman left the running board with a little bound, holding her silk scarf to her throat with one hand and gathering her skirt up with the other. Slender and long-legged, she walked with a somewhat free stride, elegant and yet slightly awkward. There were jewels beneath the scarf and on her fingers. Her painted nails looked purple under the frosted light of the marquee. She stood with her back to the street, irritated, holding a small, heavy, glittering bag. The man lingered, for some reason, in the cab.

Mary touched Leventhal's arm.

'Do you recognize her?' she whispered.

But Leventhal was trying to see her companion.

'Isn't that Yvonne Crane?'

'Who?'

'The actress.'

'I don't know,' he said, looking blankly. 'Is it?'

'She's still perfectly beautiful,' said Mary with admiration. 'How do they stay looking so young?'

The woman, after waiting awhile, turned and said in a low, harsh tone, 'Come on. Will you come out of there?'

The man inside shouted quarrelsomely, 'He took us the long way around. Does he think I don't know the city? I'm no greenhorn here.'

They did not catch the woman's next words, but they heard the driver, laconic and confident, and then the escort, crying out laughingly, 'Don't give me that . . . That's for the visiting fat boys.'

The woman opened her purse and threw a bill to the driver.

Leventhal, when he heard the voice, was certain that the man was Allbee, and, with a rigid face and a look approaching horror in his eyes, he waited for him to appear.

Then Allbee stepped to the curb, saying, 'You shouldn't have done that.' The cab started away with its open door flapping; the driver, without slowing up, reached back and slammed it.

Leventhal had a close view of Allbee as the two walked into the theater. He was wearing a white dinner jacket. A flower, pinned erratically, swung from his lapel; he pressed his hat under his arm and strode forward, his large shoulders stiffly raised, swaggering and gallant. His cheeks were red and shining. He was laughing into his companion's pretty but nervously severe face. He seemed to be pushing her playfully, and it was evident from the set of her arms that she did not wish to be pushed.

260

'I don't recognize him,' said Mary. 'But I'm sure she's Yvonne Crane. I've seen her picture a hundred times. Don't you remember her?'

Throughout the second act, Leventhal peered round at the boxes. He could see no more than the color of a face in the radiance thrown back from the stage, or, occasionally, the black shape of a head rising near the red ball of an exit light, or moving its shadow across the obscure shine of the rails. He thought that they must be sitting in a box. The woman might or might not be Yvonne Crane, though Mary was probably right. She was, in any case, a wealthy woman; and Allbee looked more than moderately prosperous in the dinner jacket and the silk-seamed formal trousers. To say nothing of the flower. The flower struck Leventhal in a very curious way as a mark of something extraordinary, barbaric, rich, even decadent. 'Yes, he's gone places,' Leventhal mused. 'And that woman, whoever she is, he's got that woman under his thumb.' None of the rumors had described him as so well off. 'And here I had him dead and buried in Potter's Field. Dead. But imagine!' He tugged a handkerchief from his breast pocket and wiped his neck and chin. The lights came to life in the arches, causing him to squint and frown. The curtain was swooping down. There was applause. He had not noticed that the act was ending. The orchestra began a march and, more hurriedly than the first time, he helped Mary rise.

He was lighting her cigarette, looking everywhere for Allbee, when, over her head, he caught sight of him on the stairs. He was alone, and, widening his eyes, he smiled at Leventhal and raised his hand with stiffly spread fingers in a gesture he did not understand. Mary spoke to him. Utterly confused, he answered something. She repeated what she had said. She was asking for her compact, which he had in his pocket. She was going to the ladies' lounge. He hastily got it out and gave it to her. His expression seemed to puzzle her, and she glanced at him sharply before turning away.

As she passed Allbee on the stairs, he gave her pregnant

figure an appraising look. Leventhal walked out of the lobby. He was aware that Allbee was coming up to him, but he did not raise his eyes until he heard him speak.

'Hello, Leventhal.'

The low, thick voice with its old tone of complicity, the big, obtrusive figure in the white jacket, disturbed him.

'Hello,' he answered nervously.

'I saw you when we were coming in.'

'I didn't think you did.'

'I knew it would be all right with you if I acted like a total stranger, so it's up to me, and I'd feel like a terrible fool if I didn't speak to you . . . You saw me, didn't you?'

'Yes.'

'And who I was with?'

'The actress? My wife recognized her.'

'Oh, your wife,' he said politely. 'Very handsome. Very fetching, even in her condition.' He began to smile broadly, displaying his teeth. With his hands on his hips, he bent forward slightly. 'Congratulations. I see you're following orders. "Increase and multiply."'

Leventhal answered him with a dull, short nod. It seemed to him that Allbee had no real desire to be malicious; he was merely obedient to habit. He might have been smiling at himself and making an appeal of a sort for understanding. On nearer sight, Allbee did not look good. His color was an unhealthy one. Leventhal had the feeling that it was the decay of something that had gone into his appearance of well-being, something intimate. There was very little play in the deepened wrinkles around his eyes. They had a fabric quality, crumpled and blank. A smell of whisky came from him.

'You haven't changed much,' said Allbee.

'I wasn't the one that was going to change so much.'

'Ah, that. Well, do I still look the same to you?'

'You still drink.'

'Ever since I saw you, I've been wondering whether you'd mention that. You're true to form.' He grinned, but he was

262

somewhat hurt. 'No, I only take it socially because everybody else does.'

'You look successful.'

'Oh,' he said lightly. 'Success is a big word. You ought to be careful how you use it.'

'What do you do?'

'Just now I'm squiring Miss Crane around. The columnists say we're friends, when they bother to mention her. She's not the drawing card she used to be. You probably know. Well, she doesn't want much public attention now, or she'd be seen with someone more celebrated. But she doesn't care. She's glad all that professional business is over for her and she can live more quietly. She's actually a very intelligent person. We're both a little lost, out there on the Coast.'

Leventhal nodded again.

'Oh, yes. She's real nobility. She's really fine. Queenly, if you know what I mean. Some of those women become loathsome when their popularity dies down. They live like criminals. They want to make up for all those years under the public eye, I guess.'

'So . . . I congratulate you too,' Leventhal murmured.

'She's not Flora, of course . . . My wife.' His continued smile gave a touch of cynicism to the sensational, terrible look of pain that rose to his eyes. Leventhal saw that he could not help himself and pitied him. 'She has qualities . . .'

His last words were lost in the braying of the taxis. Leventhal found nothing to say.

'I want you to know one thing,' said Allbee. 'That night . . . I wanted to put an end to myself. I wasn't thinking of hurting you. I suppose you would have been . . . But I wasn't thinking of you. You weren't even in my mind.'

Leventhal laughed outright at this.

'You could have jumped in the river. That's a funny lie. Why tell it? Did you have to use my kitchen?'

Allbee glanced around restlessly. The bays that rose into his loose blond hair became crimson. 'No,' he said miserably.

'Well, anyhow, I don't remember how it was. I must have been demented. When you turn against yourself, nobody else means anything to you either.' Bitterly shame-faced and self-mocking, he took Leventhal's hand and pressed it. 'But I want to say that I owe you something. I was trying to get around it when I talked about trying to kill myself only.' He spoke with great difficulty. 'I don't want to exaggerate, but I don't want to play it down either. I know I owe you something. I knew it that night when I was standing in your shower . . .'

Leventhal pulled his hand away.

'What do you do out there, are you an actor?'

'An actor? No, I'm in radio. Advertising. It's a middle-sized job. So you see? I've made my peace with things as they are. I've gotten off the pony – you remember, I said that to you once? I'm on the train.'

'A conductor?'

'Conductor, hell! I'm just a passenger.' His laugh was short and faint. 'Not even first class. I'm not the type that runs things. I never could be. I realized that long ago. I'm the type that comes to terms with whoever runs things. What do I care? The world wasn't made exactly for me. What am I going to do about it?'

'What?' Leventhal smiled at him.

'Approximately made for me will have to be good enough. All that stiffness of once upon a time, that's gone, that's gone.'

The crowd was beginning to return. The curtain bell had rung.

'Anyway, I'm enjoying life.' Suddenly he looked around and said, 'Say, I've got to run. Yvonne will send them out looking for me.'

'Wait a minute, what's your idea of who runs things?' said Leventhal. But he heard Mary's voice at his back. Allbee ran in and sprang up the stairs. The bell continued its dinning, and Leventhal and Mary were still in the aisle when the houselights went off. An usher showed them to their seats.